THE
DEFIANT
QUEEN

L.R. JACKSON

WWW.BLACKODYSSEY.NET

Published by
BLACK ODYSSEY MEDIA

www.blackodyssey.net
Email: info@blackodyssey.net

This book is a work of fiction. Any references to events, real people, or real places are used fictitiously. Other names, characters, places, and events are products of the author's imagination, and any resemblance to actual events or places or persons, living or dead, is entirely coincidental.

THE DEFIANT QUEEN. Copyright © 2025 by L.R. JACKSON

Library of Congress Control Number: 2024916887

First Trade Paperback Printing: May 2025
ISBN: 978-1-957950-62-4
ISBN: 978-1-957950-63-1 (e-book)

Cover Design by Ty Woolridge
To the extent that the image or images on the cover of this book depict a person or persons, such person or persons are merely models and are not intended to portray any character in the book.

All rights reserved. Black Odyssey Media, LLC | Dallas, TX.

This book or parts thereof may not be reproduced in any form, stored in a retrieval system, or transmitted in any form by any means—electronic, mechanical, photocopy, recording, or otherwise—without prior written permission of the publisher, excepting brief quotes or tags used in reviews, interviews, or complimentary promotion, and as permissible by United States of America copyright law.

10 9 8 7 6 5 4 3 2 1

Manufactured in the United States of America

Distributed by Kensington Publishing Corp.

The authorized representative in the EU for product safety and compliance
Is eucomply OU, Parnu mnt 139b-14, Apt 123
Tallinn, Berlin 11317, hello@eucompliancepartner.com

Dear Reader,

I want to thank you immensely for supporting Black Odyssey Media and our ongoing efforts to spotlight the diverse narratives of blossoming and seasoned storytellers. With every manuscript we acquire, we believe that it took talent, discipline, and remarkable courage to construct that story, flesh out those characters, and prepare it for the world. Debut or seasoned, our authors are the real heroes and heroines in *OUR* story. For them, we are eternally grateful.

Whether you are new to L.R. Jackson or Black Odyssey Media, we hope that you are here to stay. Our goal is to make a lasting impact in the publishing landscape, one step at a time and one book at a time. As always, we welcome your feedback and kindly ask that you leave a review. For upcoming releases, announcements, submission guidelines, etc., please be sure to visit our website at www.blackodyssey.net or scan the QR code below. And remember, no matter where you are in your journey, the best of both worlds begins now!

Joyfully,

Shawanda Williams

Shawanda "N'Tyse" Williams
Founder & CEO, Black Odyssey Media

The Defiant Queen is the second book in The Queen's World. It is recommended that you read *The Accidental Queen* to get the entire reading experience.

CHAPTER ONE

Baas

Mafachiko, Africa

I'm deep in thought as I sit in the garden, enjoying a cool, breezy night. It's quiet except for crickets chirping and the water gushing from the waterfall. The moon shines brightly, offering enough light to sip my whiskey without spilling it. I glance at my watch; it's after ten, meaning Nala should be asleep by now, and I can finally go to bed. It sounds weird, I know, waiting for my wife to fall asleep before I join her. But it's what's best. For me, anyway. If she's already sleeping, I can ignore the awkward silence. I can ignore the expectation of conversing with her. I can ignore her desire to have sex. And most of all, I can ignore the look of rejection on her face when I tell her I'm too tired to touch her.

I place the empty glass beside me and stand, shoving my hands into my pockets as I look up at the sky and think about Shaya. I wonder if she thinks about me as much as I think about her. I shake away that thought. Of course, she thinks about me. There's no way that she couldn't. Because what we had was . . . I pause before the word enters my mind. *Special.* What we had was

1

special. But as special as it was, I had a duty to the king and my country.

I take the trail back to the palace and climb the steps slowly. When I reach my bedroom door, I take a deep breath before entering. I expect her to be asleep when I walk in, but she isn't. She's reading a book. She lowers it when she hears the door close. "You missed dinner again."

I sit on the bench in front of the bed and remove my shoes. "Yeah, I had to work late."

She sets the book down on the nightstand. "You're always working late. I feel like we never see each other."

I loosen my tie. "We've talked about this, Nala. Repeatedly."

She climbs off the bed and folds her arms across her chest when she's in front of me. "I know. I just . . ." She pauses for a second. "Baas, I'm trying here."

I remove my glasses and the rest of my clothing before I grab a towel, wrap it around my waist, and then answer her. "Nala, nothing's changed for me."

She follows me closely as I walk toward the bathroom. "Is this what the rest of my life will be like?"

"What do you mean?"

"I'm your wife; yet you treat me like I'm—"

"Like, you're what? A woman I was forced to marry?"

"That's not fair."

"Isn't it, though? This is what you asked for. You wanted to be a part of the royal family, and now you are. You wanted the jewelry, the money, and the social status. You got what you wanted, and you should be happy."

"You think treating me like this makes me happy?"

I spin around with irritation. "What do you want from me, Nala?"

"What I want is for you to talk to me sometime. How's *that*, for starters? I want you to stop looking at me like you hate me. I want you to spend some time with me."

"I sleep beside you every night; that's more time than I spend with anybody."

"You know what I mean."

"No, I don't."

"Can you at least make love to me sometimes?"

"We made love last week."

"That wasn't making love, Baas. That was an emotionless fuck."

I stop in my tracks. "Are you saying you didn't enjoy it? Because if I recall, you had multiple orgasms."

She blushes. "That's not the point."

"Then what *is* the point?"

"Yes, the sex is great. But I want intimacy. I want you to *want* me. For example, last night, I hinted that I was horny, but you rolled over and ignored me."

My patience is thinning, and I'm tired of hearing her rant. I close the gap between us, breathing so hard that I feel like I will burst. Her eyes widen before I smash my lips against hers, completely surprising her. I pull them away and spin her around, lifting her tiny nightgown up and around her waist. I push her gently toward the wall, and when she places her hands against it, I yank the towel from my waist and toss it behind me. I nudge her legs apart with my foot, and my hand settles between them, finding that she's already wet. "Is *this* why you're upset? Because you're horny?" She doesn't answer me. Instead, she closes her eyes and drops her head back. I place my finger on her clit. "Is *this* what you want?"

She bites her lip and moans when I stroke it. "Hmmm. Yes, Baas."

I continue to stroke her. And when I kiss her neck, her moans grow louder. She squirms beneath my hand until she finally cries out with ecstasy. When she stills, I enter her quickly, eager to release and get this over with. She whimpers with pleasure as I drive into her, long and deep. "That feels good, doesn't it?"

"Yes. Fuck, yes."

"Want to come again?"

"Yes, please."

She screams as I fuck her harder and screams even louder when she tells me she's close. Her body immediately goes slack when she comes, and I'm able to stroke two more times before I grunt and spill inside her. We stay in position for a second before I pull myself out and take a step back. We're silent as she shoves her nightgown down, and I turn on the shower. My back is toward her while I check the water temperature.

"Want some company?" she asks.

I turn around to face her. "I'd rather shower alone if you don't mind."

She looks hurt but brushes it off. "Of course."

When she leaves the bathroom, I step inside the shower and inhale the steam. I want to yell, but I don't want to alarm her. So, I bang my fist against the shower wall instead, hoping it alleviates some of my frustration. The last thing I want to do is hurt Nala. I may not love her, but she's still my wife, and I have a duty to her. We agreed before we were married. We agreed that we weren't marrying each other for love. We were marrying for peace between our countries. She knew I could never love her because my heart was with someone else. She said that she understood. She said we were both doing what was best for our countries, and she didn't expect us to act like an average married couple. But she didn't keep up with her end of the bargain. She's demanding that I give her more than I can, expecting me to do things I don't want to do with her. I don't care about spending any time with her. I don't care to confide in her.

I have three duties to my wife: to protect her, provide for her, and respect her. And I'm doing all three. She has no idea how often I want to reach out to Shaya. She has no idea how frequently I talk myself out of flying to New York and leaving her and this life behind. Because if she knew, she wouldn't be so quick to complain. I'm holding up my end of the deal. I'm doing everything that a husband should do except for loving her. And that's something that will never happen.

After I shower, I shut off the water and open the shower door. Nala stands in front of me. "I'm sorry."

I nod before I grab a fresh towel and step out. I walk around her and go to the nightstand to retrieve my glasses. I reply to her after I shove them on. "It's okay. I understand."

"No, it's not okay. I know we agreed that there wouldn't be anything between us. I just didn't expect . . ." Shit, I know where she's going with this, but I remain quiet. "I didn't expect to feel so lonely, Baas."

"You're not the only one who feels lonely."

"So, let's stop being lonely then. Let's be true partners. Don't you care for me even a little bit?"

She's asking questions I don't want to answer. Because answering them will make me look like a jerk. I tried everything I could to avoid making her think this was anything more than it was. I've remained distant. Unemotional. I limit how intimate we are. And none of it has worked. Nala may have initially agreed to this arrangement, but it was only a matter of time before she wanted more. I don't want what she wants. And I won't lie to her. I have and will continue to be honest about where I stand.

"Yes, I care about you, but not in the sense that you'd like. Nala, you're my wife, and I'm doing my best to honor my duties as your husband. But I will never love you."

She walks closer to me. "You don't know that. Can you at least try?"

I shake my head. "No."

"You're being foolish, Baas. She's gone, and you need to forget about her. What's the point in loving someone you can never be with? We're married until one of us leaves this earth. Why not at least try to be happy until that day comes?"

She's right. Nala and I can never get divorced. And although my best friend is a king who has the power to change this law, I would never ask him to do it. Because if he does and I divorce her, we will make enemies we don't want to make. I've made my bed. Now, I must lie in it. But that doesn't mean I will be happy while doing it. If Shaya and I had never met, I would do my best to make a happy life with Nala. I would try my hardest to get to know her, hoping to fall in love with her. But I did meet Shaya. And after meeting her, my life was never the same. *I* am not the same. She made me question things I never had to question. She made me see life differently. She made me *feel*. She's the first woman I ever loved and probably the only woman I'll ever love. But I fucked up things between us and ruined our chances of ever being together. Nala stares at me curiously, wondering what I'm thinking about.

"I'm sorry, Nala. But it will *always* be her."

CHAPTER TWO

Shaya

New York

I plop down on the couch with my glass of wine and take a big gulp. Today was a hectic day. I woke up this morning in what felt like 200-degree weather because the air conditioner stopped working overnight. When I got into my car to go to work, it wouldn't start. So, I called a cab at the last minute and got stuck with a driver who drove as if my life didn't matter. Then when I got to the clinic, two people called, unable to work, leaving us short-staffed and me overworked. I grab my phone and dial the one person who will understand.

"Hey, Eb."

"Hey, you sound tired; long night?"

"More like a long day," I reply.

She laughs. "I bet you're drinking wine right now."

"Yup. And I'll probably drink the entire bottle."

She sighs. "I miss you."

"I miss you too, Eb."

"You're still coming, aren't you?"

I don't answer her because I haven't decided yet.

"Shaya!"

"Eb, you know I want to come." I struggle to find the rest of the words for my sentence.

"You can't avoid him forever. You're my best friend, and he's my husband's best friend."

"I know," I reply.

"Listen, I don't know what the two of you discussed that day at the hospital. Whatever it was, it made you hide the truth from him. But don't you think now may be the right time to tell him? Face-to-face."

She's referring to the day she gave birth. Baas and Dafari arrived as soon as they could, and while Dafari gushed over his son, Baas led me outside the hospital room to talk. My thoughts drift back to that day.

"I've been calling you."

"I've been busy."

"Shaya, don't do this. Don't sabotage us."

"That's just it, Baas. There is no us. You're marrying someone else."

"I don't have to."

"Yes, you do. You made that clear."

"No. I made my duty clear. But it's not what I want to do."

"Let's not complicate this. Go home. Fulfill your duty and forget about me."

"Forget about you? How could you say such a thing?"

"Because it needs to be said."

He closed the gap between us, breathing evenly. "Shaya, how could I ever forget about you? You're everything to me. But . . ." I anxiously wait for him to finish his sentence. "I will leave you be if that's what you want. Tell me you don't love me. Tell me what we had didn't mean anything to you, and I will walk away and forget about you forever."

My thoughts are interrupted by the sound of Ebony's voice. "Shaya, are you there?"

"Yeah, sorry. He doesn't need to know, Eb. I did what I had to do. End of story."

She exhales loudly. "Okay. I beg to differ, but I'll leave it alone if you think it's for the best."

Grief paralyzes me as her words remind me of that terrible day. It was the worst day of my life and will forever haunt me. I respond to her initial question. "Yes. I'll be there."

"Great. Dafari will send the plane for you."

"Okay. But do not send Baas with him."

"I won't."

A moment of silence passes between us. "How's he doing anyway?"

"He's hanging in there, I guess."

I want to ask more, but I change the subject instead. "How's my godson?"

"Spoiled as shit." Her answer makes me laugh loudly. "Seriously, Shaya, he gets everything he wants. I don't even think he knows what the word 'no' means."

I smile with happiness for my best friend. She has everything she's ever deserved. A great career as a counselor. A husband who adores her. And the cutest son I've ever seen. "I can't wait to see him."

I hear Dafari say something in the background, and she giggles. "I gotta go, Shaya, but I'll see you soon."

"Okay. See you soon."

We end the call, and I lie back on the couch. Tension settles in at the thought of seeing Baas after all this time. What will I say when I see him? How will I feel? Will chemistry still be there? I shake my head and realize it doesn't matter because he's married. He made his choice—and it wasn't me.

I guess I can share some of the blame. I recklessly hooked up with him, not thinking of the consequences. It was supposed to just be sex—pure fun with no strings attached. But I don't think either of us knew what would hit us. Neither of us expected to fall for the other. Especially me. I had just gotten out of a long relationship. The hurt from Jay's betrayal was still fresh. Yet, somehow, Baas managed to show me that it was possible for me to love again. But then he snatched away that love and gave it to someone else, and I was hurt for a second time. He tried calling me, but there was nothing left for me to say. He had his life in Africa. I had my life in New York. And neither of our lives involved the other.

A tear escapes me as I think about what I did. Maybe I should have told him. Maybe I shouldn't have moved on so quickly and forgotten about the love that we shared. I shake my head. No. Like I told Eb, I did what was best. I wipe my tears away with the back of my hand and take another sip of my wine. I won't cry over him. It's over, and I need to come to grips with the fact that we'll never be together. I'll fly to Africa to see Ebony and my godson. I'll be cordial to Baas and his wife, and then I'll return home and continue living my life. I'll forget about our time together. I'll forget about the choice I was forced to make. I'll eventually move on, get married, and have kids one day. It sounds good in my head. But even as I think about it, I'm not sure it's a plan I can stick to.

Mara rushes into the exam room and shuts the door. "So?"

"So what?"

"Have you swiped right yet?" she asks.

I shake my head as I laugh at her statement. "I haven't swiped at all."

She places her hands on her hips. "Shaya, I spent all that time helping you set up a dating profile, and you haven't even *used* it?"

"I didn't want to sign up in the first place, *remember*?"

It was liquid courage that made me do it. My coworkers and I went out for drinks after work one night. Two margaritas later, Mara and I are crying on each other's shoulders about how we've had our hearts broken. The outcome was that both of us joined a dating app. Since then, she's been on three dates, and I've been on zero.

"Shaya, you have to get out there at some point."

"Yeah, I know," I reply.

She checks her watch. "Shit, I've got a wounded puppy coming in a few minutes. We'll talk about this later."

She leaves the room, and I pull out the sanitizer to start my cleaning. I place it on the counter and shake my head at the brand they're using. It's not as effective as the brand I used at my clinic, but I guess it'll have to do. When I returned to New York, I needed to stay busy to keep my mind off Baas. So, I worked as a senior vet at one of the animal clinics near my new condo. I was only supposed to work here until I had the time to open my own veterinary clinic, but once I started working, I fell in love with how they treat the animals here. Plus, I get to do what I love without the stress of the business side. I no longer have to worry about finances and taxes. I don't have to worry about coming out of my pocket for expenses if my patients are low for the month. And it feels good to work with a team.

My phone dings, and I pull it out of my pocket. It's a notification that I've got a match. I view his profile, and I'm immediately impressed. He's tall. Good looking. And according to his occupation, he's a business owner. I hold my finger out, hesitant to swipe. Maybe I'm not ready. Or maybe I am ready, but

I'm scared. Mara's right. I have to get myself back out there sooner than later. I swipe right and release the breath I'm holding. Then I shove the phone back into my pocket and smile as I thoroughly clean the exam room.

Today starts my new journey. My new journey to love and happiness. I'm sick of crying every time I think of Baas. I'm sick of feeling jealous every time I think about the fact that he's with another woman. This is not how I want the rest of my life to be. And I refuse to sit back and be miserable while he gets to frolic around with his wife and live a life of happiness. No. I get to be happy too. Things are looking up for me for the first time in a long time. I have a new outlook on life. Today is just a start, but soon, I will have it all.

Baas

Mafachiko, Africa

I try my hardest to pay attention during the council meeting, but it's almost impossible. My mind is racing, and I can't turn it off, no matter how hard I try. Femi calls my name to get my attention. "Yes," I answer.

"King Juma expected an heir by now. He's getting anxious."

I lean back in my chair and meet his stare. "King Juma doesn't dictate when my wife gets pregnant."

I knew this was coming. Nala mentioned this over the weekend, and I knew the elders wouldn't let this rest. Not only were Nala and I married to join our countries, but we were also required to produce a child. Preferably a son. I knew going into this that it would be a problem, and so did she. I have no desire to have a baby with a woman I don't love, and she feels the same. What we have is complicated enough without subjecting an innocent child to the mix. So, we both agreed that we would never conceive. She's been on birth control since the day we married and plans to keep it that way.

Femi straightens his posture before he responds. "You're wrong. If we are to keep this treaty intact, we must honor the terms of the agreement."

I huff. "Femi, how about you worry about more important things? My wife and I know what's at stake, and we're taking care of it."

Dafari shifts in his seat before he jumps in. "Yes, I hardly think there's anything we can do to speed up the process. It will happen when it happens." He nods, reassuring me that he's got my back. "Let's move on, shall we?" he continues. "Baas, how's our military doing?"

"Promising. I just recruited five new soldiers last week. Strong and eager to learn." I speak firmly and with pride. "We lost a lot of men when we went to war, and although we are not 100 percent recovered, we've come a long way."

Dafari smiles. "That's good to hear. What's next on the agenda?"

I check my notes before answering him, something I've never had to do before. But with my mind being distracted, I needed to make sure I could remember the topics and not look incompetent. Many men are lined up to serve in my position. They're just waiting for me to slip so they can swoop in and "save the day." Now, of course, this will never happen. For one, I am good at what I do. I've been by Dafari's side since we were kids. And when it comes to protecting him and this country, no one can compare to me. And second, even if I did slip a little, Dafari would never replace me. He would never trust anyone as much as he trusts me. But even with knowing this, I have to stay focused. I can't look like I'm slacking. Because if I do, people will lose respect for me. And, more importantly, lose respect for Dafari. "The next item on the agenda is . . ." I stop and look up at Dafari. He eyes me curiously, and I finish my sentence. "The next item on the agenda is the memorial for Prince Enu."

The mention of Enu's name still holds a dark cloud over the palace. He was a traitor. But he was still a prince, and his mother and brother still grieve him. Although I also grew up with Enu, I feel no emotion about his death. He put Queen Ebony in danger and almost killed my best friend. As far as I'm concerned, I hope he's rotting in hell. Dafari clears his throat before he speaks. "Please send the secretary to consult with the Queen Mother. Whatever she wants to do is fine by me."

The room remains quiet before the timer rings, interrupting us. Femi is the first to stand to his feet. "See you next week, gentlemen," he says before rushing out of the room.

I stay seated as I watch the rest of the men file in a line and exit the room. When Dafari and I are alone, I speak. "I've got to do something about this baby situation, Dafari."

"There's nothing you can do," he replies.

"Marriage is one thing. I can accept that. But getting her pregnant. I can't do it."

He nods. "I know."

"You've got to get the elders off my back."

"I will think of something," he replies.

I take a deep breath. "Thank you."

He stands to his feet. "There is something I've wanted to discuss with you, Baas."

"What is it?"

"You've been my right hand for as long as I can remember."

"Yes," I reply.

"You're my brother, and I trust you with my life," he continues.

I rise to my feet. "Dafari, you're acting weird. Are you sick or something?"

He chuckles. "No."

"Then where is all this coming from?"

He walks over to his desk, opens the drawer, grabs a piece of paper, and hands it to me. As I scan the document, I see it's official paperwork appointing me as Aiden's godfather. "Life is short, Baas. Should something happen to Ebony and me, you and Shaya are the only ones we trust to raise Aiden."

"I love Aiden like he's my own."

"Yes, we know. The queen and I plan to live a long time, but we wanted to do this . . . just in case."

"I'm grateful for you both."

"For years, you stood by my father's side as well as mine. Everyone knows that you and Shaya are his godparents. But we wanted to have it in writing to avoid confusion or opposition regarding who steps in to raise him."

"I understand."

"Baas, thank you for being there for him."

"Of course."

"You may not be of royal blood, but make no mistake. You *are* royalty. You've sacrificed so much, and despite what our DNA says, you are my brother."

"It's my honor."

"I know."

He points to the paper. "If I am incapacitated or if I die before Aiden reaches adulthood and Ebony is still alive, this says that you are to act as interim king until he reaches eighteen years old. After that, he has the right and the authority to make decisions on his own behalf and that of the Royal Family." He clears his throat before he continues. "If the queen and I are both dead and, God forbid, something happens to Aiden, you will rule Mafachiko as king."

"Unless you two have more children," I add.

He smirks. "Aiden is a handful. Ebony has made it clear that one child is enough for us."

I chuckle. "I see."

I've served this family for years. I've never expected anything from it. I've never felt like it was a burden. And I've never felt entitled to anything more than what I've been given. But still, it means the world that Dafari thinks this highly of me. "*If* any of what you mentioned happens, I won't let you or the Royal Family down."

He smiles. "I know you won't."

A knock at the door interrupts us, and my personal assistant, Cora, walks in. "You're needed," she says.

She doesn't need to tell me what I'm needed for because I already know. I've been waiting for this news all day. "Dafari, please excuse me. I have an important matter I must address."

"Is everything okay?" he asks.

"Yes."

"Okay, we'll chat later."

I quickly leave the room and follow my assistant to a nearby sitting room. She hands me the phone, and my contact speaks on the other end. "She's connected with someone."

Rage fuels every blood vessel in my body. "Are you sure?"

"Yeah. They've been messaging each other for two days. They're meeting at an Asian restaurant around the corner from her place," he replies.

"Fuck!"

"What do you want me to do, sir?" he asks.

"I want you to handle it."

I end the call and grind my teeth as I try to digest what my contact in New York has told me. Dafari walks in just as I'm about to storm out.

"You left in such a hurry that you forgot your paperwork." He hands it to me, and it doesn't take him long to see that I'm furious. "What's wrong?"

"It's Shaya," I reply.

"Is she all right?"

"Yes. She joined a fucking dating app and has a date tonight."

He's quiet as he watches me with sympathy. "Baas, I thought we agreed you wouldn't keep tabs on her."

"I know. But I couldn't help myself. I called our people and put a guy on her three months ago."

"It isn't healthy to track her. You have to move on."

"I tried. I'm miserable without her, Dafari."

He places his hand on my shoulder. "I know the feeling."

It's become standard practice for people to say they know how you feel. Or that they understand. But the reality is that most don't truly understand what you're going through unless they've been in your shoes. And Dafari has been in my shoes. It wasn't too long ago that he was fighting against everything he ever believed in to be with the love of his life. "Baas, I can fix this," he adds.

"And risk another war? We're still recovering from the last one, and if we go to war with King Juma, we won't win. It will ruin us."

"We can find a way."

"There is no other way. Don't you think I've tried to come up with thousands of options? Dafari, this is the only way. Besides, Shaya made it clear that she wanted nothing to do with me."

"Then why torture yourself by keeping tabs on her?"

"Because I still need to know that she's okay."

He takes a deep breath. "Well, if she's started dating, I would say she's doing just fine."

He's right. When I got the first report, she was depressed and sleeping a lot. She was crying and barely getting out of bed. It gave me no pleasure to know that she was hurting. But it did give me pleasure that she cared enough to be as hurt by this as I am. As the days passed, the report showed she was moving on one day at a time. I guess I knew she would eventually start dating. But I wasn't prepared for how I'd feel when that day came. I gather my composure. "Has, ah, has Ebony mentioned anything?"

He shakes his head. "The queen doesn't discuss their conversations with me. She's only mentioned that Shaya asked about you."

"You're right, Dafari. I need to stop keeping tabs on her. It's only making things worse."

He grabs a bottle of bourbon, pours two glasses, and hands me one. We both take a drink. "How are things with you and Nala?"

I shrug. "About the same."

"Baas, I know I've said it already. But I'm grateful for you and your loyalty. I know this is not what you wanted, yet you did what you had to do to save our country. I owe you my life."

His gratitude is welcomed but not needed because he should expect nothing less from me as his right hand. "I'm just doing my job, sir."

We continue drinking silently while I decide the best way to pull my guy off Shaya. Dafari clears his throat, indicating that he's about to say something. "Ebony *did* mention that Shaya will be here for the birthday party next week."

My heart beats faster. "Really? I didn't think she would come."

"You know she wouldn't miss her godson's first birthday."

"Yeah, good point."

"Pretend you know nothing about her coming. Ebony will be pissed if she knows I'm telling you things about her."

I chuckle as I raise my glass. He clinks his with mine. "I won't breathe a word."

We take another gulp just as Anaya walks in. "I've been looking all over for you two."

"Is something wrong?" Dafari asks. She stares at us solemnly without responding. "Mother, what is it?"

Her eyes swing to mine. "Baas, you're needed upstairs."

I rush upstairs and enter the room just as the doctor removes his stethoscope. When he's finished, he turns around to face me.

"Well?"

"It's not looking good," he replies.

"I don't understand. She was just fine this morning."

"Brain aneurysms work quickly. No one would have seen it coming," he replies.

"What do we do now?"

"We've done all we can. She'll either pull through or . . ."

He's nervous about completing his sentence. "Give it to me straight," I demand.

"She'll either pull through or she won't. Only time will tell," he answers.

"Thank you."

"You're welcome. Give me a call if anything changes."

When he leaves the room, I sit beside the bed and stare at Nala. She looks like she's sleeping, only she isn't. I was told she passed out shortly after I left the room this morning and was found by one of her assistants. I place my hand on the side of her face, thinking her eyes will open. But they remain closed.

Dafari walks in. "I just heard the news."

"Yeah, the doctor said it's not looking good."

He stands next to me. "Is there anything I can do?"

I shake my head. "I know we didn't have a traditional marriage, but I care enough that I don't want to see her this way."

"I know. But let's not give up hope. She could pull through this."

I suddenly feel guilty about the way I've treated her. She had my respect and my loyalty, but I didn't give her what she wanted the most. My attention and my love. It's a devastating thing to see someone so full of life lie lifeless like this. But it's even more devastating knowing that the person lying lifeless didn't feel loved. I know we had an agreement and that this was a business transaction, but for some reason, I wish I had done things differently.

Dafari must sense this. "Don't do that," he demands.

"Do what?"

"Beat yourself up. There is nothing you could have done. You have nothing to feel guilty about, Baas. Your heart may not be in it, but you're still a good husband."

I nod because, as much as I know, he means what he said. But I'm not so sure he's right.

Slow music plays in the background as people gather around Nala's body. She looks angelic, wrapped in all-white linen and surrounded by flowers. I thought there was a chance she would pull through. I stayed with her. I talked to her and apologized for my behavior. But she didn't make it. She took her last breath as I held her hand. It's customary that we bury our people within forty-eight hours, so we moved quickly with announcing her death as well as her celebration of life. I watch her parents cry over her from the back of the room. Her mother wails loudly while her father, King Juma, tries his best to keep it together.

Nala was a good person. She was kind, witty, and smart. She could do math calculations in her head on a whim. It's too bad the only path her parents prepared her for was the path to royalty. The elders move everyone aside to allow room for me to say my final goodbye. I walk slowly toward the front of the room, and when I reach her, I lean down and kiss her cheek. "Goodbye, Nala. I'm sorry I wasn't a better man to you."

I turn around and nod to her parents, a gesture of my condolences. Then I take my seat next to them while Dafari steps forward to give the final speech. When he's finished, he performs the death ritual, and we all pray to the ancestors to allow her to ascend. Her body is carried away, and we all gather in the ballroom. I'm not in the mood to be here. People will expect me to be the grieving husband, and I'm not one for keeping up appearances. Don't get me wrong. I'm saddened that Nala's life was cut short, but if people expect me to carry on as her mother did, they'll be mistaken.

Dafari approaches me. "Are you up for this?" he asks.

"No. Not really."

"I'll try moving it along as fast as possible."

"No. Don't rush it. She deserves this."

He nods before he walks off. People approach me and shake my hand. They offer me condolences on the loss of my wife. Some of them knew her better than I did, which isn't surprising. I don't say much. I simply nod and thank them for their sentiments.

Suddenly, my phone rings, and it's the call I've been waiting for. It's the guy I have watching over Shaya. But the timing is wrong. It would be disrespectful for me to answer right now. So, I don't. I'll call him back another time. Right now, I have my last duty as a husband. And that is to bury my wife respectfully and with no distractions. She argued that I didn't show her much attention when she was alive. The least I can do is reserve this day just for her. I'm about to reject the call when it stops vibrating, and a text message tells me everything is in place for tonight. I don't respond. I shove the phone back into my pocket and forget I saw it.

Shaya

New York

I can't believe I'm doing this. I'm about to sleep with a man that I just met. Am I *really* this easy? Is a steak dinner and wine all that's needed to take me to a hotel and fuck me? I shake away the inner voice screaming in my head. I want this. No—I *need* this. It's been a long time since a man has touched me, and there's nothing wrong with two adults having consensual, safe sex. I exit the bathroom wearing my sexiest bra and panties. He lies naked on the bed, his eyes sweeping me from head to toe. I lower my eyes and smile with satisfaction at the sight of him. He looks like he'll get the job done and then some. I hope he's as good as I think he might be because I've been dying for an orgasm produced by something other than my vibrator.

"You're so beautiful," he says.

"Thank you." I approach the bed slowly, giving him enough time to watch me with lust-filled eyes. My hormones go into overdrive when I climb on top of him and kiss him. He flips me on my back and nestles his head between my legs, making me wetter at the thought of him tasting me. When he takes the first lick, I hiss. It feels so good to have a man pleasure me, and I don't want him to stop. I open my legs wider for him and gently place my hand on the top of his head. He teases and taunts me at first, offering slow and quick licks. Then . . . Things go downhill from there. His tongue touches every spot *but* the one that matters. I need a release and become frustrated at his lack of skill. I do my best to indirectly guide him, showing him what my body needs right now, but it's useless. He's licking everywhere *except* where I need him to lick.

I give up. I won't get the results I'm looking for, so it's best we move on before I become uninterested altogether. I slowly push his head away, and he stops to climb on top of me. His erection presses into me, and I immediately stop him.

"Do you have a condom?"

He shakes his head. "No. I thought you had those covered."

I gently move him off me. "No. I don't have any either."

He climbs off the bed and grabs a robe from the bathroom. "You keep your sexy ass right there. I saw a convenience store downstairs in the lobby. I'll be right back."

"Okay."

I rush to my phone and dial Ebony when he's out the door. She picks up on the first ring.

"Shaya, I've been calling you."

"Yeah, I know. Sorry. I was busy with work, and then I went on a date."

"A date?" She says it loudly but lowers her voice immediately. "You went on a *date*?"

"Yes. We're at a hotel, but he just stepped out of the room. Eb, we're about to have sex. Am I making a mistake?"

"I'm not sure that's a good idea, Shaya."

"I know how it looks, but it's been awhile since I've been with someone." She's quiet. "Eb, are you still there?"

"Yes, I'm here."

"Well, should I do this or not?"

"Shaya, I was going to wait until you got here to tell you, but . . ."

"What?"

"It's Baas. His wife just died."

CHAPTER THREE

Shaya

Mafachiko, Africa

"And you haven't heard from him since?"

"No. He said he was going to get condoms and never returned."

Mara sighs over the phone. "Well, maybe it was a good thing. You said you were on the fence about sleeping with him."

"Yeah, something tells me it would have been a waste. I swear the man had no idea what a clitoris is."

"Ugh. I probably would have kicked him out at that point. You got lucky, girl. You probably dodged a bullet."

"Yeah, but why would he leave his clothes behind? Was he so rushed that he'd disappear wearing only a robe?"

"I don't know, Shaya. Men are weird these days."

"Hence, why I've steered clear of dating." I look out the window at the crystal blue water. "Anyway, I'm here."

"Who knows why he left you there like that, but try not to worry about it. Block him and move on."

"Already have," I reply.

"Okay. Have fun."

"I'll try. Don't work too much."

I end the call just as the plane lands. The flight crew, which consists of two beautiful women, kindly help me with my bags and escort me down the steps and onto the runway into the scorching hot sun. A black SUV arrives with tinted windows. When the door opens, I raise my hand to shield the sunlight and get a better view. I gasp when I see him, and images of our last good time together rush to my head.

He trails a finger over my hip. "Don't go. Stay here with me."

I giggle. "I can't. Anyway, we just met. We barely know each other."

He smirks. "I know everything I need to know about you, Shaya. Especially the fact that I want you to be mine."

"Don't you think it's too soon to ask me to move in?"

"No. We've spent every second together. I've made love to you too many times to count. And you're everything I never knew I needed. So, no, I don't think it's too soon to ask. Now, will you stay?"

He rises to his full height when he steps out of the vehicle. Then he stands there for a minute, watching me carefully before he takes long strides toward me. When we're face-to-face, I study him. He hasn't changed a bit. If anything, he's even sexier than before. His smooth brown skin has a glow from the sunlight. His brown eyes are hidden behind dark shades, and his neatly shaved beard outlines his strong jaw. He's dressed in his signature button-up shirt and bow tie, and he's wearing a pair of linen pants. I want to throw myself at him. I want him to make love to me right here, on this runway, and whisper in my ear how much he's missed me. But I don't move.

He reaches into his pocket, pulls out his eyeglasses, and swaps them with his shades. His eyes meet mine, probably with more clarity now. "Shaya."

"Baas. I didn't know you'd be the one picking me up."

"Are you disappointed?"

"No. I mean, I just thought that Ebony and Dafari would be the ones to pick me up."

"They're finishing the last few touches for the party, so they asked me to come."

"Great."

We stand in uncomfortable silence before he bends down to grab my bags. "Let's get you to the palace."

"Yes, thank you."

He trails behind me, rolling my luggage carefully. When we reach the car, the driver loads my luggage into the trunk while Baas sits beside me in the back. I avert my eyes by fastening my seat belt when the driver pulls off. Neither of us says anything at first, but I should be the one to break the silence.

"I, um, I heard about your wife. I'm sorry."

He answers without looking at me. "Thank you."

There's so much more I want to say, but I hold back. Not only because this isn't the right time but also because it doesn't matter what I say to him. What we had is over, and it's best to keep things cordial.

"How have you been?" he asks.

"I've been well."

"Still saving animals?"

"Yeah, I work at a pretty good clinic near my house."

He smiles at me. "They're lucky to have you."

"Thank you."

He shifts in his seat, which means I'm not the only one nervous. I'm just better at hiding it than he is. I stare out the window, taking in the beauty of Africa. The trees stand tall and bountiful as fruit I can't pronounce hang from the branches. The flowers are in full bloom, creating fields of bright and bold colors. Red, yellow, and purple flowers blow in the wind, inviting you to smell them. Monkeys jump from tree to tree, following the SUV as we cruise through the city. I crane my neck as I spot a giraffe. It's the most magnificent animal I've ever seen.

We arrive at the palace, and it still manages to take my breath away with its perfect landscaping and historical architecture. The driver unloads my luggage, and Baas reads a text message he receives.

"It's the Queen. She's putting out a fire but will be up shortly. In the meantime, I'll escort you to your room."

I have flashbacks of our time there. If those walls could talk, they would tell how we made love for hours. They would also tell us the exact moment we fell in love. And it would be a good thing because I don't even know when that moment was. I can still remember the way my body shattered beneath him. I can still remember the way he made me feel. No other man has ever made me feel the way Baas has. As we climb the steps together, all my memories rush back, and my emotions spiral out of control.

"I think I'm in love with you."

"Baas, we agreed. Just sex."

He caresses my hair. "Are you saying you don't feel it?"

"That's not what I'm saying."

"So, you feel it too?"

"Yes," I whisper. "But we can't be together."

"Why not?"

"You know why. You're marrying someone else."

By the time we enter the room, I'm a mushy mess inside. When he closes the door, I'm angry and sad all over again. I whirl around. "Why?"

Confusion crosses his face. "Why what?"

"Why did you choose her?"

He shakes his head. "Don't put this all on me, Shaya. You left me no choice."

"You *always* had a choice, Baas."

"I called you. I sent messages. You didn't respond to any of them. So, what was I supposed to do?"

"Give me more time. I was hurt. I needed time to deal with everything."

"Your way of dealing with everything was to hop on a plane to New York and never speak to me again?"

"I never intended to stop speaking to you," I reply.

"Yet it happened."

The tension in the air is thick, and our emotions are heightened. "I was angry. The thought of you with another woman . . ." Even now, I can't bring myself to finish my sentence.

"Shaya, I made my intentions with you clear from day one. It was *you* who didn't want to be serious. *You* were the one who said it had to be just sex between us. I told you I loved you, and you pushed me away even more."

He's right. I got scared. He was in a position where he would have to choose me or his country, and if I allowed him to choose me, he would have resented me. I take a deep breath at the realization. "I guess it doesn't matter now anyway."

I turn to walk away, but he gently stops me. "What is that supposed to mean?"

"It means the damage is done."

"You caused the damage, sweetheart, then left me to deal with it."

I snatch my arm away. "You think it was *easy* for me? Do you know how many nights I cried myself to sleep? Do you know how long it took for me to get over you? While you were living the perfect married life, I was alone. You have no idea what I went through."

Anger flashes across his face. "My marriage was far from perfect. Do you *really* think I was happy with Nala? I could barely look at her, Shaya. She reminded me of what I couldn't have, and I resented her for it. I didn't even get the chance to apologize before she . . ."

He can't bring himself to say it. And I suddenly feel horrible about bringing her up. How selfish of me to do so. I didn't intend to argue with him or make him feel guilty, but I needed to get some things off my chest before we resent each other forever. I don't want that. And I don't want things to be awkward between us.

"Let's just stop. Clearly, we see the situation differently, and we need to leave it at that. I think it's best that we be cordial and move on. Besides, I've started dating someone."

I don't know why I say this to him because it's a lie. I haven't been on one date since I left Africa. Maybe it's because I want him to feel the hurt of imagining me with someone else. Or perhaps it's because I think he'll keep his distance if he thinks I'm dating. But if I know one thing about Baas, he doesn't back away from anything he's determined to have. He narrows his eyes and closes the gap between us.

"You're dating someone?" he asks.

I hold my head high with confidence. "Yes."

"Is this *someone* the guy you were about to fuck the other night?"

Baas

I'm so angry I want to bend her over and spank her to show her who she belongs to. Her eyes go wide at my statement.

"What? How did you . . ."

"Did you think I wouldn't find out?"

"That was none of your business," she replies.

"You *are* my business."

"Were you stalking me, Baas?"

I don't answer her because her question is beside the point. "I knew what room you two were in and saw everything. I was prepared to end his life the moment he put his mouth on you. But it turns out I didn't have to."

Her eyes go wide. "What? How?"

I close the gap between us and ignore her question. "Did you honestly think I would allow *any* man to touch you?"

"You had no right spying on me and interfering with my life," she yells.

"AND YOU HAD NO RIGHT OFFERING SOMETHING SO PRECIOUS TO A STRANGER!"

I roar so loudly that I swear I hear the floor shake beneath me. Had my contact not intervened, she would have made a mistake. Just knowing that guy touched her made me want to kill him. But I had to show restraint. I instructed my contact to give him an old-fashioned beat down, that's all.

Her eyes narrow. "Is that why . . ." She pauses. "Baas, what did you do?"

"I did what was necessary."

"*You* are the reason he disappeared?" she asks.

"It's better you don't know the details. All you need to know is that he was given clear instructions to never come near you again."

She laughs out loud, but not because I'm funny.

"How selfish of you. You interfere with *my* happiness, yet I'm willing to bet money that you were fucking your wife every night."

"That's not true. I . . ."

My first instinct is to deny it. But I don't lie. I always tell the truth, and she's right in a sense. I didn't sleep with Nala *every* night, but the fact of the matter is that I did sleep with her from time to time. What audacity of me to expect Shaya not to sleep with anyone. She has needs just like I do. I'm about to respond to her when the door bursts open. Ebony storms in with Dafari trailing behind her.

She goes straight for Shaya. "Are you okay?"

Shaya nods, and they both look at me like they want to tear me apart. Dafari senses the tension and steps in. "Ah, Baas, can you come and help me carry the rest of the gifts to the gift table? It'll give the ladies a chance to catch up."

I turn to Shaya. "I'm sorry for raising my voice." I don't give her time to respond. Instead, I turn around and leave the room with Dafari tailing behind.

"Well, she has a point, Baas."

We place the last of the presents on the gift table and wait for the guest of honor to arrive. The backyard is swarming with energetic kids and their impatient parents. Dafari and I are way on the other side of the yard purposely to give Shaya and me some space.

"I think the entire palace heard you yell."

"I lost my cool. I never meant for her to find out that I put a detail on her. I was just so angry; it slipped out," I reply.

He looks over at Ebony. "My wife isn't happy about this. I can tell."

"I'll make things right."

"Good. Because we don't want to be in the middle of this. You two are going to have to figure this out." The music starts, and he smiles. "It's time."

He leaves me to join Ebony. I sip lemonade as I watch my godson enter through the gate. Aiden wobbles ahead toward the cake table, but Ebony intercepts him. I laugh out loud because it's amusing, just like everything else he does. His parents don't like that I let him have his way. They say I encourage him to misbehave simply because it's entertaining to me. And they would be right. Besides, my role to the king being Aiden's godparent is my second greatest honor. I try to spend as much time with him as I can. I watch him with wonder, wondering if I'll ever have the pleasure of having a son of my own one day. The thought makes me glance over at Shaya. She's holding Aiden now and smiling. Watching her interact with him is a good look for her. It's at that moment that I realize I was an idiot earlier. Not only are our best friends married, but we also share the role of godparents with Aiden. We have to fix this so we can at least be civil to each other. I walk over to them, and when I'm at her side, she hands Aiden over to Dafari.

"Did you see his cake?" Ebony asks with excitement.

"Yes, and I can't wait until we cut it," I reply.

"It's chocolate. His favorite," she adds.

"I'm sure he'll be pleased," I respond.

Dafari walks away with Aiden, and Ebony follows suit, leaving me alone with Shaya. "I wanted to apologize for my actions earlier."

She nods, but I can tell she's still upset. "You crossed the line. What were you thinking?"

"Shaya, you have to understand. Not hearing from you drove me crazy."

Her face softens with understanding. "Please tell me he's not hurt too badly. I can't have what you did tracing back to me."

"I would never do anything to put you in jeopardy. You know I'm smarter than that. We have his address. He's married. Three kids. If he reports the attack, he'll have to explain to his wife why he was assaulted outside of a hotel wearing only a bathrobe and holding condoms. And the person who did it is long gone to London by now."

"How did you know about . . . um . . ."

She pauses, and I finish her sentence. "That you let him taste you?" She narrows her eyes as she cocks her head to the side. "That mishap at the front desk? That was my guy. He hacked into the system, making it look like they had only one room available. He had time to set up surveillance while you two were checking in."

She steps closer. "So, I'm on camera for the *entire world* to see?"

"You know me better than that. I would never allow another man to see you naked. Only I had access to the footage, and it's since been erased."

She places her hand on her forehead. "Jesus, Baas. I . . ." She's silent for a second before she continues. "You know what? Never mind."

"Are we good now?"

"Yes. We're good." She cranes her neck to look behind me. "It's almost time to sing 'Happy Birthday.'"

She walks away, leaving me breathless. I don't understand how she seems more beautiful than the last time I laid eyes on her. She's wearing a white, flowy sundress, yet you can see every curve. Her short curls are wild and frizzy from the heat, and the scent of her shea butter body lotion still lingers in the air. I join the crowd, and Ebony wastes no time giving me a piece of her mind.

"I know you and Shaya have unresolved issues, but please don't ever raise your voice at my best friend like that again."

I keep a straight face but chuckle internally because I want her to know I'm taking her seriously. It makes me happy that Ebony is protective of Shaya. I understand it because I'm the same way with Dafari. I raise my hand in surrender. "I was wrong. And it'll never happen again."

"Good. Baas, just tell her how you feel. I know her better than anyone, and she'll come around eventually."

"I will."

She smiles at me before picking up Aiden and placing him at the table's center. We sing "Happy Birthday," and he happily blows out his one candle with his father's assistance. He immediately opens his gifts, and I watch with the same pride his parents have. Dafari had other plans for Aiden's first birthday. He wanted to take him along when he went hunting and fishing. Ebony quickly derailed that idea and said her son would have a traditional birthday bash with all the extras. Live horses and elephants. A clown. Enough food for an army and a cake as tall as him. She compromised a little by telling Dafari they could plan a family fishing trip together. After he's opened all his gifts, I walk away and head inside. I need a moment to think because I'm conflicted. Shaya isn't here long term, and I need to spend whatever time I have winning her back.

But I also just buried my wife. This is both morally wrong and downright selfish. My wife's body is still fresh in the ground, and I'm already anticipating picking up where Shaya and I left off. The issue is not with my conscience. I was loyal to Nala. The problem is how people will perceive me moving on so fast. How will that make both of us look? How will it make the king look? I grab a glass and a bottle of wine when I reach the kitchen. I'd rather have something much stronger, but wine is more suitable for a day like today. I take a big sip as soon as I pour it, hoping it relaxes my mind.

Shaya

I read the official document naming me Aiden's godmother. "I'll always be here for him, Eb."

"We know. But we wanted to make it official so there's no questions should something happen to us."

"I understand." I place the document in my purse and open my suitcase to unpack. "The party was a lot of fun."

She smiles. "Yeah, Aiden wore himself out, which means he might sleep in tomorrow."

Ebony has a full staff available at her every beck and call, but she refuses to put all the responsibility on them. She's very hands-on with Aiden. She bathes him, cooks for him, and spends as much time with him as possible.

"I'm glad I came."

"Me too. We should go out tonight if you're up to it."

"If I'm up to it? You've been super mom all day. Don't you mean if *you're* up to it?"

"Hell yeah, I'm up for it. I haven't let loose since I've been here. A night out with my best friend is *exactly* what I need right now."

"Okay then. Tonight, it's just me, you, alcohol, and dancing," I reply excitedly.

We high-five each other. "I've missed you."

"I've missed you too, Eb."

"Seems someone else missed you too."

"Did you know he was keeping tabs on me?"

"No. But I'm not surprised." She stands to her feet. "I need to take a quick nap if we're going to do this. Let's be ready to leave at nine."

"Okay, see you later."

When she leaves the room, I shower and grab my phone to check my work emails. Suddenly, someone knocks at the door, and I answer it, still wearing my robe. Baas's eyes sweep me from head to toe.

"May I come in?"

I step aside and allow him in. I nervously tighten the belt around my robe after I close the door. "What are you doing here?"

"We need to talk. Like *really* talk. There's a lot I need to say."

"Okay," I reply.

"I'll start. I love you. I've never stopped loving you."

It isn't what I expected to hear, so it catches me off guard. I thought he was here to continue his disdain about my attempt to sleep with someone else.

He continues. "We come from different worlds, Shaya, and I don't expect you to fully understand how important my role is. Or why my duty to my country and Dafari come first. But I do expect you to know that what I felt for you was real. *Is* real. My marriage changed nothing."

"Baas, I do understand. But I guess some small part of me hoped I was just as important."

He closes the gap between us. "You are *very* important. There were so many other factors in place, sweetheart, but you have always been the only one for me."

I'm so glad that my robe is thick because I can feel my nipples hardening underneath it. "You really mean that?"

"Yes. But when you stopped communicating with me, you made me question if you felt the same."

Me and my stubbornness. It's a trait of mine that I wish I could eliminate. If only I had answered his calls and talked things through, then maybe things would be better between us, no matter his choice. "Did . . . Did you develop feelings for her?"

"No. But I cared about her well-being."

His response is honest, but it still stings. The thought of him caring for a woman in any capacity makes me envious. "I know it was selfish of me, but I hated knowing you were with her."

He nods. "I know. And I hated knowing you felt that way."

"It seems we both have unresolved feelings we should have addressed long ago."

"I agree. But I'm glad we're able to talk about it. So, what do we do now?" he asks.

Nothing. We do nothing. Because if I allow myself to be swept into this again, it'll make me feel even more guilty about what I've done. And if he ever finds out that I kept such a big secret from him, he'll never look at me the same again. "Now that we've put that behind us, we can be friends."

He raises a brow. "I'm sorry . . . Did you just say 'friends'?"

"Yeah. Now that we've hashed it out, it's not awkward between us. Being friends will ensure that we don't complicate things."

"Shaya, I just told you that I love you. And you're standing in front of me, wearing only a robe. Do I need to remind you that I know what's underneath that robe? The only thing that's complicated for me right now is deciding if I want to fuck you on the bed or bend you over the desk." My mouth opens, and he continues. "I can't be your *friend*."

Before I can reply, he swiftly unties the robe and kisses me. His hands slide under it and roam my body, setting me on fire. I pull away. "I can't do this, Baas."

He moves closer. "Yes, you can."

I stop him. "No."

He swiftly removes his hands and steps away from me.

I struggle to find the words to tell him why we can't go any further, but my brain is mush. He clears his throat. "I, ah, I'll let you get some rest." He hurries out of the room, closing the door behind him. And I fall onto the bed, wishing he could fall into it with me.

Chapter Four

Shaya

Ebony overslept, and we arrived at the nightclub by ten. Much later than what we anticipated. Dafari was adamant about sending security with us, but we didn't want it. We're adult women who know how to handle ourselves, and we want a normal night out without all the extras. So, we snuck out and ditched the security detail. We walked at least a mile before hopping in a taxi and going to the best nightclub in the city. We quickly head to the bar once inside. I am excited as I wait for the bartender to take our orders. When he finally gets to us, he smiles widely at Ebony and yells over the music.

"What would you like my queen?"

Her eyes narrow. "What's your name?" she yells.

"Abam."

"Abam, tonight, I'm not the queen. Just Ebony, okay?"

"Got it. What can I get you?"

"Two Long Island Iced Teas."

He nods before he turns away to make our drinks, and I pull her closer to speak in her ear. "You forgot our extra cherries."

"Shit! I did, didn't I?"

"It's okay. Next time."

He returns with our drinks, Ebony thanks him, and we find seats near the dance floor. She closes her eyes as she takes a gulp.

"Damn, girl, slow down."

She laughs. "You have no idea how stressed I've been the past few weeks planning Aiden's party."

She holds her drink up, and I hold mine up as well. "Best friends."

"Best friends," she repeats. We clink our red cups and drink to celebrate our friendship.

"So, you and Baas hash things out yet?"

"No."

"Why not?"

"Things are so fucking complicated between us, Eb."

"What's complicated about it? The man is head over heels in love with you, Shaya. You can't see that?"

We're interrupted by a waitress who hands us two more drinks. "All drinks are on the house tonight," she says.

We thank her before handing her a tip. "Ebony, we didn't come out tonight to talk about Baas and me. Tonight, it's about you and me letting loose and having fun."

"Cheers to that. Let's dance."

She grabs my hand and leads me to the dance floor. We find a spot and sway our hips to the music as we drink from our cups. We let loose. And we're singing along with the song lyrics by drink number four. I feel someone behind me, and I spin around. Blue eyes stare into my hazel ones.

"What's your name, gorgeous?"

"Shaya."

He places his hand on the back of my little red dress and pulls me toward him, dancing with me closely. "Shaya, I'm Jalees. And you're wearing the hell out of that dress."

I'm too drunk to respond. Instead, I smile at him and look over at Ebony, who's also dancing with someone but not as close. She's drunk but aware enough to remember she's a married woman. His hand glides farther, down to the small of my back, and he leans in and speaks into my ear.

"How about you and I get out of here?"

Before I can answer, he's yanked away from me with force. Baas stands between us. "Get your fucking hands off her."

The music is playing loudly but not so loud that I can't hear the exchange.

"Who the hell are you?" Jalees asks.

Baas closes the gap between them. "Do you *really* want to find out?"

Jalees glances between us before he backs away slowly. When he's out of sight, Baas turns to face me. "We're leaving—now."

"But Ebony—"

"Is with the king," he interrupts.

He quickly grabs my wrist and leads me through the crowd, causing my drink to spill. Finally, we reach his car, and he opens the door.

"Get in."

"No. Not without Ebony," I refuse.

"I just told you she's with Dafari. Now get in."

"You can't come here and tell me what to do, Baas."

He steps toward me and takes the cup out of my hand. "Either you get in, or I put you in. The choice is yours."

He's furious, but I'm too drunk to continue this argument with him. So, I huff before I slide into the seat. He slams the door and tosses the cup in a nearby trash bin before sitting on the driver's side. When he starts the car, he looks over at me.

"We have eyes everywhere. Did you two honestly think we wouldn't find you?"

"We wanted to have fun without a babysitter, Baas."

"It's not about having a babysitter. Ebony is the Queen. Do you realize the risk you two took tonight? You need security for your safety."

"So serious all the time. You're overreacting."

"And you're drunk."

I laugh and stick my tongue out at him. "So?"

"Put your seat belt on."

"I don't want to." He leans over and straps me in. The heat of his touch makes the hairs on my neck stand up and my panties moist. He freezes when I grab his hand, and his eyes bore into mine. "You are so sexy. Like the Greek god, Adonis."

It's meant as a compliment, but he doesn't take it that way. He moves away from me quickly and puts the car into gear.

"I'm not Greek. And that's the liquor talking."

"I don't need alcohol to tell you how sexy you are."

He waits until we pull out of the parking lot before he responds. "What were you thinking, letting that man touch you?"

"We were just dancing," I reply.

"That wasn't dancing. That was grinding."

"What were you doing there anyway? It's supposed to be a girls' night."

He looks over at me and quickly sweeps my body before he puts his attention back on the road ahead. "Do you think I would let you go out alone wearing that? You're half-naked, Shaya."

I huff. "You've got some nerve acting as if you own me."

"I'm keeping you safe. God knows what you would have done had I not shown up."

My body heats from anger. "We are *not* a couple, Baas. So, if I want to go home with a guy and fuck him, that's *my* business."

I don't know why I choose to add fuel to the fire. But I'm riled up. Maybe it is the alcohol. Or perhaps it's the fact that Baas showed up and claimed me, knowing I don't belong to him. He swerves the car down a dark, wooded path. The vehicle jerks as he slams on the brakes. I grab the armrest as he shifts it into park. He unlocks my seat belt and pulls me to him. When our foreheads connect, his fiery eyes dance with mine.

"Are you purposely trying to infuriate me? Because that's what happens at the mere thought of another man touching you."

I want to say something witty. Something sarcastic. Because that's the mood that I'm in. But I don't. "I—"

His lips slam into mine, and my entire body goes limp. Our tongues swirl, and I moan right before he releases me. "Is *that* what you want, Shaya? Do you want another man touching you . . . here?"

His hand slides between my legs, and he finds me wet.

"No," I whisper.

He slides his hand inside my panties. When he slips a finger inside me, I open wider for him.

"Do you feel that? Remember it, sweetheart. Remember how wet I make you?"

My head falls back. "Yes."

"Why do you defy me? Why do you push me away?" he asks.

"I don't want to."

"Then why?"

"Because I have to."

He strokes my clit while he kisses my neck, and I combust. I grip the door handle and scream with pleasure as my orgasm ripples through me. He watches me for a second before he moves his hand from between my legs. Then he leans over me, opens the glove compartment, and removes a handkerchief. He hands it to me before adjusting himself and locking in his seat belt.

We're both quiet as I wipe myself, and he shifts the car into gear. He looks at me when we're back on the road but says nothing. He seems angry, and I know it has everything to do with what I said to him. He wants answers, but he won't get them. Especially not tonight. Not when I'm too drunk and vulnerable to tell him everything. I lock my seat belt and turn my head to stare out the window. I knew it was a mistake coming here. I knew it would all come full circle when I saw Baas. Being with him makes me change my mind about telling him the truth. Maybe Eb was right. Perhaps now is the right time to tell him. I quickly shake away that thought, and a tear slides down my cheek. It's too late to tell him. The damage is done, and there's no coming back from it. I have to accept the fact that I fucked up, and it could possibly cost me the only man I ever loved.

Baas has managed to avoid me at every turn. If I walk into a room that he's in, he leaves. If he walks into a room that I'm in, he leaves. He turns around if he sees me in any area he's approaching. And I hate it. I know he's angry, but I don't know what he's angry about. Is he angry that I rejected him? Is he angry about last night? Or is it a combination of both?

Ebony adjusts her sunglasses. "I wish you wouldn't leave."

"It's best this way, Eb. Maybe you and Aiden can come and visit me soon."

"Honey, if I visit, it won't be with Aiden. Momma looks forward to her getaways."

"I bet."

"Ugh. I never want to see another Long Island Iced Tea again in my life."

I laugh. "Yeah, I'm hungover too. Was Dafari angry with you?"

"Angry? No. Upset? Yes. He gave me this huge lecture about being safe and how things could have gone bad for us last night. Especially once more people realized who I was."

"Yeah, I got the same lecture."

"You should have seen Baas's face when he saw that guy touch you. I honestly thought he was going to kill him."

"He was so mad, Eb, but he has yet to speak to me."

"How long are you two going to keep avoiding each other?"

"I don't know. But I'm leaving soon anyway, so I guess it doesn't matter."

She shakes her head. "You two are the most stubborn people I know." She thinks to herself. "No. Dafari has both of you beat. You two come in second, though."

I laugh out loud. "We had something special, but you know the old saying, 'People come into your life for a season.'"

"Bullshit, Shaya. That kind of love only comes around once in a lifetime. You're just scared of being hurt. I hope I don't have to remind you that Baas is nothing like Jay."

I admire the scenery in the garden as I agree in silence. "You know it's weird. I thought I was in love with Jay. I thought we'd be together forever. I was hurt when he cheated on me, but then I met Baas. I don't know, Eb. It felt like we were meant to be together. We fell for each other quickly, and I realized that what I felt for him was *true* love. I loved Jay. But I was *in love* with Baas."

"*Was* in love with Baas?"

I change the subject. "How's Trina?"

Ebony and Trina had the same foster family. They treated them horribly, and when Ebony managed to break free, she took Trina with her. Ebony could have left Trina behind. After all, it's much easier to be on the run when it's just yourself. But my best friend has a big heart. It's one of the many things I love about her. And I admire how selfless she is.

"On track to graduate early."

"Wow, that's amazing."

"I know. She may come and spend the summer with us." She stands to her feet slowly. "It's Aiden's naptime, and I could use one myself. We'll catch up later, OK?"

"Yeah."

"Don't go back so soon, Shaya. You know you can stay as long as you want to."

"I know."

"Don't let this thing get too out of hand with you and Baas."

"I'm trying."

We're silent for a moment before she asks her next question. "Do you think you could ever live here? I hate being so far away from you."

The tears in her eyes almost break me. Of course, I want to stay here with my best friend. I want to explore the relationship that Baas and I didn't get to have. But I can't because being this close to Baas reminds me of the worst mistake I ever made. "Maybe one day, Eb."

She smiles. "That's good enough for me."

CHAPTER FIVE

Shaya

I release a breath of air when I step foot into my room. I shed my clothes but still wear the weight of my secret. I expected to feel guilty around Baas. I've carried that guilt since the moment I made my decision. But what I didn't expect to feel was shame or betrayal. I felt it the minute Baas stared into my eyes. I plop down on my couch and let the tears stream freely down my cheeks. If only I had listened to Ebony. She told me it wasn't a good idea. She told me that one day, I may regret my decision. She was right . . . because that day has come. I wipe away my tears and straighten my spine. There's nothing I can do now, and there's no need to wallow in sorrow over it. My phone rings. It's Mara.

"Hey."

"You must be having fun because you never responded to my text message."

"I'm so sorry. It's been a little crazy around here," I reply.

"Sounds like fun. Well, you're not missing anything here at work. It's the same ole shit."

"Good to know."

"How was your godson's party?" she asks.

"It was amazing."

"Good. So, have you met any men? More importantly, do they have friends? Brothers?"

"Nope. None at all," I respond.

"Damn it. Will you let me know if you do? I'll be on the first flight smoking."

We both laugh aloud before I reply, "You'll be the first to know."

"I'll call you later."

"Okay."

I smile when I end the call. Mara doesn't know about Baas. I've tried my best to keep my work and personal life separate. I consider her a friend, but I don't choose to share this part of my life with her. All she knows is that my best friend lives in Africa with my godson. I'm on edge and need something to calm me. So, I grab a bottle of wine and pour myself a large glass. It's just what I need to relax.

It's now nighttime, and I'm on my second bottle of wine. And it feels good. I feel light. I feel free. I feel . . . horny. Visions of Baas swirl in my head. They clash with the memories of him touching me. I shake my head, attempting to forget. Only I can't. This suite is a constant reminder of him making love to me. I gulp the rest of my glass, turn off the television, and head to my bedroom. When I reach it, I grab the vibrator from my suitcase and climb into my bed. I'm already wet by the time I turn it on. My eyes close the minute it touches me. I moan with pleasure as I change the speed and think about Baas making love to me.

"Holy shit!"

I'm close. So close to having a mind-blowing orgasm. I increase the speed and spread my legs wide. "Oh God."

I'm right on the edge. Tension builds as I imagine Baas flicking his tongue over my clit. I bite my lip and slide my free hand under my T-shirt to rub my breast. I'm about to explode in one, two . . .

My eyes fly open as I'm interrupted by loud pounding. I jump off my bed, throw on my panties, and rush to the door, not realizing I'm still holding the vibrator. I slide one hand behind my back and fling the door open with the other. I'm prepared to give whoever this is a piece of my mind. One for interrupting a much-needed release. And two for knocking so loudly. My mouth opens wide at the intruder.

"Baas, it's late. What are you doing here?"

He doesn't answer. Instead, he brushes past me and walks right in. I close the door and spin around quickly before he can see what's in my hand.

"We need to talk."

"About?" I ask.

"Us . . . avoiding each other."

"Don't you mean *you* are avoiding *me*?"

"I haven't been avoiding you," he replies.

"Really? Because you won't even look at me."

"I was angry with you. Seeing that man so close to you after you had just rejected me made me lose my mind. I can't stand being around you right now. Being near you and unable to touch you is driving me crazy."

"But you *did* touch me. Last night in the car."

"That was an appetizer, sweetheart. I want the entrée."

Shit! Why does he choose to do this now when I'm hot and horny? "I didn't reject you. I wanted you just as bad."

He cocks his head to the side. "Really? Because I was two seconds from being inside you, and you told me to stop."

"I know. I just . . . I mean . . ."

"Talk to me, sweetheart."

"I told you to stop because I don't want to mess things up any more than they already are," I explain.

He steps forward. "That wouldn't have happened."

"You don't know that. The wounds are still fresh. Emotions are still strong. If we would have had sex—"

"It would have been the highlight of my fucking night," he answers.

I almost hug him. But I remember what I'm holding. Fuck! I need to walk away and ditch it. He looks down at my hand behind my back.

"Are you hiding something?"

I shift uncomfortably. "No."

He takes another step. This time, it brings him so close I can feel the heat of his breath. "You're lying." He holds his hand out. "Let me see."

Embarrassment creeps in, and I shake my head, refusing to let him see what I'm holding. His eyes search mine before he takes a step around me. I shut my eyes tightly, humiliated that he's standing behind me, staring at my vibrator. He moves closer to me and gently removes it from my hand. I feel the heat of his breath in my ear.

"Were you using this before I got here?"

My chest rises and falls as I struggle to answer him. He slowly drags the vibrator up to his nose and sniffs.

"Answer me," he demands.

I'm no longer embarrassed. I'm turned on, dying for him to finish what I started. I spin around to face him with every intention of answering his question . . . but words fail me.

"Tell me. Were you thinking about me as you played with your pussy, Shaya?"

Holy shit! I'm so horny right now that I could come with one touch. "Yes."

There's no need to lie. Baas knows his effect on me. Even if I tried to say otherwise, he wouldn't be convinced. He takes a step forward, and I take a step backward. We repeat this three times until my legs hit the back of the couch. His hand grabs the end of my thin T-shirt, and he smirks.

"Do you want me to finish the job . . . properly?"

My nipples are so hard that they hurt. The heat between my legs is hot enough to start a fire. Everything in me is saying this is *not* a good idea. Because once we start, I know we won't stop. He'll want more. He'll want to consume me. And that can't happen. But he looks irresistible, standing before me, his eyes burning with desire for me.

"Shaya . . ."

"Yes?" I answer.

"Tell me what you want."

I don't hesitate to answer him this time. "You. I want you."

He yanks my shirt, ripping it off me. He does the same with my panties, and I stand naked before him . . . dying to be touched. He sheds his clothes quickly, grabs me by my waist, and plants his lips on mine. He spins me around until his back is facing the couch. Then he pulls away and sits in the middle of it. His eyes drag from my head to my toes.

"Jesus, you're so fucking beautiful." I straddle him, grinding against his hard dick. "You feel what you do to me, Shaya?"

"Yes." Moisture pools between my legs and drips on him. I grab his dick, gently rise, and place it at my entrance. His eyes meet mine right before I ease it in. I hiss, and he grabs my ass, squeezing it as I ride him. He allows me to take him as I wish while guiding me in the process. "Oh my . . ."

"That's it, sweetheart. Take it. Take it all."

As instructed, I take him deeper. "Baas . . ."

"Talk to me, baby."

"I . . ."

He leans forward and takes a nipple in his mouth. His tongue swirls around it, setting me off. "Oh God."

I explode, releasing around him until I have nothing left. He grips me as he comes inside me, grunting so loudly I'm sure people can hear. When he's finished, he grips me tightly and stands to his feet with me still wrapped around him. "Let's get you cleaned up."

Baas

I wasn't sure if coming to Shaya's suite was the right decision. At first, I thought it was best to leave her be. Things got tense between us after I made her leave the nightclub. I was so angry with her that I couldn't face her. But then I remembered what happened the last time we ignored each other. I was miserable. So, I had to see her. Even if it meant settling the dust and moving on with no hard feelings. We'll always be in each other's lives; the last thing I want is for us to be enemies.

I stare out her window as I sip my cup of coffee. I smile as flashbacks of last night creep into my brain. That smile disappears when I suddenly realize something. I've gone soft. I'm a trained warrior. I don't take shit from anyone, and I don't chase women. Women usually chase me. I don't let my feelings get in the way of logic. I don't spend time worrying about anything other than the king, his family, and my country. Shaya changed all of that.

My phone rings, interrupting my thoughts. It's Dafari. "Hey."

"Hey. You good? We missed you at this morning's meeting."

"Yeah, I'm good. I had some business to handle with Shaya."

The truth is that I'm not sure if we worked anything out. We had sex. But that isn't enough to fix our issues. We still have a lot to discuss.

"It's about damn time," he replies.

We both laugh. Before I ask the question, I check behind me to ensure she's still sleeping. "How did you deal with this, Dafari?"

"Deal with what?"

"Love. You, of all people, know I'm as tough as they come. But when it comes to her . . ."

He finishes my sentence. "You're vulnerable? Can't think straight without her? Can't imagine life without her?"

"Yes."

"I know this is all new to you. Hell, I'm shocked even to hear you say you love her."

"Tell me about it."

"I know you two have a lot to sort out, but if you're in love with her, you can fix this."

Shaya walks into the kitchen.

"I'll check in later."

I end the call and grab a mug from the cabinet, then pour her a cup of coffee, black like she likes it, and hand it to her.

"Thank you," she says softly, taking it from me.

She's blushing. Her hair is propped on top of her head in a bun, and she's wearing a T-shirt covering everything but her thighs. I get hard again but try my best not to act on it. "Are you hungry?"

She shakes her head. "No, but thanks for asking." She takes a sip of her coffee and places her cup down before she speaks. "Baas, about last night."

I grab her hand, not giving her the opportunity to finish. "I know what happened doesn't erase the past. I know we have things to figure out. But I want you to know that I'm here, Shaya. Whatever it takes."

She smiles before she responds. "I can't place the blame all on you. I take accountability for my role in the situation."

It feels good to hear her say it. She finally owns up to pushing me away. I bring her hand up to my lips and kiss it gently. She moves a piece of hair behind her ear and blushes again.

"Is that why you came here last night, to sort things out?" she asks.

"Yes."

"And what if I turned you away?"

"Then I would have respected your decision," I answer.

"That easily?"

I release her hand and lean against the counter. "Yes, that easily. I love you, Shaya. But that doesn't mean I'm going to continue chasing you. Especially when I've made my intentions clear."

I expect her to say something, but she doesn't. She rises to her feet and throws her arms around my waist, burying her head in my chest.

"You're right. I've been such a bitch."

I kiss the top of her head. "I never want to hear you call yourself that again."

She pulls away with tears in her eyes. "I'm so sorry, Baas. You asked me to stay with you. You asked me to let you figure out an alternative, and I . . . I ruined everything."

Her tears are falling at a rapid speed, and she's sobbing loudly. It's not my intention to make her feel worse than she already feels. So, I try my best to console her. "Hey, it's okay. You're here now, and we've had a chance to talk."

She shakes her head. "But you don't understand. I've ruined *everything*."

I have no idea what she means or why she's crying like someone just died. I'm about to probe further when my phone rings. It's Naomi. I let it go to voicemail and put my focus back on Shaya. I place both hands on her cheeks and look into her eyes. "What's wrong, sweetheart?" A flicker of pain flashes in her eyes, and she bites her lip. Something's wrong. Something not related to the fact that I married Nala. My phone rings again, and I don't even look at the caller this time. "Whatever it is, you can tell me."

She averts her gaze for a second, and my phone rings a third time when she opens her mouth to speak. Naomi has called me back-to-back, which means something must be wrong. But Shaya needs me right now. She takes a step back and wipes away her tears with the back of her hand. "You should get that."

"Nothing is more important than you right now," I respond.

"No. It's okay. I'm fine."

I want to push, but I don't want to upset her further. So, I answer the call, hoping to resolve whatever the issue is quickly. "Yes."

"Baas." Naomi sounds frantic.

"What is it?"

"It's Saleem."

CHAPTER SIX

Baas

I stare at the bright lights in front of me and the small boy on the stretcher. "How did this happen?"

"He fell from the tree."

"Naomi, you know the rules. The kids are not allowed to climb the trees."

"I know. I turned my back for one second."

I whirl around. "He could have died."

She squeezes her eyes shut. "I'm sorry."

"Do you have any idea how this makes us look? I pride myself on keeping a safe environment, and now . . ."

"It was an accident."

"One that could have been prevented."

"You know how overwhelmed I've been lately, Baas. I'm doing my best."

I realize I'm being too hard on her. Naomi does a great job running the place; she loves these kids as much as I do. I exhale loudly. "I know. And you do a great job, Naomi. But if you needed more resources, you should have told me. We can talk more about it later, but right now, I want to make sure Saleem is okay."

"So, I'm not fired?"

"No."

She throws herself at me and wraps her arms around me tightly. "Thank you. You're a good man, Baas."

I look up at the sky and roll my eyes. I don't have time for Naomi's flirty shenanigans, but I also don't want to be mean. I pat her back gently. "You're welcome."

She looks up at me. "I'll go check in with the paramedic."

She walks away, and I look up at the tall tree that Saleem fell out of. I then look over at the other two trees. I've always kept them to provide a shaded area for the kids to play in, but now, I'm contemplating cutting them down. I turn around at the sound of footsteps. It's Dafari. "I got your message. What happened?"

I shake my head. "Saleem fell out of that tree." I point to it.

He narrows his eyes. "Ouch, is he hurt badly?"

"I don't know yet. But I thought you should know. I know you care about the kids as well."

"Yes, of course. Thanks for letting me know." He looks around. "You've done one hell of a job with these kids, Baas."

"Thank you."

"Have you brought Shaya here yet?"

I shake my head. "No."

"What are you waiting for?"

"I don't know."

"Baas, if she's important to you, she must know everything about you. Including your history with this place."

I tap the pen on the table as one of the elders disagrees with Dafari about a law he wants to change. I'm too distracted to weigh in because my mind is overloaded with thoughts of Shaya and the orphanage.

"You're going too far with some of these changes," says Femi, our oldest elder.

"I disagree. I work hard to maintain our country's traditions, but times are changing, and sometimes, a country has to change with the times if it wants to grow," Dafari explains.

Femi shakes his head. "Not if it completely contradicts what we stand for."

Dafari looks over at me. "Baas, what do you think?"

I have no idea which topic they're discussing. My mind wandered somewhere between the legal age to drink and education requirements. Dafari must sense this because he stands to his feet.

"Let's add this to the next meeting's agenda. Thank you, gentlemen." We all rise from the table. Dafari calls after me when I reach the door. "Baas."

I turn around to face him. "Yes."

"You seem distracted. Are you okay? Is it Saleem?"

I shake my head. "No. He'll be fine. Just a broken arm."

"Then what's troubling you? I usually can't get a word in during our meetings, yet today, you were quiet."

I take a second to shut the door before I tell him what I'm thinking. I take a few steps toward him and shove my hands into my pants pockets. "I'm going to ask Shaya to marry me."

He's quiet at first. But then he smiles. "Are you sure?"

"I'm positive."

"When? Should I have the staff arrange something special?"

"No. But thank you. I'm going to ask her before she leaves for New York."

"Your life is here. What if she doesn't want to give up her life in New York?"

"That's what's been on my mind, and I think I have a solution."
I take a seat and gesture for him to do the same. "Dafari, we need
to talk."

Shaya

Baas received a phone call and took off in a hurry. I decided to take
some time for myself in the garden. I have a lot to think about.
Like, am I making a mistake by walking away from him again?
I take a sip of wine as the cool breeze and sound of the waterfall
relax me. Suddenly, I hear someone behind me, and I turn around.
It's him.

"I thought I'd find you here."

"Hey."

"I'm sorry I ran off like that. I had an urgent matter to attend
to," he explains.

"Is everything okay?"

"Yeah, everything is fine." He pauses for a moment. "Shaya,
last night, you seemed . . . upset. You were going to tell me
something before we were interrupted."

Shit! I almost forgot how vulnerable I was last night. I was
close to telling him everything. "It's nothing, really."

He watches me with scrutiny. "Are you sure?"

"Yes."

He inches closer. "The thought of not having you in my life
drives me crazy."

"I feel the same. I want you in my life too."

"I'm glad to hear you say that because . . ."

I interrupt him. "But I also know that as much as we may
want to be together, we still have so much that we don't know
about each other. A lot of time passed when we were apart."

"I don't care about any of that. I know what I want. And that's you."

Shit! My brain can never find the right words when I need them. He watches me, waiting for me to reply, but I can't think straight right now. My core tightens, and my breath quickens. I want this man so badly I can't stand it. Right here. Right now. Forever. But . . . I can't have him like this. Not while I'm hiding things. I reply in barely a whisper. "I'm going back to New York soon."

"Don't go. Stay."

What I wouldn't give to do as he's asked. The thought of staying here with Baas and my best friend fills me with happiness. But that happiness wouldn't last. Because at some point in my life, my past might catch up to me. And if it does, I can't be here with him. I shake my head. "I can't."

"Why not?" he asks.

"I have a life back home. I have a job. Responsibilities."

"Those don't sound like real reasons to me. Talk to me, sweetheart."

"I just . . . I'm not sure if this life is for me, Baas."

He places his hand over mine. "Come with me. I want to show you something, and then you can decide."

I'm relieved that the conversation has been cut short, so I rise and follow him. The driver is waiting for us at the end of the driveway. He opens my door, and when I'm safely inside, Baas joins me. I look over at him and smile. "Where are we going?"

He smiles back at me before the driver pulls off. "Someplace special."

We drive in silence for about ten minutes before we finally come to a stop. The driver opens my door for me, and when I step outside, I stare ahead at the brick building in front of us. Baas holds his hand out.

"Come on."

I place my hand inside of his, and we walk. I hear children laughing as we approach the building, but we don't enter through the front. Instead, Baas guides me to the backyard, where a playground is nearby. There are swing sets, sliding boards, and seesaws. The children run around the yard and play. Finally, one of them sees us.

"Baas."

We enter the gate, and he runs to us. Baas swoops him up. "What's up, little man? You doing okay?"

He slightly tickles him, and the little boy squirms and laughs loudly. When he stops, he looks over at me.

"I want you to meet someone very special to me. This is Shaya."

"Hi, what's your name?" I ask.

"Kenu."

Baas sets him down, and he runs off to play. "Baas, what is this place?"

"It's an orphanage."

"Oh."

"And it's also where I grew up."

I'm stunned. "You were . . ."

"An orphan? Yes."

I think of ways that Baas could go from being an orphan to being part of the royal family. I'm about to ask when a woman approaches us.

"Baas, it's so good to see you."

She hugs him tightly, and I frown. She's very pretty. Curvy, straight white teeth, and high cheekbones. They break away, but her hand lingers on him a little too long for my taste.

She looks at me. "Who do we have here?"

Baas holds his chin high. "This is Shaya."

She holds her hand out. "Hi, I'm Naomi."

I shake it quickly, trying my hardest not to show that I'm bothered by her interaction with Baas. My body is tense and hot, but I flash my biggest smile. "It's nice to meet you."

"Likewise," she replies.

"Is Saleem resting?" Baas asks.

"Yes, just as the doctor ordered," she responds.

Baas's expression turns serious. "What do the numbers look like this week?"

Naomi shakes her head. "It's not looking good. Only two kids were adopted."

He nods. "Anything else you need me to do?"

She blushes. "No. You've done enough. But thank you."

Something tells me they have a history, which makes me angry. My teeth grind, and my pulse quickens as I watch her lustfully stare at him. He's oblivious to it, or at least he's acting like it.

"Thank you, Naomi."

"Sure. Shaya, it was lovely to meet you."

Yeah, right. "It was lovely to meet you as well, Naomi."

I scowl as she walks away.

"Is something wrong?" Baas asks.

"No. I'm fine."

"Take a walk with me."

We walk the grounds with the children laughing behind us. "We shared a lot with each other, Shaya. But I never shared this side of me."

"Why not?"

"I don't know. It's not something I hide, but things moved quickly between us, and then you were gone. I guess I never got the chance. I asked you to stay here with me. And if you take me up on my offer, I need you to know me *and* my past."

"Okay."

"I grew up poor. My parents had little money, but they did their best. Unfortunately, they died when I was eight years old."

I stop walking. "Baas, I'm so sorry."

He turns to face me and continues his story. "When they died, I was sent here." He pauses to think before he continues. "I was angry at the world. I was angry at God for taking my parents away from me."

"How did they die? If you don't mind me asking."

"We had an outbreak. Some virus that was untreatable and incurable. My parents caught it and died."

"And you didn't catch it?"

"Yes, I did. But I survived." He clears his throat. "I felt guilty that I survived, and my parents didn't. I started many fights here. I was always getting myself into trouble. My temper was uncontrollable, so the teacher signed me up with a martial arts trainer. It helped release my anger, and it helped me focus. One day, the king was visiting. He happened to walk by right in the middle of training. He was impressed. He invited me to the palace to be a playmate for Dafari, but it turned into more than that."

"That's how you two became friends?"

"More like brothers. The king took notice of this and took me into the family."

"Why didn't he formally adopt you?"

"Adopting me would have made me first in line for the crown. I'm older than both Dafari and Enu. Not by much, but still."

"Oh."

"I come from poverty, Shaya. I'm blessed to be a part of the royal family, but I never forgot where I came from. The first thing I did when I was able was to come back and take ownership of this place."

This explains why Baas is so humble. I place my hand inside his. "Thank you for bringing me here."

Naomi chooses this moment to interrupt us. "There you are. I'm sorry to interrupt, but I wanted to catch you before you left."

"Is everything okay?"

"Yeah, everything's fine. It's just that the contractors will be here next week to start the pool, and I was wondering if you were stopping by."

Jesus, this woman doesn't give up. Baas nods. "That won't be a problem."

She blushes. "Thank you."

When she walks away this time, I shake my head.

"What is it?" he asks.

"You don't see it?"

"See what?"

"Naomi. She clearly wants you, Baas."

He takes a step forward. "Naomi and I have a history."

"I knew it."

"And that's exactly what it is. History."

"Did you sleep with her?"

"Yes."

For some reason, I didn't expect him to answer me so quickly. But that's Baas. Always honest. Always up front.

"It happened twice. And before I met you."

I take a deep breath. "Well, it seems you left a lasting impression."

His mouth curves in a smile. "Are you jealous, sweetheart?" When I don't answer, he closes the gap between us. "You have nothing to be concerned about."

I flash a silly grin right before he leans in and kisses me. When we break apart, the kids point and tease us, and Naomi frowns as she attempts to get them to calm down. Baas chuckles. "Come on. There's one more place I want you to see."

We drive back to the palace but don't go inside. Baas takes my hand, and we walk together for at least a mile, taking a path lined with bricks. We stop when we reach a brick home. It's large and lined with beautiful flowers and shrubbery. The trees in the backyard are tall enough for me to see from the driveway. "Who lives here?"

"No one yet."

The door isn't locked, and we walk right in. It's fully furnished and immaculate. I look around with amazement at how beautifully decorated it is. We enter the living room, and he heads straight to a picture on the mantle. I join him. "Who's that?"

"My parents."

I look closer at the picture and see the resemblance to his father. They have the same facial features and height. I look closer at his mother and see that he has her eyes. And eyesight, as she's wearing glasses.

"I bought this place for us, Shaya."

My eyes widen with surprise. "What? When?"

"Right before things fell apart between us. When I asked you to stay, I anticipated you would say yes. I wanted us to have some privacy outside of the palace."

"But I didn't stay. And you kept this place all this time?"

"Yes. I had hoped that one day, we would get a second chance. I want a future with you. Marriage. Kids. If you choose to stay, we can build our own life here in our home."

Every woman wishes to meet the man of her dreams, marry him, and create a family. It was also once my dream. But that dream faded away when I took matters into my own hands and went against everything I wanted.

"Baas, this is a lot. Your wife just died and—"

He interrupts me. "I had concerns about that too. But I don't care what people think anymore. I did right by her, and that's all that matters. I deserve to be happy now. *We* deserve to be happy."

This is overwhelming. I wasn't prepared for this, but this man never ceases to amaze me. Suddenly, I'm teary-eyed. My heart swells with emotion. He's done all this for me, and I didn't have the decency to tell him the truth. I try not to think about it because the guilt is eating at me so badly that I'm scared the truth will slip out. I fling my arms around him and press my lips against his. He wraps his arms around my waist and pulls me close to him. I pull away and pull my dress over my head, tossing it to the floor. Fire dances in his eyes as I slide my panties down. "I want you—now."

He undresses quickly, picks me up, places me gently on the couch, then removes his glasses. Jesus, this man is gorgeous. He places soft kisses all over my body, starting at my breasts and ending between my legs. I'm panting and so sensitive that the slightest touch sets me off.

"Do you have any idea how many nights I dreamed of this?" he asks.

I shake my head right before he takes the first lick. "Do you know how long I've waited to taste you again?" he continues.

He licks me gently before flickering his tongue in a rapid movement that makes me scream for more. I'm so wet I can feel my love box dripping. I want to savor this feeling forever . . . in case there's a chance I'll never feel it again. I grip the throw pillow behind me and cry out as I come. He rises and hovers over me before he enters me. I receive him, opening my legs wider for him to take all of me. "Baas . . ."

"Yes, baby?"

"I love you too."

How cliché to tell him I love him while we're having sex. But I feel vulnerable enough at this moment to do so. He grips me tighter.

"It's me and you, Shaya. Always."

"Yes, me and you."

Baas makes love to me, and it feels like nothing I've ever felt before. I feel closer to him this time—more in sync. We touch. We kiss. We grind, trying to meld our bodies together. He takes his time with me, savoring every single touch, kiss, and stroke. And when the end is close, he rises a little and looks me straight in the eye. I lose control and let go. "Oh God . . ."

"That's it, baby."

"Baas, I'm close."

"Let it go, sweetheart. I'm right there with you."

I moan loudly, squeezing the pillow in the process. He moans softly right before I feel him release inside me. He rolls to the side, breathing heavily and holding me tight. He kisses the top of my head.

"I know you have a life in New York. But I want you to know that I'm willing to give up my life here and join you if that's what it takes for us to be together."

"You mean that? You would give up all this . . . for me?"

"In a heartbeat. I've spoken with Dafari about it, and I would still advise him . . . from afar."

I grow quiet, and not because I have nothing to say. Instead, I'm in utter disbelief that Baas would be willing to make a life with me in New York.

"Do you want to take a nap? We can go upstairs to the bedroom," he asks.

I pull his arm around me. "No. The only place I want to be right now is in your arms."

Baas

I never thought it would be possible for me to fall in love. I didn't date much, and I put little effort into a woman other than making her come. There was no need to because I knew one day my wife would be chosen for me. It's how things are done in the royal family. I may not be royal blood, but I am still a part of the royal family. When I met Shaya, things changed for me. She swooped in and turned my life upside down. She showed me that I had a heart. That I could be vulnerable with her. My line of work is tedious and aggressive at times. I must always be on point and can't let my guard down. Because of this, I learned to suppress emotions and feelings. Because being emotional can get you killed. It remains a mystery how one could fall in love with someone quickly, but I have no intention of solving that mystery. The fact of the matter is that it was love at first sight. From the moment I met her, I wanted to make her mine. And one can't argue with facts. I'm whistling when Dafari walks into the room.

"Someone's in a good mood. I assume things went well when you took Shaya to see the house?"

I'm a gentleman. I don't kiss and tell. "Things went well. I'm just glad that we're on speaking terms again."

"So, did you pop the question yet?"

The ladies walk in before I can answer him. "Sorry, we're late. Aiden had a tantrum," Ebony says.

Dafari smiles at his wife. "I told you about spoiling him, Princess. It'll only get worse."

She waves him off as he pulls the chair out for her. I do the same for Shaya. When she's seated, we sit and wait for the servers to bring us dinner. I glance over at her, and she blushes. "I'm starving," she says as the servers enter and place her dish before her.

She doesn't know it yet, but she has a surprise under the lid. When she removes it, she grins. "Fried shrimp. My favorite."

During her brief time here, I remembered her craving fried shrimp. She said it was one of her favorites, especially with cocktail sauce. I made sure the chef made homemade cocktail sauce with the finest ingredients. She pops one into her mouth and savors the flavor as she slowly chews. It pleases me to know that she's satisfied. The rest of us dig into our meals, consisting of stewed chicken and roasted vegetables.

"Shaya, it's good having you here," Dafari says from across the table.

"Thanks, Dafari."

"Whatever you need, let us know. Our home is your home. I hope you know that."

She nods. "Thank you."

I look around the table as we all break bread together. This is what life is about. Family. Love. My eyes land on Shaya, and I know my life here won't be the same if she leaves for New York. I dread the thought of it and hope that after everything I showed her today, she'll consider staying. She doesn't need to be in New York to work. She can tend to the animals here just like she did before.

We laugh, talk, and joke as we eat our meals. Shaya and I steal glances across the table, and she blushes when I smile at her.

After dinner, I rush to my room to shower and change my clothes. I have a date planned for us. I planned it two days ago and can't wait to see her face when we arrive. I wanted to take her someplace nice, outside of the palace walls.

We arrive in front of the building, and security recognizes me. They allow us to skip the line and walk in. We take our seats right in front of the stage, and she looks at me curiously. "Are we seeing a show?"

I smirk. "You'll see soon enough."

The lights dim, and the performer walks on stage. He grabs the microphone, thanks us all for coming, and then the music starts. I can feel her energy shift as soon as he begins to sing. She grabs my hand and squeezes it tightly. The smooth, baritone sound of his voice has her in a trance. I lean over and speak in her ear. "Do you like him?"

"Yes. I don't understand what he's saying, yet I *feel* every lyric."

"He's our top artist. He just crossed over the charts, and soon, every household in the world will know his name. He's professing his love for a woman. She's the love of his life, and he's saying there is no one else on this earth for him but her." I know the feeling all too well. And if I could sing, I'd join him on stage and sing the song to Shaya myself.

When the show is over, my driver picks us up. Her cell phone rings, and when she answers it, no one replies. She disconnects the call, guessing it's the wrong number. We arrive at the palace, and I walk her to her room.

"I had fun tonight, Baas. Thank you."

"We didn't have much time to date before. I want to change that if you let me."

She nods. "I'd like that."

I want to invite myself in, but I'm unsure if she's up to having company, so I patiently wait while she unlocks her door.

"Would you like to come in?"

"Yes."

She opens the door, and I follow her in. I look around her suite, and my eyes land on the suitcase tucked in the corner of the living room. A reminder that she'll leave me at some point. Her phone rings, and again, there is no answer on the other end. It does it again three more times.

"Did you try calling the number back?" I ask with concern.

"The number is restricted. I hate when people decide to play on phones. It's irritating."

"Are you sure it's not someone you know?"

She turns around and smiles. "If you're asking if it could be another man, the answer is no." She kicks off her shoes. "Spend the night with me."

She doesn't have to ask because there was no way in hell that I would be leaving this room tonight. I would have slept on the floor if I had to.

"Okay."

"Good. Let's take a shower."

Before I can answer her, someone knocks at the door. She answers it, and one of the staff members walks in.

"I'm sorry to bother you so late, but you're needed in the stable."

Her brows narrow with concern. "What is it?"

"It's Claire, ma'am," he replies.

Shaya grew to like Claire during her time here. She bonded with her more than any of the other horses, and if she had the option to take her back to New York with her, she would have. "Is she okay?"

"We don't know," he replies.

"Let's go," I demand.

She rushes out of the room, and I quickly follow her. We exit the palace, and she jogs toward the stables. When she reaches them, she unlocks the gate and walks inside. Claire is lying down, and Shaya kneels beside her. Her caregiver joins us.

"Have there been any changes in her behavior?" she asks.

He nods. "Yeah, she's been less active. Not wanting any of us to touch her."

Shaya continues to stroke her softly. "She's lost weight. Has she been eating?"

"No. Not much," he answers.

She stops stroking her and examines her hair more closely. "Her skin is peeling a little. How long has she been this way?" She shoots to her feet with anger, and the caregiver becomes nervous.

"We . . . We've been caring for her to the best of our ability for two weeks. So when we heard you were back, someone suggested that you come to see her. We thought that maybe if she saw you, it would boost her spirits a bit."

I take a step forward and turn to the caregiver. "Thank you. I'm sure you all are doing all that you can."

He nods before he walks off, and Shaya stands before me with tears falling. "She's dying, Baas."

I carefully open the gate and walk inside. "Do you know what's wrong with her?"

She shakes her head. "Not offhand. But even if I did, it's too late to save her."

I pull her to me closely. "What can I do?"

"Let's just sit with her, so she's not alone."

We sit on each side of her. Shaya sits on the side where Claire can face her. She rubs her gently and speaks softly to her, assuring her that she's not alone. Claire groans a little but keeps her eyes on Shaya.

"She remembers you."

"Yeah." She looks over at me. "It's almost time."

I place my hand on the side of Claire's belly. Shaya does the same. Claire takes one big breath . . . and then stops breathing.

Shaya sighs. "Goodbye, sweet girl."

"Are you okay?"

She wipes away her tears. "Yes."

We rise to our feet just as the caregiver walks in. Shaya tells him that Claire has died, and he tells us that he and his team will take care of it. I'm escorting her out when she stops.

"What will happen to her?" she asks.

I take a minute to think before I answer her. "I'm not sure, sweetheart."

She turns and speaks to the caregiver. "What will happen to her?"

"We will cremate her," he replies.

"What? No, you can't," she replies.

The caregiver looks at me for guidance. "Bury her properly. I'll speak to the king about locations," I instruct.

"Yes, sir."

We leave the stable, and Shaya places her hand in mine. "Thank you for staying with me."

"You're welcome. I'll make sure she's taken care of, okay?"

She nods. "Okay."

"It's late. Let's go back inside."

When we enter her suite, we take the shower we were supposed to take earlier. Only this time, I don't touch her. She's deep in thought, and I'm sure she's not in the mood. I need to be a gentleman right now, but fuck, it's hard. I love animals just as much as the next person. But it's different for Shaya. She gives her heart to every animal she cares for, which affects her deeply when she can't fix them. I may not be as sad as she is about losing Claire, but I love this woman. So, when she hurts, my job is to be here for her. We've finished our shower and are both drying off in the bedroom. My back is facing her while I text Dafari. I don't want to call and wake him, so I text him about tonight's events and suggest a few places that are big and safe enough to bury Claire. Shaya calls my name right after I hit send.

"Baas."

I spin around. "Yeah?" My mouth drops open at seeing her naked. I put the phone on the dresser and take two big steps toward her. Still, I don't touch her as much as I want to. "Are you okay, sweetheart?"

She closes the gap between us. "Make love to me."

I pick her up, and she throws her arms around my neck. She wraps her legs around my waist and kisses me intensely. My erection becomes strained under the towel around my waist. When we reach the front of the bed, she gives me one last kiss before she unwraps her legs from around me. She lands on her feet and drags her hands from my chest to my waist. Then she yanks the towel from around me and tosses it to the side. She lowers herself slowly until she's on her knees before me. Her eyes stare into mine as she opens her mouth and wraps her lips around the tip of my dick, swirling her tongue around it.

"Jesus . . ." She wraps her hand around my shaft and takes the rest of me in. My hand rests on her head, and we don't break eye contact. I get harder and harder watching her suck me, and if I'm not careful, I'll come too soon. "Fuck, Shaya . . ."

"Mm-hmm."

I grip her hair, but I'm careful not to hurt her. "Move your hand." She drops it, and I step closer to her. "Open wider." She opens her mouth wider, and I guide myself deeper inside. She doesn't flinch. Her head moves back and forth as she sucks me harder and faster. "I'm close, baby. If you don't want me coming in your mouth, I need you to stop right now."

She doesn't stop. Her lips glide to the base of my dick, and I still. My head falls back with pleasure as I come. Finally, I release the grip I have on her hair and gently pull out of her. She rises to her feet and falls back on the bed, waiting for me to join her. I climb on top of her, placing my hand between her legs. "You're soaked."

"And waiting."

I'm hard again. I got that way the minute she fell on the bed, waiting for me to make love to her. "Well, I don't want to keep the lady waiting."

She moans the minute I enter her. She quickly grips me tightly and pulls me as close to her as possible. She needs to feel me in more ways than one. I make love to her gently and slowly, savoring every minute of it. And when we both come, we come together. Then she cuddles up next to me, resting her head on my chest.

"You know, I could get used to this."

I smile. "Oh, sweetheart, that's exactly what I want to happen."

CHAPTER SEVEN
Shaya

I open my eyes the following day, feeling anew. I turn over, and Baas is already awake, watching me.

"Good morning, sweetheart."

I will never get used to his accent . . . to the base of his voice. "Good morning, handsome."

He kisses me on the lips and tries to roll on top of me, but I stop him. "Before you go there, I'd like to shower first."

He looks taken aback. "Why shower if I'm just going to get you dirty again?"

I laugh out loud. "You're something else. You know that?"

He searches my eyes. "Have you thought about what we discussed?"

I have thought about it—a lot. I came here with a plan. I was supposed to be cordial to Baas. I was supposed to spend time with Aiden and Ebony, then head back to New York and live my life. But nothing happened according to plan. I didn't expect to reconnect with Baas. I didn't expect for my buried feelings to rise to the surface. Yes, my life is in New York. It's where I call home. But what I've learned is that there is no home without Baas. "Yes, I've thought about it."

"And?"

I can feel his heart beating fast with anticipation of my answer. I can also see the worry on his face. "Yes."

"Yes?"

"Yes. I'll stay."

His eyes light with excitement, and he smiles widely. "You've made me a very happy man."

"But I still need to go home and gather some things."

"You have all you need here. If you need anything else, I'll take care of it."

I giggle. "Baas, I still have to terminate my lease, shut off all the utilities, and say goodbye to my parents."

He strokes the side of my cheek. "I can have all that taken care of for you, but I understand you want to say goodbye to your parents. How about we plan to see them together? I'd love to meet them."

I'd rather take care of my business in person, but as I stare into his eyes, I see why he's reluctant to let me go. The last time he let me go, I ran and cut contact with him. He's afraid I might do it again, although he won't admit it. I give him a quick and tender kiss before I respond. "Okay."

He instantly relaxes. "I'll take care of it right away."

I smile. "Okay, thank you."

"I want you to be comfortable, sweetheart, so tell me, where would you like to live?"

The palace is beautiful. The staff is friendly, and I love being under the same roof as Aiden and Ebony. But I also like the idea of Baas and me having our own space. A place that the two of us can call home. "I'd like to live in the home you bought for us."

"I was hoping you'd say that."

His alarm rings, and he grabs his phone. He takes a deep breath before turning over to face me. "I've got to go, sweetheart. I have a meeting in twenty minutes."

"Okay."

"I have a busy agenda today, but how about you go shopping? You can get the things you need. Then I'll meet you at the house for dinner, OK?"

"Yes. Sounds good."

He kisses me once more before he rises from the bed. I lie back and stare at the ceiling as he walks away to shower. I've chosen to stay and have a life with Baas, meaning I may have to tell him the truth about me at some point. But I can't worry about that right now. For now, I want to keep the past behind me.

Baas gave me money, and I've been out shopping all day. I purchased all my hygiene products and some clothes until mine arrive. I also got some items for the home we'll share. The place is already decorated, but I'd like to put my spin on it and make it my own. I changed the curtains, put down a few area rugs, and added throw pillows to the living room. I kept the color scheme neutral, adding colors like beige and cream. I love the wall art, so I decide to keep it the way it is. I plan to redo the kitchen and our bedroom at some point.

While I was out, I also purchased groceries. Baas mentioned he would arrange for us to have dinner, but I texted him that I have it covered. I used to cook a lot, but when Jay and I split, I lost my passion for it. No way will I live in this gorgeous home, in this beautiful country, and not cook for my handsome man. I contacted the palace chef, Keo. I asked him to help me make one of Baas's favorites. I know nothing about cooking African food, and I wouldn't dare try it without help from a native. He was kind enough to come over and help me. He tastes a spoonful of the stewed goat, and I wait for his feedback. He chews it slowly, then swallows it before he places the spoon down.

"Perfect," he says.

"Are you sure I added enough of the curry?"

"Yes, he doesn't like it too spicy."

I look down in the pot. "Are there enough tomatoes?"

"Ms. Shaya, it's perfect."

"It should be. You stood here and guided me through it."

"And you did wonderfully. You followed my directions to the letter, and it's obvious you know your way around the kitchen."

"Thank you," I respond. "And thank you for making the jollof rice. I'm not ready to tackle that yet."

He chuckles. "It's easy to make. I can show you next week."

"Sounds good."

After we set the dining room table, he removes his apron. I follow suit before washing my hands at the kitchen sink. When we hear the front door close, Keo turns to me.

"We finished just in time."

I grin. "I can't wait for him to try it."

Baas enters the kitchen and stops. His eyes shift from me to Keo. "What's going on here?" he asks.

I step forward. "I made dinner for us tonight. Keo was nice enough to come over and help me."

His eyes soften. "You really didn't have to cook, sweetheart. But I appreciate it just the same. Keo, thank you."

Keo nods, says his goodbyes, and leaves. Baas closes the gap between us when we're alone and kisses me. He holds me tightly as his tongue explores mine. We finally come up for air, and he speaks.

"Suddenly, there's only one thing I'm hungry for."

I take a step back. "Oh no, you don't. I worked hard on this meal, and we *will* eat it."

He chuckles. "Okay. I can't wait to taste it." I cross my arms, and he raises his hands in surrender. "The food, I mean."

I give him a peck on the lips. "You can taste *it* for dessert. How about that?" I say in almost a whisper.

"Can't wait."

He washes his hands, then pulls out my chair for me as I sit at the table. He takes a seat across from me and looks down at the food.

"This looks delicious."

"Let's hope it tastes as good as it looks."

He takes a forkful of the stewed goat and shoves it into his mouth along with a small portion of the jollof rice. He watches me as he chews his food slowly. I don't touch my food because I'm on the edge of my seat waiting for his opinion. Keo gave it a thumbs-up, but his opinion doesn't count, even if he is the chef.

He leans back in his chair. "It's perfect."

My eyes grow wide. "Really?" He doesn't answer me. Instead, he smiles. "Right, you don't lie."

"Exactly. But if you need reassurance, yes, really. It's delicious, Shaya."

I'm happy with his answer, so I take a bite of my food, allowing the explosion of flavor to satisfy my taste buds. It's quite spicy, so I gulp my water after I swallow my food. "I've been thinking."

"About?" he asks.

"I'd like to become involved with the orphanage."

"I didn't know you had a soft spot for kids."

"I love kids," I reply.

"Really?"

"Does that surprise you?"

"No. It's just that we never discussed kids."

"We never got the chance."

He nods. "Good point. And I would love for you to help. Naomi needs all the help she can get right now."

I'm not happy about spending time around her, but I'm willing to put my feelings aside for a good cause. The orphanage is special to Baas. And if it's special to him, then it's special to me.

"Shaya?"

His voice snaps me out of my thoughts. "Yes."

"I said, do you want kids?"

My throat tightens at the thought. I'm not capable of motherhood, especially after what I've done. I was selfish and put my own needs above what was right. Baas loves children. I saw it when he took me to the orphanage. He probably wants a house full of them. But if he ever found out about how horrible of a person I am, he would change his mind about wanting me to carry his child. I chew my bottom lip before I answer him. "Yes. One day."

"Good. Because I can't wait to make one with you."

I feel the sweat gathering in my armpits and chest as anxiety rushes through me. "We have lots of time to think about babies, Baas. Right now, it's just you and me. I want to enjoy it before we add a little person to the mix."

I speak fast, hoping to get my point across quickly. When I'm finished, he smiles at me from across the table.

"I'd like that too, sweetheart."

Relief sets in that he's on board with waiting to have children. But maybe he'll change his mind once he sees how active I'll be at the orphanage.

We eat the rest of our meal while I rave about my decorating plans for the house. He watches me with a smile on his face, happy that I'm making this place a home for us. He tells me about his day and the important matters he needs to consider this week. This feels good. I feel at peace here with Baas. I feel safe and secure.

This man loves me. I can tell with every longing gaze. I can tell with every subtle touch. And there's no other feeling like it. Baas is my person. He's my soul mate. And as scary as it was for me to uproot my life and move to another country to be with him, I'd do it all over again. I'd follow him anywhere because I know he'll never steer me wrong. One day, I will tell him. I will tell him about the mistake that I made and beg him for forgiveness. I just hope and pray that when that day comes, he shows me mercy.

I shake away my thoughts. I'm getting emotional, and I don't want Baas to notice. This is a romantic dinner; spoiling the mood isn't on the agenda tonight. We finish our meals, and I'm just about to do the dishes when he approaches me from behind and wraps his arms around me.

"Housekeeping can take care of that," he says in my ear.

The deep rumble of his voice sends chills down my spine. I slowly spin around and throw my arms around his neck. "We don't need housekeeping. This is our home now, baby. I take pride in that."

"So, no help?"

"No. Only if I need it. But I got this."

He grabs the small of my back. "Why did that just turn me on?"

I giggle. "I don't know. But I like it."

He scoops me up gently and carries me up the stairs and into our bedroom. When he lowers me to the floor, I stand on my toes and place my lips against his. My body grows warm as he grips me by the waist. Finally, he pulls away from me and watches me seriously.

"Shaya, we're in this now. No matter what happens, we will get through it."

"Yes, I know."

"No running this time, okay?"

I smile. "I'm not going anywhere."

Baas

I'm in great spirits this morning. Yesterday, I came home to the woman of my dreams in the home we'll grow old in. Shaya and I have made our intentions clear with each other, but there's still a tiny part of me that fears she'll leave me again. And I hate it. I fear no one. I fear nothing . . . except for the thought of losing her. It's my weakness. I want her to be mine and take my last name officially. Shaya Osei.

I've been trying to find the right time to propose, but every time I plan to, I get cold feet. And not because I think she doesn't want to marry me. It's because I want it to be special. Unforgettable. Initially, I planned a lavish dinner with Ebony, Dafari, and members of the royal family. I quickly changed my mind and decided to make my proposal more intimate. My lady is simple and would have it no other way.

When we arrive at the orphanage, Shaya takes a deep breath and looks around. "How many kids are here again?"

"Right now, we have around 100 kids."

"That's a lot."

"Not really. We had more than that when we first started but were able to place them in good homes."

My heart swells at the idea of Shaya helping me oversee the orphanage. It makes me happy to know she'll be by my side as we fight to place these kids with loving families. She grabs my hand and squeezes it tightly when we walk inside.

"They're all so young."

"Yes, they are," I reply.

"Did their parents give them away?" she asks.

I nod. "Most of them, yes. The others lost both parents and had no other families." I grow angry as I say it. "I don't understand it. How could a parent not want their own child, especially a mother?"

Her hand grows sweaty before she releases it. "We never know what a person is going through. They could have had a good reason. Besides, isn't it better for them to be here than with parents who can't care for them?"

She makes a good point, but I stand firm in my thoughts on the matter. "In some cases, yes. But despite how well a family can love and care for them, most of these kids will grow up feeling abandoned and rejected because their parents gave them away."

She's about to respond, but Naomi walks in. "Baas, I'm so glad to see you." She bats her eyes at me and smiles before she turns to Shaya. "Shaya, nice to see you again."

"You too, Naomi," Shaya replies dryly.

"Naomi, Shaya will be joining me in overseeing the orphanage."

Her smile quickly turns to a frown. "Oh, I was under the impression she was only visiting the country for a bit."

"That was the case, but she agreed to stay. We're officially together again." I put my arm around Shaya as I reply to Naomi. For this to work, she needs to understand how important Shaya is to me and that she has zero chance of me ever sleeping with her again.

She places a piece of hair behind her ear. "Oh, well, that's such good news."

Shaya narrows her eyes, and I feel the anger rolling off her. She's not fond of Naomi. I knew it from the moment they met. And if it comes down to firing Naomi and making my lady feel comfortable, Naomi is out of here. "I'm going to take her to my office and go over some things with her before I head to the palace."

I guide Shaya down the hall with me and to the first office on the right. Once inside, I lock the door behind me to avoid interruptions. She looks around the room before she walks toward the window. She stares out at the kids playing in the back.

"They look so happy here."

I join her. "That's the goal. To see them happy and full of life."

She turns to face me. "So, what can I do?"

You can be my wife. That is the first thing that comes to my mind. But this is not the place to pop the question. "We need someone to be the face of the orphanage. Dafari and I have advocated for these kids, but I don't think we're relatable enough."

"What does that mean?" she asks.

"We need someone out there speaking about the importance of adopting. Someone who doesn't come from a royal background. Someone the people can connect with. I think that's you, sweetheart."

She nods. "I could do that. I don't think people understand how much you can change a life by giving a kid a loving home."

"I agree. In fact, I considered it myself."

She parts her mouth in shock. "You have?"

"Yes. I mean, I want us to have kids biologically. When you're ready, of course. But wouldn't it be wonderful to give a home to one of these kids as well?"

She laughs nervously. "How many kids are you talking about, Baas? I envisioned just one."

I kiss her on the top of her head. "If it were up to me, we'd have as many as this orphanage has. But I'll settle for two or three."

She looks up at me with soft eyes. "You would be an amazing father."

I pull her in and hug her tightly, never wanting to let go. If I keep this up, I'll have her on my desk, legs spread, and waiting for me. But we have business to take care of. "Let me show you the file where we keep the kids' profiles. This will help when deciding if a home is a good fit."

"Okay."

I turn on my computer and give her the password to all my files. I open the folder that has all the information on each kid. She points at one of the photos. "She's beautiful."

I enlarge the profile. "That's Nari. She's seven months old," I respond.

"She's just a baby."

"Yeah, I know." I spin around when I hear her sniffle and see the tears slide down her face. "Baby, what is it?"

She doesn't answer me. Instead, she wipes the tear with the back of her hand before she runs out of the office and down the hall.

Shaya

What was I thinking? I shouldn't have gone there. Seeing those kids and knowing I may never have any of my own triggered me. I couldn't handle it, no matter how hard I tried. I had to get out of there. So, I left and asked the driver to bring me back home. I needed time to get myself together. Time to calm the panic attack I was having. I hear the front door slam and the sound of Baas's footsteps. He rushes into the bedroom and searches my face.

"Are you okay?"

"Yes. I'm okay."

"Baby, what happened back there?"

I can't tell him the truth. Not now, and maybe not ever. "I . . . I got overwhelmed."

It's partially true. Seeing those kids back there stirred emotions I tried hard to bury.

He looks confused. "Overwhelmed? Because of the work? The kids? Talk to me, sweetheart."

"Baas . . ." *Don't do it, Shaya. Don't tell him.* "Seeing all those kids that need homes is just emotional is all. I didn't think it would affect me that way."

He releases a breath before his expression turns serious. "You can't just run off like that, sweetheart. I was worried."

"I'm sorry. I shouldn't have done that."

"Will you be okay? Do you still want to help with the orphanage? It's perfectly fine if you don't."

"Yes. I still want to help. I'll be fine."

He pulls his phone out of his pocket and sends a text. "Won't you lie down for a bit? I'll stay with you."

"But I thought you had a long day ahead of you?"

"I did. I'm texting Dafari to tell him I'll meet him later for an overview. Right now, you're more important."

Guilt sets in as I realize I'm interfering with his role. Baas is an advisor and the right hand to the king. Which means he doesn't get to blow off important matters. He needs to be present and always ready.

"No. I'll be fine. Please don't skip out on important matters because of me. The last thing I want is for people to think I'm affecting your reliability."

He chuckles. "Sweetheart, since when do I give a damn about what people think? I'm a very confident man, and I'm secure in my role to the king. So I can afford to skip a day and ensure my lady is cared for."

My heart melts instantly. I don't deserve this. I don't deserve him. I'm not worthy of any of the love and loyalty he's showing me because I'm hiding a secret from him. But I accept it just the same because it pains me not to. He guides me to the bed and helps me take off my socks. He slowly undresses me until I'm fully naked. "I thought we were lying down."

He smiles. "I said *you* need to lie down." He jerks his head to the bed. "Go ahead."

I do as he says and climb into the bed, lying on my back. "Are you joining me?"

He removes his tie and unbuttons the first two buttons of his shirt. "Not yet."

"Why not?"

He smirks. "Open your legs." I open them on demand. "Wider." When he's satisfied. He steps toward me and pulls me to the edge of the bed. "Let me relax you, baby."

He falls to his knees, and my head drops back when he places his face between my legs. I moan the minute his tongue makes contact. I grip the sheet as his tongue swirls and teases my clit. My legs grow weak, and my breathing is uneven as he fills me with pleasure. "Oh God . . ." my legs are wrapped around his neck, and he holds my thighs with sturdy hands. He's driving me crazy, and it doesn't take long before I'm close to the edge. "I'm close . . ."

He flickers my clit faster, and I lose it. I arch my back as the orgasm ripples through my body.

Finally, I deflate when he rises to his feet. "How do you feel?" he asks.

"Much better."

"Good."

He sheds his clothes, and I move to the middle of the bed. He climbs on top of me and kisses me passionately. My juices coat his lips and his beard. I can taste myself on him, making me want him more. I open my legs and pull him to me. He pulls his lips from mine and stares into my eyes as he enters me. He moves in and out of me with ease. Our bodies are close, yet I cling to him tightly. He makes love to me slowly and gently, allowing his body to speak for him. He's intense. He's focused as he pleasures me. And it doesn't take long for me to explode. My core tightens, and I cry out as I come. Then he comes right behind me. He kisses me once more before collapsing beside me. I inch closer and lay on his chest.

"I have plans for us tomorrow," he says.

"Really? What plans?"

"I can't tell you. But it's something special."

I smile. "You know I hate surprises, Baas."

"Yeah. But this one is worth it."

He kisses me, and I relax on his chest, wondering what his plans for tomorrow are. I bet it's another romantic date. Excitement fills me as I look forward to our alone time tomorrow. "I love you, Baas."

"I love you too, baby."

The sun peeks through the curtains, causing me to shield my eyes from the bright rays. "Good morning, sweetheart."

I turn over and see Baas staring at me. "Are you watching me sleep?"

"Yes."

"Why?"

"Because you're beautiful when you sleep."

I turn on my back and yawn before I reply to him. "I wouldn't say all that now."

He chuckles. "I have a spa day arranged for you. Ebony will be here to get you in a few hours."

"Is that my surprise?"

"Part of it."

My phone rings loudly, but I ignore it.

"Do you need to get that?" he asks.

"No. They can leave a message."

He's on top of me in an instant. "Good. Because there's nothing I want more than to be inside of you right now."

My phone rings again, and I stop him. "I'd better see who's calling. That might be my job. I haven't told them yet that I'm resigning."

"Yes. That's important. You need to let them know."

I climb off the bed and grab my phone. The number is showing as a restricted number, but I answer it. "Hello."

"We have Bailey." The voice speaks low and firm.

I grip the phone tightly. "Who is this?"

"We want $10 million, or she dies."

The line goes dead, and I drop to my knees. "No! No! No!"

Baas is at my side quickly. "What's wrong?"

I don't answer him. How can I when I haven't told him the truth? I'm hyperventilating and shaking, and I can see that it's frightening him.

"Shaya, what is it?"

This is the moment of truth. I can no longer hide this. Because if the person on the other end of that phone were telling the truth, I would need his help. "Baas, she's in danger."

"Who's in danger?"

"Our daughter."

CHAPTER EIGHT

Shaya

We're silent as we dress. I slip his shirt on, button it quickly, and roll up the sleeves. He swipes his pants off the floor, and a tiny velvet box falls out of his pocket. My eyes go wide. *That can't be what I think it is, can it? Is this what he had planned for me today? Was he going to ask me to marry him?* Tears sting my eyes at the realization. He slides the pants on, grabs the box, and shoves it back into his pocket. His expression is serious, but he remains speechless. "Baas, say something."

"Did I hear you correctly? Did you just say . . . *our daughter?*"

Tears fall as I nod.

"You were pregnant and didn't tell me?" he asks.

"I wanted to tell you."

"Why didn't you?"

"Because it wouldn't have mattered."

"I can't believe this." He paces the room.

"Baas, I'm sorry."

He stops. "You said she's in danger. Is she hurt?"

"I'm not sure."

"Where is she?" he asks.

"I don't know."

"I don't understand. What do you mean you don't know?"

"I didn't keep her. I couldn't keep her," I reply.

"Shaya, I need you to explain—right now."

"I gave her up for adoption."

His body stiffens. "Adoption?" I can see the wheels spinning as he thinks about my answer. "Is this why you ran off yesterday? You were thinking about our daughter the entire time we were at the orphanage?"

"Yes."

He shakes his head as he stares at me, making me feel more horrible than what I already feel.

"We created a life together. And you decided to give our baby away without *telling* me?"

"I thought it was the right thing to do."

He's quiet before he asks his next question. "Her name is Bailey?"

"Yes. Bailey Baas Osei."

Now that it's out in the open, I decide we've talked enough about why I did what I did. Right now, we need to save her. "The person on the other end of the phone said they have her. They said either we pay them $10 million, or she dies."

He spins around. "The money is no issue. I won't let them hurt her."

I exhale with relief. "Oh, thank God." I move to hug him, but he jerks back. A painful tightness forms in my throat, and my eyes water. "Baas, I never meant to hurt you."

He shakes his head. "You took something special from me, Shaya. I don't know how I can ever forgive you for this." His statement breaks me. My shoulders droop, and my mouth drops open, but no words escape me. Instead, he stares at me, and I can feel his anger and his pain.

"*How* could you do this?"

My head lowers with shame, and the tears fall. "I made a mistake, and I'm sorry." I think I see tears in his eyes for a quick second, which almost shatters me. "Baas, you have to understand how hard it was for me. I didn't want to raise her alone."

This seems to anger him more. "Do you really think that I would have left the two of you in New York to fend for yourselves? You think *that* low of me, Shaya?"

"No. That's not what I think at all. I knew you had responsibilities. Duties you couldn't get out of. I didn't want to make things difficult for you. I thought adoption was the best way."

"When was she born?"

"December 8. A year ago."

"Ebony flew to New York that week to see you."

My mind flashes back to that painful day.

"She's so little."

Ebony smiles. "She's beautiful, Shaya. It's not too late to change your mind. Are you sure about this?"

Tears fall from my eyes and drip on the white and blue baby blanket that cradles my daughter. "I have to do this, Eb. Baas has moved on, and there's no way I'm fit to be a single mother."

She rushes to my side. "Don't say that. You will be a great mom. This could change things, Shaya. Just . . . Call him."

I shake my head. "No."

The nurse walks in, and I know my few minutes with Bailey are ending. This is the one and only time I'll ever see my daughter again unless she chooses to seek me out when she's an adult. I take a few minutes to scan her face one last time. To take in all her features. She looks like Baas, which makes this even more painful. The nurse smiles at me. "They're ready for her."

I look over at Ebony, who's also fighting back tears but trying her hardest to be there for me. She pulls her phone out of her pocket and looks at the nurse. "Can we take a picture? Just one."

The nurse nods. I wipe away my tears with the back of my hand and pull Bailey closer. She stirs but doesn't cry. Ebony positions the phone to capture Bailey and takes one last look at me to make sure this is what I want. When I nod, she presses the button and snaps the picture.

"Ebony was with me when I gave birth. She was there to help me through the process. But please, don't be mad at her, Baas. I made her swear not to tell anyone."

"I'm not mad at her. I'm just glad someone was with you since you didn't trust me enough to call me."

"It had nothing to do with trust."

He stands tall with his chin held high. "I'll find our daughter, Shaya. And when I do, we will do everything possible to get her back. I don't care how attached the people are who adopted her, and I don't care how solid the paperwork is that you signed to give her to them. She does not belong to them."

"What if—"

He interrupts me. "There is *no* what-if. I will search the ends of the earth to save her and bring her home."

I've cried for hours on Ebony's shoulder. My eyes are wet and heavy, and time feels like it's slowed down with everything that's happened. "He's barely speaking to me, Eb."

"Shaya, he just found out some life-changing news. He needs space."

"I messed up big time."

"You did what you thought was right."

"I should have listened to you. I should have told him."

"You can't change the past. All you can do is move forward."

Dafari walks in, and I wipe away my tears. "What did he say?" I ask.

"His focus right now is finding Bailey. We've been on the phone all morning with our contacts in the FBI and CIA."

"You know people in the American government?"

He smiles. "Kings can't be successful without allies in other countries. Both my father and I have had strong ties with the American government. We've traded favors for years."

Ebony nods. "What are they saying?"

"Since it's a ransom, they won't go public. It'll risk her being harmed. They want to be more discreet about it."

"Okay."

"You and Baas will travel to New York tonight."

"We should go with them," Ebony says.

Dafari shakes his head. "Princess, I think it's best that we stay here for now."

I can tell that he doesn't want them involved in the mess I've created with Baas. And I can't say that I blame him.

"But we'll be on standby if you need anything, Shaya," he adds.

He nods at Ebony before he leaves the room. She turns to me. "If you need me, just say the word."

I shake my head. "I always need you, Eb. But right now, Baas needs me, and I need him. So we have to get through this together, just me and him."

Tears stream down her eyes. "Just know that whatever happens, you'll always have me."

Baas

New York

We make it to the hospital right after Ebony gave birth, and I watch Dafari swoon over his newborn. I'm happy for him. I really am. But right now, I can't focus because I'm too busy convincing Shaya to give us a chance. We're standing outside of the hospital room. She stands close to me, yet I feel she'll run again.

I close the gap between us, breathing evenly. "Shaya, how could I ever forget about you? You're everything to me. But . . ." She anxiously waits for me to finish my sentence. "I will leave you be if that's what you want. Tell me you don't love me. Tell me what we had didn't mean anything to you, and I will walk away and forget about you forever."

"Dafari and Ebony are safe now. You promised to put him and your country first, and now you must honor it."

"Dafari will understand. I can get out of this. Baby, just . . ." I'm suddenly speechless. I can feel her slipping away from me with every word I speak. "Shaya, I love you. You're all that matters. We can get through this together if you give us a chance. I will find a solution to this."

Her mouth quivers, and a tear slides down her cheek. "I can't do this, Baas. I'm sorry."

That was the last time I saw her. It was the last time we spoke. And I had no fucking idea that our baby was growing inside of her.

Nostalgia sets in as I step foot in the same penthouse suite I did over a year ago when Dafari and I arrived in New York. I tip the concierge after he sets our things down and send him on his way. When I close the door, Shaya speaks.

"I don't have to stay here. I can go to my place."

"No, you can't. Because whoever this person is could come after you next."

Words can't describe how furious I am. How could she do something like this? She made a selfish decision, taking away my choice and the opportunity to raise my daughter. If this had never happened, would she have told me? Would I have left this earth never knowing that I had a child?

"Baas, I understand you're angry with me . . ."

"Angry? I'm not just *angry*. I'm disappointed, Shaya. I'm . . ." I take a second to stop myself from breaking down. "I planned to ask you to marry me. To build a life with me. Now . . ." I take a minute to gather my thoughts. "You broke my goddamned heart."

I don't know how to feel about her right now. And I honestly don't know where we go from here. But it's not something I can think about at this moment because there's something more important I need to handle. And that's finding our daughter. A knock at the door interrupts us. When I swing the door open, Dafari and Ebony walk in. She rushes toward Shaya.

"Did you really think I would let you go through this alone?" she asks.

She hugs her tightly as she sobs in her arms. "Thank you, Eb."

"I love you, Shaya. We're family, and that's what family does. We stick together."

She looks at me when she says it. But I look away and turn to Dafari. "Thank you for coming."

He pats me on the back. "We took off thirty minutes after you two did. I wanted to give you both your space while you handle this. But someone reminded me we're brothers, and I need to be here." I look on as Shaya and Ebony speak softly. "Any news yet?" Dafari asks.

"Not yet. Right now, they're trying to see if they can trace the call that came through." We're silent before I say my next statement. "I'm a father, Dafari."

He smiles. "Yeah, you are."

"I have to save her."

"We will." He looks over at Shaya. "You two have had a long flight. Ebony and I will let you get some rest. We'll be right next door if you need us."

Ebony hugs Shaya one last time. Then she walks over and pulls me in tightly. She whispers in my ear. "We'll find Bailey."

Dafari clears his throat, and she releases me, smiling at me before they walk out. I spin around and face Shaya. "You should rest."

She shakes her head. "I won't be able to sleep knowing someone has her."

Fuck! I want to hold her as I rock her to sleep. I want to assure her I'll move the moon and the sun to find our baby girl. But I can't offer her the comfort she needs from me right now. So, I do the next best thing. I take a deep breath and offer her reassurance. "I will bring her home safely. Finding Bailey is what's important right now, and in order to do so, I need to focus. I can't focus if I'm also worried about you."

She places both hands inside of mine. It's our first physical contact since she told me the truth. I don't pull back this time because maybe, in a sense, I need this too.

"I'm scared, Baas."

Shit! This cracks my heart wide open. Watching her stand in front of me in pain and with eyes full of tears makes me hurt even more. I pull her in and hold her as she breaks down.

"I'm so fucking sorry. This would have never happened if I didn't give her up."

"You don't know that. Stop blaming yourself," I respond.

"You must hate me."

I pull away from her. "I could never hate you. I love you. More than anything in this world. It's just . . ." I break physical contact this time because I'm too vulnerable right now. I don't do vulnerability well. In fact, I don't recall being this vulnerable since my parents died. She watches me quietly, unsure of what I will say next. "I'll call for something to help you rest."

She nods before she walks toward the bedroom. I call the front desk and have them bring a bottle of melatonin. I pour a glass of water and take it to her. When I enter the bedroom, she's wiping tears. I hand her the glass and pill, and she gulps it down right away. Then she turns to face me when she places the glass down.

"Will you sleep with me tonight? Please, Baas. I don't want to be alone."

I'd love nothing more than to curl up beside her and hold her. I want to kiss the top of her head as I stroke her back and tell her how much I love her and the baby I've never met. But I have too much on my mind. Too much pain and pressure to rest comfortably with her. "I can't."

She nods. "I understand."

"Get some rest. I'll be here if you need anything."

She turns over to her side with her back facing me. Her body shakes as she sobs silently. I feel like a jerk for turning my back on her when she needs me the most. I'm acting like an idiot, and I don't want to hurt her any more than she already is. I move toward her but halt. Something inside me won't allow me to go to her. My mouth opens to offer some comfort, but I don't trust the words that may come out. So, instead, I do nothing. I turn around and walk out.

CHAPTER NINE

Baas

My phone rings, awakening me from a deep sleep. It's
Dafari. "Yeah."

"Any news?" he asks.

"No. Not yet. We're waiting to see if they call back."

He pauses. "How's Shaya?"

I take a deep breath. "She's hurting."

"And so are you. Cut her some slack, Baas."

"She's the one who lied."

"I'm not saying what she did was right. She should have told
you about the baby. I'm saying that we all make mistakes. Right
now, put your anger aside and be there for her."

"Okay. I'll let you know if I hear anything."

"Okay."

I end the call and stretch my body. This couch is big but not
big enough for me to sleep on it comfortably. I scroll through my
phone, check my emails, and confirm that I don't have any missed
calls. Shaya enters the room.

"Good morning."

She's wearing one of my T-shirts. Her hair is messy, and her eyes look puffy. "Good morning. Did you get any rest?"

She shakes her head. "No." She takes a seat across from me and folds her legs underneath her. "Any news?"

"No. Not yet. But keep your phone close in case they call back."

"Okay."

"You should eat," I suggest.

"I'm not hungry."

I pat the seat next to me. "Shaya, we need to talk."

She nervously sits beside me. "Okay."

"If we're going to find Bailey, it's important that I know everything. Can you start from the beginning?"

She nods. "Yeah. Of course."

She crosses her ankles before she begins. "I found out I was pregnant shortly after leaving Africa. But I was angry with both you and Ebony. I know she was only doing what she had to do to save Dafari at the time, but I was hurt. I thought I had lost you and my best friend. I ignored your calls and messages because I had no intention of ever speaking to either of you again. By the time I found out what had really happened and why Ebony had to send me away, I had already signed the adoption paperwork, and you were already set to get married. I figured you had moved on, and it was time for me to do the same."

This is harder to hear than I expected. But I allow her to continue without interruption.

"I was going to call you, Baas, I swear. But when I spoke to Ebony, and she told me you had gone through with the wedding, I . . . I changed my mind."

It's taking everything in me not to yell at her. To scream at her for not believing in us. Not believing that I was a good enough man to make this right. "Go on."

"Abortion was never an option for me. So, I had two choices. Raise Bailey alone or give her up for adoption."

I shake my head. "You had a third choice but chose not to take it."

"I know. I almost didn't go through with it. I fell in love with her from the moment they placed her in my arms. But I had already agreed, and the paperwork was in place."

"Who are the parents?" I ask.

"I don't know. It was a closed adoption. But . . ."

"But what?"

"I have a picture."

She leaves the room and returns with a picture in her hand. She hands it over, and I take it from her gently. My eyes water when I stare at the photo. Two tiny, brown eyes stare back at me. She's wrapped in a baby blanket with only her deep brown skin and curly hair exposed. "She's . . ."

She's beautiful. But I can't even bring myself to say the words without choking. This is my baby. A piece of me that I created with the woman I love. And I failed her. I failed both of them. Fuck! I can't take this. It's too overwhelming. I hand the picture back to Shaya and stand. "I need to shower."

"Baas, wait!"

But it's too late. By the time she calls after me, I've already disappeared down the hall.

The four of us listen to our agent, Telly, as he tells us how to help us get our daughter back. Shaya is listening, but I can tell her mind is too overloaded with grief to take in what he's saying. Ebony takes notes and consoles Shaya in between. Dafari and I listen to every syllable and explore every option. "Have you found the adopted parents yet?" I ask.

"Actually, we have."

"You have?" Shaya asks with surprise.

"Yes. Although, we had to pull some major strings to get this information," he responds.

"What are they like? Are we sure they had nothing to do with this?" Dafari weighs in.

"They're model citizens. Dad's a coach, and Mom's a teacher. They have no criminal history, not so much as a speeding ticket. The agency also vetted them before the adoption and labeled them as the type of parents every child should have," Telly replies.

"They're not her parents. We are," I reply angrily.

Telly watches me cautiously. "That may be, but legally, you two have no parental rights."

"But we will. We'll bring her back home," I say with confidence.

He looks between Shaya and me before he speaks. "Listen, I know how hard this must be for both of you. But I want you to understand that it will be extremely difficult to make any decisions on behalf of Bailey. Technically, you're *not* her parents."

If I hear him say that again, I'll punch him. Shaya gave birth to her. *She* is her mother, and *I* am her father. So I don't give a damn what any paperwork says.

"Well, maybe that's where we need to start," Ebony says. "Maybe we should talk to the parents."

Dafari shakes his head. "That may not be a good idea. We shouldn't interfere with police work, and speaking to them will only expose us."

"He's right. We're handling this case discreetly. Until then, we shouldn't contact them," Telly replies.

Shaya's phone rings, and we all jump. She looks down at the caller. "It's them. Should I put them on speaker?"

"No," Telly answers. "They'll know someone is listening."

She nods before answering the phone. Helpless, I watch as she speaks with the person on the other end.

"Yes. Uh-huh. Where? When? Okay. I won't." She pauses before she asks her next question. "Can I see her, please? I need to know she's okay. Fine."

When she ends the call, she takes a deep breath.

"They'll call me back soon with instructions on where to meet. They're also going to send me a picture."

Telly stands to his feet. "Now that we know the number they call from is untraceable, we must resort to plan B. Do you have the money ready?" he asks me.

"Yes, every cent," I reply.

"Okay. We'll arrange for the drop-off," he responds.

"I don't want Shaya to go. It's too risky. Dafari and I will go. Whoever this is, they're no match for us," I explain.

"No. If I don't follow their instructions, they could hurt Bailey," Shaya replies.

Telly looks between me and her before speaking. "How about I let you two talk? Give me a call once you've decided."

"Okay," I reply.

Dafari and Ebony follow suit. They both hug Shaya and tell us they'll check on us later. When Shaya and I are alone, I repeat myself. "You're not going. I can't put you and Bailey in danger at the same damn time."

"I'm going to do whatever it takes to make sure she's not harmed," she argues.

Her phone dings from a notification, and she checks it. She smiles and places her hand over her heart.

"It's her. They said they would text me a picture of her to show me she's okay."

She hands the phone over to me, and I view the picture. She's bigger now and looks just like her mother. "Shaya, she's . . . She's beautiful." I plop down on the couch. "How is it possible to love someone I haven't even met more than I love myself?"

She sits beside me. "Parental instinct."

We're staring at the picture together when she receives another notification—this time from her dating app. I frown as I read the message from the stranger, asking to get to know her better.

"Oh, sorry about that. I didn't get the chance to delete the app," she says as she grabs the phone from me.

I don't like what I just saw. But I'm too exhausted to argue about it now. Not while we're trying to save our daughter. Right now, things are off between Shaya and me. I don't know if we'll pick up where we left off or if this situation is too much for us to return to the way we were. But I do know that even while I'm angry with her, I can't stand the thought of another man giving her attention. It makes it even more complicated because even if we don't make it through this, I will always consider her . . . mine.

Shaya

I think about what Baas said to me. He said he *wanted* to marry me. He was direct and clear when he used the word in the past tense. My suspicions were correct when I saw that little black box fall to the floor. It contained a ring. A ring I'll never get the chance to wear. Baas was going to ask me to be his wife. And now, that will never happen. I pick at my food while I sit across the table from him. He ordered lunch and pretty much demanded that I eat something, but I'm tired. Both physically and mentally. All I want to do is curl up in bed and sleep.

"We need to go see your parents."

I look up from my plate, giving my attention to him. "Why?"

"To tell them about Bailey. And to put proper measures in place to ensure they're safe."

"How about I just call them?"

"And give them news like this over the phone? Shaya, I think you should tell them face-to-face."

He raises a good point, but I don't feel like explaining to them who Baas is. When I told them I was pregnant, they wondered who the father was. I told them that it didn't matter and that I would most likely never see him again. They assumed it was Jay, and I didn't confirm otherwise. Baas interrupts my thoughts.

"You don't want me to meet them? Is that what this is about?"

I shake my head. "No. It's not that. This is just a lot to deal with."

He nods. "I understand. Are you and your parents close?"

"Yes. I'm the only child."

"Did you have a good upbringing?"

"Yes, I did."

We're quiet for a second before he asks his next question.

"When we first met, we spent a lot of time together, talking and getting to know each other. But we never mentioned kids. It's probably a little too late to ask you this, but did that have something to do with you choosing adoption? Were you being dishonest when you told me a few days ago that you eventually wanted kids?"

"Before you, I never wanted kids. I considered myself too selfish to be a good mother. But then I met you and wanted everything with you. Marriage. Kids. The house with the picket fence. Baas. When I found out I was pregnant, I was happy at first. Each kick made me want her more. Each sound of her heartbeat made me want to be the best mom I could be for her. But I also had to be realistic about the situation. I was messed up inside. I was heartbroken over you. I was still figuring out what my next career move would be. She deserved a stable home and stable parents. Not two parents who live on separate continents."

It pains him to hear me say it. I can tell by his expression.

"Bailey deserves two parents who love her, regardless of their circumstances. And that's us," he responds.

It's an accurate statement. I never stopped loving Bailey. And I know Baas loves her too, even though he's never seen her. Not a day goes by that I don't think about my daughter. But I also find comfort in knowing that she's with parents who don't come with all the complications we come with. Baas isn't seeing the big picture. In his mind, Bailey is his. And he won't stop until he has her. "When they find her. Do you really want to fight to get her back?" I ask.

"Of course I do."

"And what about us?"

"What about us?" he asks.

"Will we be together, and if not, how will we coparent? Will we split weekends and holidays with her? Fly her back and forth between New York and Africa?"

"What are you getting at, Shaya?"

"What I'm getting at is that it's not fair to pull her out of her home when we can't even get our shit straight. It would be selfish and mean."

He takes a sip of water before he replies. "We may not have things figured out between us yet, but we'll find a way to make this work."

He doesn't get it. And I'm done arguing with him about it. I jerk to my feet, sending my chair flying over the tile. It hits the wall with a bang as I storm out of the room. When I reach the bedroom, I fall into bed and cry. I hear him enter, and the bed dips as he sits on the edge of it. He places his hand across my back.

"I didn't mean to upset you."

I don't reply because I'm too busy crying.

"Shaya, I'm sorry . . . for everything. This whole situation is just as much my fault as it is yours. I didn't make you feel secure, and you had every right to question my love for you and my loyalty."

I rise to look at him as the weight of some of my guilt sheds piece by piece. "Baas, you have no idea how much I needed to hear you say that."

He embraces me, and I cling to him tightly, dreading the moment I must let him go. My eyes close as he kisses the top of my head. I exhale my breath when he strokes my back, offering me comfort. I let myself go in his arms, allowing him to carry me and my pain. My eyelids become heavy, and my arms go limp as I drift off to sleep. I try my hardest to fight it, but I'm losing. So, I give in. But not before I hear him speak to me.

"I love you" is the last thing I hear before I fall asleep.

CHAPTER TEN
Shaya

My mom pulls me in an embrace. "Oh, honey," she says.

I sob heavily, wetting the crook of her neck with tears. She squeezes me tightly, allowing me to let it all out. When she releases me, she wipes the tears away.

"It's going to be okay. We will find her."

I look across the room just in time to see Baas staring at the family photos above the fireplace mantle. When he spins around, his eyes meet mine. They swirl with sadness, but only I notice it. Baas is great at hiding his thoughts and feelings but can never hide them from me. I know him too well. I take a step back so I can make a proper introduction. "Mom, Dad, this is Baas. He's Bailey's father."

My father extends his hand and offers Baas a firm handshake. My mother, however, is a bit more informal.

She pulls him in a hug. "Oh, you poor thing."

He goes along with it but glances at me when he pulls away. Then he clears his throat. "I want you both to know that I'm doing everything in my power to find Bailey."

"What are the police saying?" Dad asks.

Baas shakes his head. "We haven't involved the local police."

Confusion crosses my mother's face. "Why not?" she asks.

Baas shoves his hands in his pockets as he answers her. "I have my own people. They're helping us."

My dad chuckles but stops when he sees that we're not laughing. "You're serious?" he asks.

Baas nods. "Yes. This isn't something to joke about."

My dad asks his next question. "What kind of work do you do that gives you personal access to law enforcement?"

I answer for him. "Dad, please, not now."

I can tell he and my mom want to probe more, but they don't. And I'm grateful because this is not the time to explain. Baas takes a deep breath before he speaks.

"I'm sure you both have questions. And I'll be more than happy to answer them . . . once we've found Bailey. Right now, my focus is on saving her and keeping you all safe."

My dad nods and folds his arms. "We didn't get the chance to meet her. But she's still our granddaughter."

My mom stands. "Let's take this into the kitchen. I think we could all use some coffee."

"Thanks, Mom."

We follow her into the kitchen. My father and I take a seat, but Baas remains standing. "Would you like any help?" he asks.

"I've got it. But thank you," Mom replies.

Baas takes a seat next to me and places his hand over mine. My mom smiles when she catches a glimpse of it. She pours four cups of coffee and takes a seat across from us. I take a sip and close my eyes, hoping the caffeine will kick in quickly. Although I could sleep a few hours last night, I still feel like I'm running off fumes. My mom breaks the silence.

"Baas, thank you for looking after Shaya. I can only imagine what you two are going through."

"It's my honor to look after her," he replies.

"You have an accent. Where are you from?" she asks.

"Africa."

"Do you live here, in New York?" she continues.

"No. He lives in Africa, Mom."

She looks between us. "When on earth did you visit Africa, Shaya?"

"It's a long story. I'll fill you in when things settle a bit," I reply.

"Is that why you two decided to give Bailey up for adoption? Because of the distance?" Mom continues.

I almost spit my coffee out. My inquisitive mother has no idea of the wounds she's reopening by asking that question. I lift my mug to my lips but glance at Baas as I drink. He's wearing a poker face right now, and I have no idea how he will answer her question. Hell, I don't even know how to answer her question. The backstory is much too detailed and complex to get into right now. And if I tell my mother the short version of it and admit that Baas only just found out he had a daughter because I gave her up without his knowledge or consent, both of my parents will be extremely disappointed with me. And they would have no problem letting me know that right here in front of Baas. Baas looks at me and opens his mouth to speak.

"There were many reasons why it was a good idea at the time. But now, we're reconsidering the decision."

I shift in my seat. This couldn't have been easy for him. Baas is one of the most honest and genuine men I've ever met. He takes pride in telling the truth, even if he knows it will hurt someone to do so. But just now, in front of my parents, he did the one thing he avoids at all costs . . . He lied. To protect me. My eyes swell with tears as I'm reminded of just how much I've fucked things up. I jeopardized my daughter's life, and I've lost the love of my life. I suddenly need some air. I place my mug down and rise to my feet. "Excuse me."

I rush out of the kitchen and onto the front porch. By the time the door slams, I break down in tears. The screen door squeaks as it opens, and Baas steps onto the porch.

"Are you all right?"

I can be stubborn. I'm as strong as they come. And when people ask me if I'm okay, my answer is almost always yes. But right now, I don't want to be strong. I don't want to hide how I'm feeling. This is not the time to be a superwoman. This is the time to hang up my cape and accept that I'm losing my shit. I shake my head. "No, Baas. I'm a mess."

He pulls me in an embrace. "I know."

"Thank you for what you did back there. I know lying goes against what you stand for."

He pulls away gently and looks me in the eyes. "Shaya, I might not like what you did, but I know you had your reasons. You can tell your parents about it when you're ready."

His eyes suddenly avert over my shoulder, and he cranes his neck a little. I turn around to see what he's looking at and notice a black SUV with tinted windows parked two houses down. When it slowly moves forward, Baas opens the door and shoves me in.

"Lock the doors. Get your parents and hide."

Panic fills me. I slam and lock the door but don't follow his orders. I'm too worried about him. Instead, I rush to the window. I see the car speed past with Baas running behind at top speed. My hand flies to my mouth when he pulls a gun from his waist. The car swerves around the corner and disappears before he can fire it. He tucks the gun back into his waist and grabs his cell phone. He makes a call as he runs back toward the house. I quickly unlock the door for him when he steps on the porch. He walks right in and grabs me, searching my eyes.

"Are you okay?"

"Yes, I'm okay."

My parents walk in at that moment, and confusion sets in when they see the look on Baas's face and me.

"What's going on?" Dad asks.

Baas turns to face them. "You're in danger. I need you both to come with us. Now."

I'm still on edge from the events that transpired earlier. Baas said I could be in danger, but seeing it up close and personal made it real to me. What's worse is that I have no idea how much danger Bailey is in. But if given the chance, I'd gladly trade places with her. Baas paces back and forth as he listens to whoever is on the other end of the phone. He's giving one-word responses.

"Yes."

"Uh-huh."

"No."

"Okay."

"Thanks."

He stops pacing when he ends the call. "Your parents are somewhere safe."

"Where?"

"It's best you don't know. But they're safe and have everything they need until we get to the bottom of this."

"How would someone know where my parents live? Do you think the person behind this is someone I know?"

"Is there anyone out there that would want to hurt you?" he asks.

I shake my head. "No. Before you, I lived a very boring life."

He takes a deep breath. "Then whoever this is knows more about you than we thought."

I check my phone. "They haven't called back, Baas. I'm worried. I'm so scared for Bailey."

He slides his hand down the front of his face, anger etched in every crease and crevice. "Fuck!" he says in a voice laced with frustration.

The next thing I know, he knocks everything off the nearby accent table—a vase, books, and a lamp crash to the floor.

"FUUCCKK!" he yells.

I hurt for him because I know how he's feeling. Baas is an overachiever. A fixer. He's always had power at his fingertips. But in this situation. A situation that's between the life and death of someone so precious to him, he's powerless. I move to comfort him, but he holds his hands up.

"Just . . . Give me a minute."

I step back, and he storms down the hall and slams the bedroom door.

Baas

I'm feeling a lot of emotions right now, and they're all crashing into me like a tsunami. My helpless baby daughter needs me right now, and I have no fucking clue how to save her. If something were to happen to her, I'd never forgive myself. I grab my phone and call Telly. I don't allow him to finish saying hello before speaking. "Any leads?"

"Not yet."

"My daughter is out there, Telly. She could be hungry, sick, or hurt. I need you and your men to find out who the fuck has her and where they're located so I can go there and slice every one of their throats . . . slowly."

"Baas, we're on it."

"Obviously not. It's been a whole goddamn day, and you mean to tell me you guys *still* don't have shit?"

"I assure you this is our top priority. We will find her soon. I'm sure of it," he responds.

"You'd better. Because if anything happens to her because you didn't do your fucking job, all of you will have to deal with me. And trust me. You don't want that."

I end the call and toss my phone on the bed right before someone knocks lightly on the door.

"Baas."

I take a few deep breaths to calm myself enough to open it, but Shaya walks inside before I get the chance. I pace the floor, angry at the world and ready to kill anyone in my path.

"You shouldn't be in here right now, Shaya."

She walks toward me slowly, and when she reaches me, she gently places her hand on my forearm. I stop and look at her, and when our eyes meet, she nods.

"It's okay." She slowly flings her arms across my shoulders and lightly rubs the back of my neck. "I'm here. No one is here but you and me."

I don't know what she means right away, so I stare at her, wondering what the hell she's talking about. But then it hits me. As I stare into her eyes, I don't see sadness this time. I don't see fear. I don't see panic. I see strength.

She's being strong. Long enough for me to . . . *feel.* As this exchange of internal strength happens, I break. I've only cried once in my life, during my parents' funeral. When the first tear falls, she pulls me in tighter.

She speaks softly and gently. "It's okay. I know you're hurting."

I squeeze her tight. So tight, I fear I'm hurting her. And I let it out. I don't all-out sob. And I don't soak her with tears. But I shed enough to release my pent-up pain and frustration. It lasts a second before I remove her and wipe the tears away with my hand. She watches me with tenderness and affection, and I watch her with renewed wonder. I had no idea I could fall more in love with her than I already am. She showed me what it means to feel safe enough to be in your most vulnerable state. She showed me what it means to offer yourself to someone in your most raw, unfiltered, purest form . . . and have that person love you anyway. She brings out sides of me I didn't know existed. She brings forth emotions in me I didn't think I could feel. How hard it must have been for her to hold her own emotions in. To hold herself up and allow me to have a weak moment. I don't take what she just did for me lightly. "Shaya . . ."

She shakes her head. "Shh, you've been holding me up this entire time, Baas. It was time for me to do the same for you."

I yank her to me and place my lips on hers. Fireworks explode between us, and not in a sexual way. I think we're both too mentally occupied to think about that right now. But sparks burst between us as we connect once more since she first told me I have a daughter. We hold each other tightly. We kiss. We find comfort in each other. And it feels so fucking good.

Shaya

I knew what I needed to do. I could see it. He was minutes from exploding because he was holding his emotions inside. Baas has been the strong one throughout all of this. He's kept it together and allowed me to fall apart. And by doing so, it made him bottle up what he was feeling and lash out. I had to do something. I had to show him I could be strong for him, if only for a minute. This way, he could feel. He could vent. He could release without fear of me crumbling with him.

There's this rule in our community that men can't cry because it makes them look weak. And I'm willing to bet money that Baas has never cried in his life. But for a situation like this, where his baby daughter's life is in jeopardy, he said fuck the rule. He cried for his daughter. He cried for the pain that both of us felt. And not only do I respect him for it, but I'm also grateful that he trusts me enough to allow me to see that part of him.

We're lying in the bed, fully clothed and intertwined. Silence fills the room as he softly strokes my hair. Neither of us is tired. Neither of us knows what to do right now other than wait. Wait for the next phone call from the kidnappers. Wait for an update from Telly. And it's killing us both.

He breaks the silence. "I want her back, Shaya. I want the chance to be a good father to her."

I look up at him. "Me too."

I don't address the pending issue of our relationship. I don't ask questions about how it would work with us living on opposite sides of the world because none of that matters right now. Baas yearns to see and get to know his daughter. Honestly, I'm yearning for the same.

"We need to speak to the adopted parents. I need them to know what my intentions are. But not until we find her. I don't want them to know we're looking for her. Technically, we're interfering with the NYPD's investigation and could be arrested."

"And when we find her? We can't just run off with her. We could be arrested for that as well," I remind him.

"We'll deal with that when the time comes."

It's a sore subject. I feel bad about giving Bailey to two loving parents who provided a stable home—only to ask for her back. But I also know I made a horrible mistake. Either way, it's something that needs to be addressed sooner than later. "Okay."

He continues stroking me softly, and I say nothing more. I'm in deep thought about how all this will play out. I have a feeling this won't go over well with the adoptive parents. It could be drawn out in court for months or even years. Are we prepared for that? Are we prepared to get Bailey back only to lose her again if the judge denies our request to reverse the adoption decree? What if the adoptive parents get so angry with us that they refuse to let us see her? Baas senses I'm worried.

"What's on your mind?" he asks.

"Nothing in particular. I'm just worried about her."

He takes a deep breath. "Yeah, me too."

We both grow quiet again, and I close my eyes, hoping to catch a few hours of sleep. My mind and body are both exhausted.

"Shaya?"

"Hmm."

"How long were you in labor?" he asks.

"Six hours."

"Were you in a lot of pain?"

"Yes, but the pain meds helped," I reply.

"How much did she weigh?"

"Five pounds, eight ounces."

I swear I hear his mouth curve in a smile as he imagines me giving birth. I tell him a few more details. "She made a huge fuss. The nurses said she's feisty."

He chuckles. "Like her mother. You're feisty. And sometimes, downright defiant."

"True. But she looks so much like you."

He doesn't reply to me. Instead, he pulls me in tighter and kisses me on the top of my head just as I close my eyes to try to remember the scent of my newborn baby girl.

CHAPTER ELEVEN
Shaya

I review the paperwork closely, paying close attention to the fine print. It's a must when making one of your life's toughest decisions. When I'm done, I look up at the intake counselor. "So, I'll never get to see her again?"

She nods. "That's usually how a closed adoption works. Once she's with her new parents, all contact between you will cease unless they decide to involve you."

It hurts just to think about it. The idea of giving my daughter away to strangers and never seeing her again doesn't sit right with me. But do I have any other choice? The counselor senses my hesitation.

"Shaya, I know this is tough, but you don't have to decide immediately. Won't you go home and think about it?"

I shake my head. "No. This is what's best."

"And you're sure you don't know who the father is?"

For a split second, I think about calling Baas and telling him everything. But he's married now, and the last thing I want to do is cause commotion after everything they've sacrificed to become a peaceful country. I shake my head. "No. I don't know who he is."

My response makes it final for me. I grab the pen and quickly sign the adoption agreement before I can change my mind.

The loud knocking interrupts my dream and causes us to jolt out of our sleep. Baas jumps out of the bed and rushes out of the room. I follow him and arrive just in time to see Dafari, Ebony, and Telly enter the living room. Ebony hugs me.

"How are you holding up?" she asks.

"I'm trying my best," I reply.

Dafari and Telly nod, and we all sit. Ebony grabs my hand and holds it.

"Tell us what you know," Baas orders.

"Took us awhile, but we were able to get a trace on the text message they sent," Telly responds.

Baas shoots to his feet. "Okay. Let's go."

Telly holds his palms out. "Not so fast, Baas."

"We know where it came from, so what are we sitting around talking for?" Baas asks.

"I've dealt with these kinds of cases thousands of times. You don't just go barging into an unknown situation. It could jeopardize your life and Bailey's," Telly explains.

"I don't give a damn about my life right now. All I care about is hers," Baas argues.

"Baas." Dafari says his name calmly. "Let's hear what the plan is. If it isn't solid, you and I will go ourselves."

This seems to calm him a little. He looks over at me before he plops back down on the couch.

"Okay. What's the plan?" he asks with irritation.

"We think the best thing to do right now is surround the area. We'll wait until they call back. I'm sure that will be soon. You make the drop, and then we move in," Telly replies.

"No. There's no guarantee I'll get Bailey back once they get their money. And I can't have you guys rushing in guns a-blazing with Bailey in the vicinity," Baas counters.

"Then we negotiate when they call. They bring Bailey out, and you make an even swap. Once you have Bailey safely in your arms, we move in," Telly suggests.

As if on cue, my phone rings. I gasp when I see the caller. "It's them."

Telly leans forward. "Put it on speaker."

I hit the answer button and then hit the speaker. "Hello."

"235 Mansion Park Road. Seven p.m. Bring the money," the nameless person demands.

"Wait—" The call ends before I can say anything further.

Dafari speaks. "Is that the location you traced it to?"

Telly looks through his notes. "Yup."

Baas stands. "Good. Then it's confirmed. Let's put the plan in place."

I pull Ebony in in a tight hug. "We found her."

She releases me and nods. "I knew we would," she replies.

I stand to my feet. "I'm going with you."

"Shaya, no," Baas responds sternly.

"But I need to be there—"

"No. It's enough that I have to worry about Bailey's safety. I can't worry about you both."

"Baas, they want *me* to deliver the money. If they see anyone else, it could upset them, and they could hurt Bailey."

Telly nods. "She's right, Baas. She has to be the one to deliver the cash."

"I don't want to take that risk," Baas replies.

"But we have to." Dafari weighs in. "It's the only way this plan will work without them getting suspicious."

Baas shakes his head. "I don't like this." He looks at me, then back at Dafari and Telly. "But I guess I have no other choice."

Ebony places her hand on my shoulder. "I'll be right here waiting for you to get back."

Baas nods. "OK, it's settled. Let's get ready. We'll meet you downstairs."

Telly stands to his feet. "I'll instruct my men to proceed. The van will be outside to pick you up at six."

Ebony stands and gives me a big hug. "Please be careful, Shaya." She looks over at Baas. "And you too, Baas."

He nods. Dafari takes her hand. "I'll take her back to the suite and get her settled. I'll be back shortly."

As soon as they're out the door, Baas faces me. "You ever shot a gun?"

I sit nervously in the driver's seat of the Chevrolet Malibu. The tiny piece in my ear is foreign and slightly uncomfortable. "Shaya, can you hear us?" The sound of Telly's voice enters my ear loudly.

"Yes. But it's loud. Will they be able to hear you speaking in my ear?" I ask.

"No. But the volume must be loud enough to hear each other over any commotion. Did you enter the address in the GPS?" he asks.

"Yes."

"Okay. We'll be right behind you, but we'll veer off the closer you get. We don't want to alert them."

Fear creeps in. "But where will you be if something goes wrong?"

"We won't be far from you. We found a hidden area close to the location where no one can see us park. Besides, the building is surrounded, remember?"

"Oh yeah."

"You ready?" he asks.

I look in the rearview mirror at the black van parked directly behind me. "Yes."

I hear a bit of commotion. Then Baas's voice enters my ear. "I'm right behind you, sweetheart. Don't worry."

"I won't."

"I love you."

"I love you too," I reply.

"Let's go get our daughter."

A second goes by when I hear Telly's voice again. "Remember, stay calm. Do what they say, and let us handle the rest. And if you need to . . . shoot any threat that comes your way."

I shift a little in my seat at the reminder of the gun tucked in my waist. "Okay."

"Ready?"

"Ready."

My heart beats fast as I turn down a side street. The black van is no longer behind me, so I know I must be close. I glance at the GPS, which tells me I'm one mile from the location. It's less occupied in this part of town. Abandoned buildings surround the area, and hidden alleyways replace busy streets. The GPS alerts me that I'm here, and I stop. But I don't see anything. Not a building. Not a house. Nothing. I speak, hoping they can hear me. "I don't see anything."

Telly's voice enters my ear. "Look to your right." I do as he says. "You see that gate?"

"Yes."

"Open it, then take the long path."

"Okay."

I open the door, looking around for any sign of life. But there's nothing around me. I'm on an empty, hidden street with an old, rusted gate to my right and a vacant lot to my left. I approach the gate, look around again, and grab the padlock. It isn't locked. I remove the padlock and pull the gate as hard as I can. As soon as it's open, I hurry back to my car. "It's open."

Telly speaks but much quieter this time. "Okay. Take the path. Don't speak into the mic after this. We can't risk someone seeing your mouth moving and wondering who you're talking to."

"Okay."

I drive slowly onto the path, nervously tapping the steering wheel with my thumb. As I get farther to the end of it, I see a building. There are two cars parked in front of it. I come to a complete stop.

Telly speaks. "Grab the bag of money in the backseat. Do not give it to them until they give you Bailey."

I almost reply, but I quickly remember I can't speak. It'll give us away.

I look around. Telly mentioned that his men surround the area, but I don't see how. I see no one on the roof or anywhere near the building. I exit the car slowly, open the back door, and grab the bag of money. The door opens, and out walks a tall, slender man. He takes a few steps toward me, then stops.

"Where's the money?" he asks.

"It's right here." I lift the bag. "But first, where's my daughter?"

"She's inside."

"I want to see her."

"That wasn't part of the deal."

Baas

This is pure torture. I sit idle, waiting for Shaya to retrieve Bailey. It's taking everything in me not to exit this van, run over to that building, and shoot every single person in the way of me and my daughter. But I also know that I can't be reckless, or we all could be killed, including Shaya and Bailey. Telly listens in as Shaya exchanges words with the unknown criminal. I whisper. "What is going on?"

He silences me. I shake my knee, attempting to calm my nerves until I get clarity on the situation. I don't like this. I don't like the fact that I can't hear what's happening or that I'm not by Shaya's side. Suddenly, Telly stands.

"We've got a problem," he announces.

I don't hesitate. I don't ask questions. Before he can tell me what's happened, I burst through the back of the van door and run rapidly toward the building. As I round the corner, I see a man shove Shaya into a car and drive off. I grab the gun tucked in my waist, aim, and fire. I fire again—and again. But I miss. The car disappears, and I run back toward the van. Telly is running toward me.

"She's gone," I yell.

"Shit!"

"What the fuck happened back there? I thought your men were on it."

"They didn't have a clear shot. We didn't want to risk Shaya being hit," he replies.

"Someone should have followed them then. How the hell will we know where they've taken her?"

"Baas, calm—"

I whirl around and interrupt him. "Don't you *dare* fucking tell me to calm down. The love of my life and my baby are both gone."

He nods. "I understand."

"Are you married, Telly?"

"No."

"Do you have kids?"

"No."

"Then you *don't* understand."

We're back to square one. Only this time, matters are far worse. The two people I care about most in this world are missing, and we have no leads. "I knew it was a bad idea for her to go by herself."

Ebony sniffles. "Baas, you know it was the only way."

Her red, swollen eyes meet mine, and I look away quickly. I'm already on edge, and seeing Shaya's best friend this upset adds to it. Dafari hands her a handkerchief and kisses her on the head before he walks over to me.

"What are Telly and the team saying?"

His question angers me because I blame them. They should have stepped in. They should never have allowed them to take her. "This is all their fault. They should have done something."

"And risk hurting Shaya?" he asks.

"No. I mean . . ." I think about his statement for a second. "I didn't expect them to take the shot if it wasn't clear. But I was the only one who ran to help her. One of them—*any of them*—should have beat me to it."

"I understand, but it was too risky. She could have been hit. Is that what you want, Baas?"

It's not what I want. I don't want to do anything that makes these criminals so angry that they hurt Shaya or my baby girl. I shake my head to answer Dafari's question. "No."

"Listen, I know this is a lot. I know what you're feeling."

"Um-hmm."

"Baas?" he says my name in a raised voice to break my trance.

"Yeah."

"I *know* what it feels like to have someone you love to be in harm's way."

I hold his stare as I allow his words to digest. Dafari gets it. It wasn't that long ago that Ebony was in danger, and he felt helpless trying to save her. I plop down on the couch and run my hand down my face. "I can't lose them, Dafari."

"I know. And you won't," he replies.

I nod, and he continues. "That pain you're feeling, that anger and rage, hold on to it. It'll fuel you. It'll drive you to do whatever is in your power to get them back."

At that moment, Telly walks through the door. "Guys, we've got something."

CHAPTER TWELVE
Shaya

I was drugged sometime between being shoved in the back of a car and arriving at the destination. Now, my eyelids flutter open, and it takes me a minute to gather the strength to keep them open. I look around but don't recognize where I'm at. But it's someone's home. The bedroom isn't decorated; the only items inside are the bed, nightstands, and dresser. I rush to the door and try to open it, but it's locked from the outside. I run over to the window and slide the curtains open, but the window is boarded up. I reach into the pockets of my jeans to check for my cell phone. It's gone, and so is the gun. Whoever kidnapped me took them both.

"No," I say as I sit on the edge of the bed.

This wasn't supposed to happen. I was supposed to hand him the money and walk away with Bailey. I try to remember what happened, but my memory is foggy. Suddenly, the doorknob jiggles, and I fearfully shoot to my feet. As the door slowly opens, I back farther away from it and closer to the window. My eyes go wide when he steps inside.

"Jay?"

He smiles and closes the door behind him. "Shaya, it's been awhile."

"What . . ." I have so many questions, but I'm too speechless to ask them. Is this revenge for me breaking up with him? It can't be because he's the one who broke my heart. I loved him. I wanted to have a family with him and spend the rest of our days sitting on a wraparound porch, drinking lemonade, and holding hands. But that plan went out of the window when he betrayed me. He takes a tiny step toward me.

"You're probably wondering what I'm doing here."

"Yeah. Jay, what's going on?"

He cocks his head to the side. "You haven't figured it out yet?" I take too long to answer him, so he continues. "I'll go first. Let's start by me admitting that it was my fault we broke up."

"Yeah. You cheated on me."

He holds up a finger. "I'm not done talking. I messed up, I know. But I apologized. I was willing to work things out and would have done anything to regain your trust. But no. You rejected me. You and that bitch Ebony decided to humiliate me in front of her new boyfriend."

"You? *You're* behind this?"

"I said, I'm not done talking. I was going to give you your space. Give you time to come to your senses and see that we could work this out. But you disappeared, and I couldn't find you. I searched everywhere. I started to give up my search. I started to come to grips with the fact that we would never get back together. But then something happened."

"What happened, Jay?"

"You had a baby."

"How did you find out?"

"Did you forget that my sister works at the hospital where you gave birth?"

"Mika?" Fuck! I squeeze my eyes tightly. I had utterly forgotten that Jay's sister is a nurse in the labor and delivery department. I was so upset and stressed about my situation with Baas that it never occurred to me that Jay would find out I had a baby. And even if I did think he would find out, I would never think in a million years that it would bother him. "Of course. Mika told you."

"*Ding. Ding. Ding.* I thought the baby was mine. I thought for sure that this would be the thing that brought us back together. But Mika snuck down to where they keep the babies and snuck a little DNA. She tested her. The results showed there was zero chance she could be mine. Which means you fucked someone else. Just like that, as if I never meant anything to you."

I try to reason with him. "But it was after we broke up. Jay, let's just talk about this."

"We're past talking, Shaya." He walks closer to me, breathing heavily, with his fists balled to his side. "I wanted to know who the father was, and luckily, my sister got me information from the birth certificate. Bailey's middle name is named after him. Baas, is it?"

"Yes."

"One internet search and I found him. He was mentioned on the Wikipedia page for Dafari, the king of Mafachiko. He's a member of the royal family, which means he's rich."

"So *that's* what this is about? You took my daughter for money?"

"Yes. What better way to demand ransom money than from royalty?"

"How did you find her? It was a closed adoption."

"Easy. Mika was with your attending nurse when it was time to give Bailey to them."

Never in a million years would I think that Jay is behind something so sinister. I lay next to this man for years. I made love to him. We shared our darkest secrets. At one time, we were planning a future together. Was this man evil the entire time? The answer doesn't matter now because I'm running out of time.

"What do you want?"

"Revenge."

"You hurt me, Jay. Not the other way around."

He sneers. "You humiliated me."

"Can I see my daughter?"

"No."

"Jay, please," I beg.

He cocks his head to the side. "Funny."

"What?"

"It's funny that you didn't want her when she was born, but now, you're pretending to be the mother of the year."

His words sting, and I choke with tears. And not because he hurt my feelings but because he's right. What kind of mother gives her child away? I should have chosen to keep my daughter. I should have told Baas I was pregnant from the beginning. If I had, then maybe we wouldn't be in this situation, and Bailey would be safe. When I don't respond, he chuckles.

"Get some rest."

He turns around and walks out the door, leaving me shattered and speechless. I plop down on the edge of the bed and bury my face in my hands to catch the tears that fall. This is it. This is how I die. This is how I will be remembered . . . as the irresponsible mother who gave her baby away and allowed a monster to kidnap them both and kill them. I will never kiss Baas again. I will never get the chance to see my daughter again. He will never get the opportunity to meet her. He'll have to bury us both by the time he finds us.

A sudden calm washes over me. Maybe it's me coming to grips with my demise. Or maybe it's exhaustion. I lie across the bed and stare at the ceiling, wondering what is going through Baas's head. Bailey and I are the ones kidnapped, but my heart hurts knowing he's out there worrying. Panicking, wondering where we're at and if we're safe. My eyelids become heavy, and I close my eyes, hoping this is all just a dream when I wake up.

I expected Jay home an hour ago, but he said he had to stay late to see a last-minute Yorkie who hadn't eaten in days. I decided to surprise him by making him a picnic lunch. I haven't cooked much because I've been busy with our upcoming wedding. But it's something I'm really trying to work on getting better at. I pulled out all the stops. I managed to find an easy recipe for one of his favorite dishes, pepper steak and rice. I made a homemade iced tea, and I baked cupcakes from scratch. And to top it all off, I'm wearing nothing but a thong under this long peacoat. It looks weird, I know, wearing a peacoat in early fall. It's still technically warm outside. But that's the benefit of living in New York. You see many things weirder than a person wearing a coat in warm weather. I walk inside the door of the vet that we own together. It looks dark and empty. "Jay," I call out as I flip on the light.

He doesn't answer. I check the time to make sure that I didn't arrive too late and miss him. I walk down the hall, and that's when I hear it—a female moaning. I stop in my tracks. There's no way I just heard what I thought I heard. I walk closer to the end of the hall, and when I reach the last door to the left, I hear it again. I stand there for a minute, scared to death of what I might find when I open the door. I shake away that thought. Jay would never. He loves me, and we're getting married. This has to be someone else. Maybe one of the assistants. Or perhaps he's watching a movie. My hand grabs the knob, and I turn it slowly. I gasp when the door opens. The picnic basket I'm holding drops to the floor.

"*Shaya . . .*"

They untangle themselves and scurry to find clothing. I'm suddenly embarrassed, and I yank the peacoat toward me tightly. "This is what you stayed late to do?"

"Baby, it's not what—"

My hand moves on its own accord and slaps him in the face before he can finish his sentence. "Don't you fucking say it. It would be an insult to my intelligence because I know exactly what I just saw."

"I'm sorry."

I look past him and at our assistant. "I trusted you, and this is how you repay me?" Tears fill her eyes, but I don't care.

"How could you do this to us?" I ask him.

He's at a loss for words but can't deny that he's been caught. "Shaya . . . I love you."

My dream ends, and my eyes pop open. I look at the clock, and it's two in the morning. Seeing Jay just now caused me to dream about the night I caught him screwing our assistant. I should have known then that he wasn't who he said he was. He's a liar. And liars are capable of anything. This is the second time he's deceived me, and I swear on everything holy that if I make it out of here . . . He *will* pay.

Baas

I had to apologize to Telly and his men. I labeled them as useless and incompetent. But as of this morning, they've redeemed themselves. One of his men was smart enough to snap a picture of the car's license plate that sped away with Shaya. Now, I'm waiting to see to whom the car is registered. Shaya's parents have been calling me, and I lied, which is totally against my beliefs. They haven't been able to reach her, so they got worried. I assured them that she was okay. I told them that she was tired and needed some time to decompress. I can't tell them what has happened. I gave them my word that I would keep their daughter safe, and I can't bear to hear the heartbreak in their voices if I tell them otherwise. For now, it's best that they don't know.

I stare at the photo in front of me. This is him. This is the man who is responsible for jeopardizing my family's life. Dafari stands next to me and observes the picture. He leans closer and grabs the photo out of my hand.

"Wait a minute. That's . . ."

"Jay. Shaya's ex," I answer for him.

"*He's* behind all this?" he asks.

"It looks that way. The car is registered to him. He was stupid enough to use his own car when they took her."

Dafari shakes his head. "I have no idea how a piece of shit like him could be capable of something like this."

I turn around to face him. "Tell me what you know."

He shakes his head. "Not much. He came to the penthouse begging for her forgiveness. I didn't like that he got a little aggressive with her and Ebony. I escorted him out and told him that he'd regret it if he ever spoke to either of them that way again. I also forbade him to contact Shaya. I told her she would call him if she wanted to speak to him."

"Forgiveness for what? What did he do to her?" My blood boils at the thought of him hurting her, but I need to know. It's vital if I'm going to save my family. Dafari places the photo back in my hand.

"He cheated on her."

I think back to when Shaya and I first met. I was instantly drawn to her, but she was wearing a ring. When I mentioned it, she blew it off and made it clear that she was single. She never spoke about who or why. And I didn't ask because I only cared about her being a free woman. Free to be mine. I slam the photo down on the table. "I'm going to kill him."

I say it slowly, calmly, and without hesitation. Dafari remains quiet because he knows I mean it. When I see Jay, there will be no words. I will spare no mercy as I take his life quickly and without hesitation. I open the fridge and grab a cold bottle of water. I open it and take a sip, allowing the water to cool the burning inside me. I'm so angry that my blood feels like it's boiling. I wipe the sweat from my brow and take another sip.

Dafari finally speaks. "What's our next move?"

"I'm waiting for an address. Unfortunately, the address the car was registered to is an old address. It's the home he shared with Shaya."

He nods. "Okay. I'm going to check on Ebony. Call me as soon as you have something."

"I will. Thank you."

When he's out the door, I stand silently and stare out the window. This is my fault—all of it. I gave up too quickly. Mafachiko has always been home. I love my country; protecting it has always been my top priority. But in this case, it shouldn't have been. I should have put Shaya first. Had I done so, I would have known she was pregnant, and none of this would have happened. I slide my hand inside my pants pocket and grab the photo of my daughter. I smile as I stare at her. "I will save you and your mother, Bailey."

I shove the picture back into my pocket and grab my phone to dial Telly. We're running out of time, and I need an update. Just as I'm about to dial his number, the doorbell rings. I walk to the door, the phone still in hand, and swing it open. Telly steps inside.

"I was just about to call you."

He turns around to face me. Then he smiles. "We found them."

Shaya

I pick at my food as I sit across from Jay at the dining room table. He eats in silence and occasionally looks up at me. I drop my fork purposely to allow it to clink against the plate to get his attention. He chews his last bite and then places his fork down as well.

"Do you have something to say?" he asks.

"I want to see Bailey."

He smirks from across the table. "People in hell want ice water."

My anger gets the best of me, and I'm close to clearing everything off this table with one swipe. But I quickly remember that I have no idea what this man is capable of. I can't do anything to put myself or Bailey in danger. I take a second to calm my breathing before I respond. "Jay, please."

He takes a sip of his orange juice before he replies. "What's in it for me?"

My hands grip the sides of the table as I think about his question. I want Bailey back badly. Which means I'm willing to do whatever I must to make it happen. I shrug. "What do you want?"

His eyes narrow. "You know what I want."

"More money?"

"Not just money."

Confusion sets in, and I shake my head. "Then what?"

He chuckles. "You really don't know?"

"No."

"You. I want you, Shaya. In exchange for Bailey."

Tears prick my eyes. "No. Anything but that."

"Why not? You want her back safely, don't you?"

"Yes."

He leans back in his chair and folds his arms across his chest. "Then it's a no-brainer. Besides, we were in love at one point."

"That was different, and you know it. That was before I learned you were a piece of shit!"

He takes a deep breath and unfolds his arms. "I'm going to let that slide. That's my offer, Shaya. You give up your life with him and join me in exchange for Bailey."

I shake my head. "Jay, I—"

"The choice is yours."

My head spins as I weigh my options. I have to save my daughter, and it would be so much easier to get us both out of here if she's already with me. But if I do what Jay proposes, I'll betray Baas. I've betrayed him once already and can't bring myself to do it again. We were supposed to have a life together after this.

"Anything but that, Jay. Please."

He rises instantly and bangs his fists on the table. "You can take it and be reunited with your daughter—or don't take it. Your choice."

My hands tremble beneath the table, and a tear slides down my cheek. "Okay," I answer softly.

He smiles widely. "Well, all right then."

I burst into tears, but they do not affect him. He stands with his phone in his hand and walks toward me. He looms over me and speaks firmly. "I'll arrange for you to say goodbye to your daughter before we leave."

CHAPTER THIRTEEN

Baas

My heart is thumping loudly as we wait. The house is surrounded, but we're being cautious before storming in. First, we need to make sure that Shaya and Bailey are inside. And if they are, we must get to them before they're harmed. I can be impatient. It's something I've been trying my best to work on but right now, all that goes out the window. I have no patience. And I don't give a fuck. I want my family back, and I want them back *now*.

Telly whispers beside me. "We've got movement but can't confirm if it's them."

"I'm tired of waiting. Let's go in," I reply.

Dafari holds up his hand. "Baas, we have to do this right."

I'm spiraling on the inside, but somehow, I'm managing to keep it together on the outside. "If we wait any longer, my family will be dead. Is that what you want?"

I speak in a low whisper, but it's loud enough for them to know I'm irritated and angry. Dafari's eyes narrow when they meet mine.

"You know that's not what we want, Baas."

I shouldn't have said it. Shaya is like a sister to Dafari, and he's always treated her like family, even before I fell in love with her. I take a deep breath before I reply to him. "I know. I'm sorry. I just—"

He nods. "You don't have to explain. I get it." He turns to Telly. "What's the plan?"

Telly glances between us when he speaks. "They've got movement in the main area. Most likely the living room. We think it's them."

I grab my gun. "Are we ready to move in?" I confirm.

Telly says something in his earpiece, listens, then turns to face me. "My men can handle this, Baas. Trust me."

I don't want to trust him. And I don't trust anyone to save my family but myself. Telly's men don't love them as I do. They wouldn't die for them as I would. But I don't want to waste time arguing with him about it. He's about to walk away, but I grab him by his arm tightly. "If *anything* happens to them—"

He interrupts me. "Baas, I know."

I release him, and he's out the door quickly, gun in hand and speaking in his earpiece. Dafari and I stay behind in the van, praying they have Shaya and Bailey with them when they return. I suddenly feel claustrophobic. I become hot and sweaty as anticipation rushes through me. I pace back and forth.

"What if they are harmed?"

"They won't be," Dafari replies.

I shake my head. "I was so cold to her, Dafari. What if I don't get a chance to make things right?"

"You will. Shaya loves you, Baas."

Shots fire, and we freeze. We listen carefully to Telly speak to us as best as he can over the loud commotion.

"We're in," he announces.

"Do you see them?" I ask.

He doesn't respond. I hear him breathing hard as he runs through the building. I hear more gunfire, and I panic. "Telly, give me something," I shout into the earpiece.

The commotion and noise stop, and then I hear silence. I look over at Dafari with fear in my eyes. I'm about to jump out of the van when Telly's voice speaks into the earpiece.

"We got her," he replies.

I push through the doors of the back of the van and run toward the building. I don't care what's there to greet me. I run full speed ahead with Dafari on my heels. One of Telly's men carries a child out of the building. He walks down the steps toward me. When I reach them, I stop in my tracks. He hands her over to me, and I look down at her. She's wrapped in a blanket and in a deep sleep. My heart cracks wide open at the sight of her. I pull her in and kiss her forehead.

"Hi, baby girl. I'm your daddy."

I grab her tiny little finger, and she squirms before tightening it around mine. She's so tiny and fragile. So innocent and beautiful. And she's mine. Now that I have her back, I'm never giving her up again. Shaya and I . . . I stop when Shaya enters my brain. I look around, but I don't see her. I was so taken by Bailey that I didn't take the time to see if Shaya was okay. I hold Bailey tightly and securely as I approach the building. Dafari speaks to Telly, but they stop when I reach them. "Where's Shaya? Is she okay?" I ask.

Telly glances at Dafari before speaking. "She's not here, Baas."

"What?" I look down at Bailey, realizing I'm speaking too loudly while holding her. "What do you mean she's not here?"

"One of the men came clean before one of my guys killed him. He said Shaya fled with Jay. They ran off together," he responds.

"She would *never* agree to something like that. And she certainly wouldn't have left our daughter behind," I say it through gritted teeth.

Telly nods. "We agree. And we're going to get to the bottom of this."

"No," I say firmly.

"You don't have a choice," Telly reminds me.

"I just got her back, and you want me to give her up again? No. I'm *not* doing it."

I refuse. I don't care what the police say or the judge. This is *my* daughter. I didn't go through hell and back to save her, only to give her back to two incompetent people who couldn't keep her safe. "And what if he decides to come back for her, huh? She's safer with me."

Ebony stands, carefully holding Bailey. "Baas, Shaya is still out there. How will you save her *and* care for Bailey?"

I hadn't thought of it, but her question does make me stop and think. She continues. "Baas, please. Shaya needs you right now."

She's right. Shaya is still out there somewhere, and I must find her. But how can I find her if I'm in the courts fighting for Bailey? How can I find her if my focus is on getting our daughter back? Pain cripples me as my eyes shift to the tiny human Ebony's holding. This decision isn't easy, and I feel like I'm being forced between fighting for my daughter or saving her mother. It's a choice I don't want to make but need to make because time is of the essence. I rub the back of my neck to ease some of the tension. "Fine. But when we find Shaya, we're coming for our daughter."

Telly nods. "I know."

Soft cries interrupt us. Ebony looks down, then looks back at me. "She's awake."

Telly stands. "I'm going to see if we have any leads. I should be back in an hour. After that, we'll have to return Bailey to her adoptive parents."

He leaves the penthouse, and I stand in place, feeling like a failure. The goal was to save my family, not one over the other. Ebony walks over to me and hands me Bailey.

"Spend some time with your daughter."

Shaya

I didn't get to see Bailey, but I'm relieved she is safe. She was left in the care of two of Jay's men until he gave them further instructions. He somehow knew Baas was coming and demanded we flee right away. His men were supposed to leave Bailey safely in a playpen before they joined us. But they didn't get the chance. Telly and his men stormed the building, killing them before they could run. I saw it all unfold on the hidden camera Jay installed. I cried tears of joy when I saw Telly pick up my baby and rush out of the building with her. I didn't see Baas or Dafari on camera, but I knew they weren't that far behind.

I look up at the tall trees and cover my eyes to shield them from the sunlight. It's hot and sticky here. I shoo away the bugs eager to bite my skin and kick the sand with my right foot. This is a beautiful island. An island I would enjoy spending time on under different circumstances. Knowing that I'm stuck on this island alone with Jay makes this place seem like a prison. It doesn't matter that the water is a pristine blue. Or that the sand is clean and white. I don't care that this place looks like a tropical paradise. The only thing I care about is finding a way to escape. I join Jay on the porch.

"Beautiful, isn't it?" he asks.

"It's okay," I answer him nonchalantly because I don't want to give him any indication that I want to be here. "Where are we anyway?"

He chuckles. "I won't tell you. All you need to know is that this is your home now. *Our* home now."

I whirl around angrily. "You expect me to live with you and pretend you didn't break my heart and kidnap my daughter?"

"Yes. You'll forgive me over time, and we can return to how we were before."

I shake my head because I'm in disbelief. I can't believe that Jay is crazy enough to think that I could ever love him again. The waves crash against the shore, calming the rage growing inside me. I turn and look out at the ocean; there's no land in sight. Wherever we are, it really does seem like a deserted island. And I'm stuck here with a man who has gone mad. Even if I wanted to try to escape, I have no idea how. I can't swim. In fact, I fear large bodies of water. I see no nearby boats. I have no phone to call for help. And it seems there are no other people on the island but us. Jay inches next to me, and I quickly move away from him.

"Jay, I may be stuck here with you, but we will *never* return to how we were. We will simply exist in each other's company. Don't expect conversation. Don't expect walks on the beach. And if you even think about touching me, I will kill you."

The thought of killing him crosses my mind regardless of whether he touches me, but he doesn't need to know that. I can't give him the advantage of knowing any of the moves I'm contemplating.

He laughs at my statement. "Still feisty. It's one of the things I loved about you." He straightens his back. "I'm going to take a shower. You're welcome to join me if you'd like. If not, we'll catch up afterward."

He walks away, leaving me to my thoughts. I take a deep breath and survey my surroundings. Eventually, I'll have to venture out and tour the island. It's the only way I'll get out of here. But right now, I'm too tired. I have no energy, mentally or physically. I walk to the end of the porch of the bungalow-style home, climb into the hammock, close my eyes, and think about Bailey and Baas as I drift into a deep sleep.

The sound of voices wakes me, and I rise quickly, almost falling out of the hammock. I steady myself and allow my eyes to come into focus. The sun has set, and the breeze has gotten cooler. I carefully climb out of the hammock and stretch my body. I take small steps toward the front door, and when I reach it, I open it slowly. The home smells of coconut and fruit. It's an open space with clean, hardwood floors and large ceiling fans that run at high speed. I walk past the fully furnished living room and into the kitchen, where the voices are. Jay's back faces me, and he's speaking into his phone.

"I need the deposit to be untraceable," he says.

"It will be. I've opened a cryptic shell account. The chances of the money tracing back to you are highly unlikely," the unidentified male says.

He has the man on speakerphone, and I want to yell and plea for whomever he is to come and save me. But I know that won't happen. Jay hears me behind him and turns around. "Okay. Let me know when the funds are available." He ends the call and shoves his phone in his hand. "Don't sneak up on me like that."

"I wasn't sneaking. If you wanted privacy, you shouldn't have had your phone on speaker," I reply.

He walks away. "Are you hungry?"

"Not really."

I'm starving. And it's causing me to become dizzy and fatigued. But I'm too anxious to eat. I'm also nervous that he's put something in the food here. I've been drugged twice since he took me. My stomach betrays me and growls. He smirks.

"Your stomach says otherwise." He opens the refrigerator, grabs an apple, and tosses it to me. "Here."

I catch it and inspect it. I don't see any tiny holes poked into it or any indication that it's been tampered with, but I'm still hesitant to eat it. But holding it makes my stomach growl louder, and my mouth waters at the thought of tasting this beautiful red apple.

"Shaya, you need to eat," he says.

That's what makes a psycho complicated. They make you fear them all while showing concern for you. It leaves you confused and on edge, not knowing which version of them you're going to get. But he's right. I need to eat something. So I take the risk and bite the apple, savoring the sweet, robust taste. He grabs his phone out of his pocket and texts while I finish it. When I'm done, nothing is left of it but the core. I toss it in the nearby trash can and lean against the counter. "This place is remote. How will we get food? Water? Toiletries?"

If I successfully plan my escape, I won't be here long enough to find out. But before that happens, I need to discover everything about this place and its inner workings. "Good try," he replies.

"If I'm going to be here, don't you think I should know these things?"

"We've got enough food for a month and enough toiletries for three months. You let me worry about what happens when we run out," he responds.

He's not buying my concern. And he's unwilling to give me any information about this place, so I have to find answers another way. Maybe I can steal his phone and call for help. But what if he has it locked? If it is locked, I could dial the emergency number and tell them I've been kidnapped. But I don't know where I am. And I'm not sure if they could trace the call here. The sound of his voice pulls me out of my thoughts.

"Huh?"

"I said stop."

"Stop what?" I ask.

"Stop thinking you can escape. I see the wheels spinning in your head, and it's useless. The sooner you realize our life is here now, the better."

Chapter Fourteen

Baas

I stare at Bailey's picture, wishing she was with me. Telly returned her to her adoptive parents this morning, and I didn't get much time with her outside of feeding her once and changing her diaper twice. I think about how she smiled at me as I struggled through it. Ebony wanted to help, but I wanted to do it alone because of the many diaper changes I missed. Sadness washes over me as I think about other stuff I missed, such as playing with her and rocking her to sleep. I haven't gotten the chance to watch her grow and display characteristics passed down from her mother and me. It kills me because I'm unsure if I'll ever get the chance.

I was miserable when she had to go. But Telly assured me this was best and that if I had any chance of getting her back, I couldn't just steal her. He explained the situation to the police but told them he had received a tip concerning Bailey's whereabouts. He didn't tell them about me or Shaya. We didn't want them probing into our affairs or plastering our faces across every television screen in America. Telly explained that the media in America are like savages. They would ignore reporting the story about the rescue of a kidnapped child and shift the focus to the fact that said child is the product of royalty. Imagine what would happen if word got out. Every criminal alive would think they could steal our children for money. I watched from afar as my daughter was handed to them. The mother cried endlessly and held her tightly while the father smiled and wiped away his own tears. They look like good people. I can tell that they love her. But that doesn't change the fact that she belongs with me and Shaya.

We have no idea where Shaya is. The only vital information we received was that she ran off with Jay, which I know is untrue. She was forced. And my guess is that she did it in exchange for Bailey's safe return. Anger grips me. And I feel the urge to burn every city in America until Shaya is found.

I head to the kitchen and pour a much-needed shot of bourbon to take off the edge. I look around the empty penthouse as I swallow the smooth liquid. With Bailey being safe and no leads on Shaya, Dafari and Ebony returned to Mafachiko to attend to Aiden for a few days. Dafari has been checking in often, and I know that if I need him, he'll return with no question.

Telly assures me he has his hands full when it comes to finding Shaya. He's giving me frequent updates but hasn't given me anything of substance. I'm alone right now. With nothing but worry and a lack of patience. I take another shot of bourbon, then grab my phone to call him. He answers on the first ring.

"Baas, I have no update."

"Why the hell not?"

He exhales loudly. "I'm doing my best."

"We have to find her."

"I know, and we will."

"Do we have addresses for Jay's family and friends? I can visit them," I ask.

"Baas, let us handle this."

I hate hearing those words. I'm not the kind of man to let other men handle anything for me. But I'm also smart enough to know that this is Telly's territory, and his men specialize in these matters. We do things differently in Mafachiko. We don't have police forces and government agencies. Had something like this happened there, we would have hunted the criminal down and gutted him without question.

"Fine. I'll stand down. But if you don't have anything in the next forty-eight hours, I'm doing this my way."

"I understand."

We end the call, and I dial Dafari next. I speak as soon as he answers. "I've given Telly forty-eight hours to give us something."

"Okay," he replies.

"After that, I do things my way."

"What do you need?" he asks.

"I'll need the Seer."

He's silent before he speaks. "There are consequences with that, Baas. Why do you think I didn't use her to find Ebony?"

"I know. But I'm willing to take that risk, Dafari. Tell me, what other choice do we have?"

The Seer is Mafachiko's most dangerous weapon. Her ability to use spiritual insight allows her to see what the future holds. She's our best-kept secret. At 103 years old, she doesn't skip a beat. The issue is that the elders heavily guard her. She's not easily accessible and can only be consulted on matters they approve. And it's usually a decision that's between life and death. In my lifetime, I've only known her to be consulted four times. Dafari takes a deep breath.

"You're right. She's our last resort without any information from Telly. But . . . Are you sure you're willing to risk the consequences?"

There's a price to be paid when you tap into a different realm. It's a world unknown to us. Common folk and spirits don't like it when a person crosses over into their world. They don't take too kindly to their peace being interrupted by the curiosity and greed of worldly people. When the Seer taps into their world, she sometimes needs to provide an exchange. It can be as serious as one life for another. The loss of someone dear. Or the loss of a needed body function like sight or hearing. It's usually a heavy exchange and could completely alter my life if I go through with this. And I *will* go through with this because if it saves Shaya, I'm willing to pay any price. All I want is to have her back safely. I want her and Bailey to live a good life, even if it means I don't get to live. I grip the phone tightly when I reply to Dafari. "Bailey and I need her back, no matter the consequence."

After a long lecture, Dafari convinced the elders to allow us to use the Seer. Shaya didn't spend much time with them while she was here, but she's the best friend to the queen and the future king's godmother. So, she is of great importance to the royal family. I watch the camera patiently while waiting for Dafari to join the team's meeting. Two minutes remain, but I joined early because I'm eager to get answers. Finally, I hear a ding, and Dafari's face appears.

"Can you hear me?" he asks.

"Yes."

I hear some movement and watch the camera move in another direction. That's when I see her. I had never laid eyes on her before now. I only heard about her in stories. She looks regal. Her back is straight, and her head is held high. Her hair is wrapped in a yellow silk scarf, and she's wearing yellow earrings that dangle from her ears. Her skin is a smooth caramel complexion and has a soft glow. Her eyes are closed shut, and I wonder why. After all, she's the Seer. How can she see anything if her eyes are closed?

Dafari finally has the camera at the right angle, and he speaks. "Okay. We're ready."

We're all quiet, especially me because I don't know what to say or where to start. Do I ask her questions? Do I introduce myself first? Or do I allow her to speak first? What is the proper etiquette when in the presence of someone like this? She speaks first.

"Baas."

"Hi, Ms. . . ."

I realize I don't even know her name because no one has ever called her by it. For as long as I can remember, she's always been the Seer. She laughs lightly.

"I sense that you're nervous. Don't be."

"I'm sorry. I hope that I haven't offended you," I reply.

"No," she responds. A moment of silence goes by. "I remember when you were a young boy."

My eyes go wide. "You do?"

"Yes. Your father came to me."

Thoughts of my father enter my mind. What business would he have that required him to see her? She continues speaking.

"He sensed something was coming. He was worried about what would become of you."

My chest tightens when I hear this. "Are you saying my father knew he was going to die?"

She smiles. "I'm saying that he knew something was coming and needed to be at peace. I assured him that you would be okay. I told him that his son would be in the presence of royalty."

"I need your help. Please," I plead.

"I know."

I don't respond to her because if she already knows, then there is nothing more for me to say.

"I may be blind, but I see all," she replies.

Now it makes sense why her eyes are closed shut. "If you see anything that can help, please tell me. I'm running out of options."

She's quiet. And I don't know if it's because she's doing her thing or if she's thinking about what to say next. But when she nods, I know she means business. Her facial expression changes. It shifts from peaceful and relaxed to tense and strained. I immediately think something is wrong. I want to ask, but I don't want to interrupt her. It would be rude and break her concentration. Her breathing picks up but not so heavy that she's gasping for air.

"I feel pain. Lots of pain," she says.

I rub my forehead. She feels pain. But what kind of pain? Physical pain? Emotional pain? I need to know. She continues speaking.

"But also, love. Intense, unconditional love."

This makes me feel better. If she feels pain and love, she must be referring to an emotional state rather than a physical one. I wonder whom she's feeling these emotions from. Shaya? Me? It makes more sense that she would be feeling these emotions from Shaya. Emotional pain from losing Bailey. And unconditional love for her daughter. She speaks again.

"There's water. Everywhere. She's surrounded by it."

Anxiety rushes through me. I need more. What does she mean? She's surrounded by water? Did he toss her body in a river somewhere? I drag my hand down my face as I wait for her to continue with what she's seeing. This is not at all what I expected. I expected her to close her eyes, give me an answer, and be done with it. But instead, I'm getting pieces bit by bit in cryptic messages. This leaves me wanting more and worrying more. I decide to speak softly. I don't know if it's allowed, but since she didn't mention anything, I assume it's okay for me to do so.

"Is she okay?" I ask.

That's all I want to know. It's all I need to know. Everything else can come later, but right now, right this second, I just need to know if Shaya is still alive. She doesn't answer me right away, and for a second, I don't think she will answer me at all. But she smiles and responds.

"She's strong."

It's not a flat-out yes. But I take it as such because how can Shaya be strong if she's dead? She has to be alive. I'm relieved and couldn't be more grateful at this moment. Then her smile turns to a frown.

"Let her go," she says.

There's a shift in her expression, and I know that this is the end. This is all I will get. I don't know what she means by her last statement. *Let her go*. Let who go? I have no plans to let Shaya or Bailey go, so this leaves me confused.

"Let who go?" I ask.

She smiles again. "I have seen all I will see."

Dafari appears before the camera. "I'll check in with you later."

He leaves the video, and I immediately dial Telly. I don't get an answer. I need to tell him that Shaya is still alive and that wherever she is, she's near water. My mind swirls with questions. *Let her go*. What does she mean by that? I think hard about it, but I've got nothing. Then my phone rings, and it's Dafari.

"Hey."

"Hey. Can't say that I've ever experienced anything like that. And I'm the king."

"It seems that Shaya is alive and near water. I tried calling Telly, but I couldn't reach him."

"This is good. At least we have something to give him."

The line goes silent for a second. "What do you think she meant by 'let her go'?"

"I don't know, Baas."

"It just doesn't make sense. Who would I let go? Certainly not Shaya or Bailey."

He takes a deep breath. "That's the difficulty with these things. Sometimes, you have no idea what she means. You have to know that she's right 99 percent of the time and that if she tells you to do something, it's for the greater good."

"Hmmm."

It still weighs heavily on my mind, but I decide to let it go because I need to focus on finding Shaya.

"Dafari, thank you for setting this up. I appreciate it."

"Of course. Let me know when you reach Telly."

"I will."

I end the call and grab a bottle of water from the refrigerator. I take a long gulp as I think about nearby bodies of water. Now that I think about it, New York is surrounded by water, so it makes sense that she sees Shaya surrounded by it. Wherever she is, I'm sure there's a river or lake not too far away. This makes it harder to narrow down. I'm getting frustrated. I'm getting more worried by the day. I know that there was nothing I could have done to prevent this from happening since I was unaware that Bailey existed, but I feel responsible for them both. I can't help but think how different things would have been if I had rejected my marriage arrangement. I would have married Shaya instead, and I would have known that she was pregnant.

But I can't waste time harping on the past. What's done is done, and all I can do now is deal with the hand that is dealt. I have mixed feelings about my meeting with the Seer. On the one hand, I did get some answers. On the other hand, I was left with more questions. But something is better than nothing.

I'm about to head to the bedroom when I feel lightheaded. I grip the corner of the kitchen cabinet to steady myself. My vision becomes blurry, so I shake my head to try to focus on my vision. I put one leg in front of the other in an effort to walk straight, but I sway from side to side. I don't know what's happening to me, but I need to get upstairs to the bedroom.

I don't make it. I take another step . . . then everything goes black.

I feel numb. And I'm not sure if I'm still awake or asleep. My body feels awake, but my mind feels asleep. I try to speak, but I can't. I try to move, but I can't. I see visions. Visions of Shaya and a little boy. They look happy together, playing in a backyard under the bright sun. I don't see myself, and I wonder why. It's like I'm hovering over them, watching them with a smile. I reach out, but I can't touch them. I call her name, but she doesn't hear me.

They continue to run around the yard, but he trips and falls. Shaya is at his side, consoling and kissing him on the cheek. She cradles him as she looks up at me. Tears fall from her eyes as she stares at me. Can she see me? Does she know I'm here?

"I miss you," she says.

I can hear her loud and clear. It's as if she's right next to me. Why does she miss me? Why am I not there with her? I hear her voice again.

"Baas, if you can hear me, I love you."

My eyes pop open, and I gasp for air. I rise from the floor, dripping with sweat and my head pounding. I look around my surroundings to make sure I'm still in the penthouse, and I am. What just happened? Was I dreaming? No. I couldn't have been dreaming because you dream when you're asleep, and I was not sleeping. I collapsed in the kitchen. But why? I suddenly remember something else the Seer said. She said my father had visions that he wouldn't be here. Is that what just happened to me? I've never had visions or the ability to predict the future. Until today, I never knew my father had that ability. But what I saw was as plain as day. Shaya was alive and well. And it looked like I was not. Is this the consequence of speaking with the Seer? Or is this my destiny?

Will I suffer the same consequences as my father? The little boy's face is etched in my mind. Who is he? Is he one of the kids from the orphanage? I don't have answers, but if it means that Shaya and Bailey will go on to live a happy life, I'm at peace with it.

I stand and grab another water bottle. This time, I drink the entire bottle. After that, I grab my phone from my pocket and go to my notes section. I type in what I just witnessed, and when it's added, I place my phone back into my pocket and head upstairs to rest.

I didn't sleep last night. How can I when my mind is preoccupied? I yawn loudly but shake my head to relieve some of the exhaustion. I need to focus today, even if my body doesn't want to cooperate. Telly points to the right of the globe.

"This is where the signal was lost."

I lean in and look closer. "The Seer was right. There are two islands in that area."

He nods. "Yes. At this point, we have no idea which one they could be on. My sources tell me that the plane disappeared somewhere in this area."

He takes a pen and draws a big circle around a large body of water and the island to the right of the map.

"How the fuck could he get a plane and fly out of the country undetected?"

Telly shakes his head. "We don't know, but he did."

"Were you able to trace the money he got away with?"

"No. Not yet."

"I don't understand this. You and your team are the most skilled men I know. Combine that with me and Dafari, and we're unmatched. Yet, this amateur seems to be two steps ahead of us."

Telly scratches his head. "Yeah, it makes no sense to me either."

"So, when do we leave?" I ask.

"My men are making arrangements now."

"Good. I'll call Dafari."

Shaya

I've walked this island most of the day, and I'm no closer to finding a way out of here than when I first started. I wipe the sweat from my brow and take a second to catch my breath before moving on. I'm in the thick of the trees, strolling. I'm careful not to step on any of the beautiful flowers sprouting from the ground. Unknown plants and healthy, wet soil surround me. I don't like being so far out of reach. And not just because I'm stuck on the island with Jay. But because neither of us knows how to live on a remote island. Yes, we have food and toiletries, but what happens if one of us gets sick? What happens if one of us hurts ourselves? There are no doctors here. No hospitals or medical centers that could help.

Suddenly, a noise interrupts my thoughts, and I stand still, listening to where it came from. I hear the rustle of leaves, and I look up. I gasp when I see it. I make no sudden movements because I don't want to scare it away. Silently, I take two steps closer.

"Hi," I say softly and gently. It looks at me before it swings from one branch to another. "You're beautiful."

It makes a noise but continues to observe me. I don't know if it's a male or a female. I'm a veterinarian, but I rarely see monkeys, especially monkeys from other countries. It's a little thing, and I wonder if it's still a baby or just a small breed. Curiosity gets the best of me, and I slowly lift my hand to pet it. It jumps to another limb and makes a sound like a laugh. "Are you teasing me, little one?"

I place my hands on my hips and smile. It's the first time I've smiled since hearing about Bailey. It stands on its feet, then leaps into my arms. I laugh out loud. "Hi there. Where did you come from?" I look around, searching for other monkeys on the tree, but I don't see any.

"Are you all by yourself?" It leans in as if it wants to kiss me, and I quickly dodge it. I may love animals, but this is a wild animal. I have no idea where it's been, what it's been eating, or what diseases it may be carrying. I can't risk getting sick with no medical resources here. I peek between its legs and quickly determine that it's a boy. "Do you have a name?"

He gets closer to me, sniffing my face and neck. "Of course you don't." He's communicating with me, and I don't know what he wants. He may be hungry, but I don't know what monkeys eat. "I'm going to name you Lou."

I don't know why that name pops into my head, but it's fitting. Lou is small, but his personality seems big. He's being feisty and making it clear that this area belongs to him and not me. His coat is multicolored. A mix of black, white, and brown. His beady eyes look jet black, and his tiny fingers probe my hair. He's cute, and I instantly fall in love with him. "You're my only friend on this island, Lou." He takes one more look at me before he leaps and runs away.

"Lou, wait." It's silly of me to call after him. He doesn't know his name, and he's probably scared. I doubt he interacts with humans much, and seeing me left him both curious and afraid.

I look around to ensure I left no area untouched and conclude that I haven't. I've searched all day, and so far, there's no evidence of other people living here. There are no hidden boats anyway or any kind of transportation to get me off this island. I deflate with disappointment as I turn around to walk back toward the house. I take the trail that got me this far, but then I stop. I don't want to go back right now. I don't want to be forced to talk to Jay and act civilized. I'd rather be here. Out in the woods in solitude. I think more clearly here. I feel free here. I find a nearby tree trunk and sit at its base to rest my feet. I take a deep breath as I think about Baas and Bailey. I smile as I imagine us as a family. I envision her first steps. Her first words. My smile fades when I realize that I will most likely miss all of that—because I may die here. And even if I don't die here and somehow make it home, the judge may not give me my baby. Soon, I hear footsteps walking toward me, and Jay appears before I stand to my feet.

"There you are."

I rise and wipe the debris from the back of my jeans. "What do you want, Jay?" I'm irritated and want to be left alone. He's delusional if he thinks we will hang out like friends.

"You can't go off like that and not tell me where you're going, Shaya. Anything can happen."

"I can do whatever the hell I want. I held up my end of the deal, and I'm here, right? Sticking up your ass wasn't part of the agreement. I need space, and if I want to take a walk, I will take a walk."

He doesn't reply right away. Instead, he watches me for a few seconds before he looks up at the sky.

"It's going to storm soon. Come on."

He walks away, and I follow him, but not without looking at the sky myself. The sky is dark, and the clouds are fluffy. The wind picks up as we maneuver our way through the forest. We reach the house right before the downpour. But unlike Jay, I don't rush to the front porch to escape. I remain standing under the open sky and allow the heavy rain to wash over me. Jay is yelling something, but I can't hear him due to the rain and thunder. I look up at the sky and close my eyes, trying my best to release some of the anxiety and fear I've been holding since I stepped foot on this place. But it's not working. I feel a grip around my arm that snaps me out of it, and Jay stares at me angrily as his grip grows tighter.

"Enough of this. Let's go," he demands.

I yank my arm out of his grip, step around him, and stomp toward the house. I burst inside and go straight upstairs to the room I'm sleeping in. I slam the door shut and lean against it, breathing heavily. Then I slide down and take a seat on the floor. Tears stream down my face as it becomes more and more evident that I won't get out of here.

Jay knocks softly. "Shaya . . ."

"Go away," I yell.

"Listen, I didn't mean to be rough with you. Please, just come out. I made dinner."

"No. What part of 'we are not friends' do you *not* understand? Jay, I don't want to be here."

I've said this repeatedly, yet he still insists on making this into something that it isn't. He can try to force it all he wants, but I will never bend. When he doesn't reply right away, I think he's left. But then he speaks in a firm voice.

"I understand this will take some time to get used to, so I'll leave you alone tonight. But starting tomorrow, you *will* do better. I won't tolerate defiance, and if you keep this up, I'll—"

"You'll *what*?" I interrupt.

He bangs the door loudly with his fist. "Goddamit, Shaya."

I hear him walk away, and I bury my head in my hands as the feeling of hopelessness sets in. Then I look up at the ceiling and speak out loud. "God, if you're listening, please help me. Please help me get out of here and get back to my family."

I sit silently, waiting for a sign that he's heard my prayer. And when I don't see one, I stand to my feet and plop onto the bed. I stare ahead at the window, twiddling my fingers as I try desperately to think of a plan to escape.

CHAPTER FIFTEEN

Baas

I'm going to save Shaya. And because it's a dangerous situation, I decide to see my daughter one last time, in case I don't make it back alive. The easy choice would have been to allow Telly and his men to save Shaya. Because if she didn't make it, at least Bailey would still have one surviving parent. But I can't do that. I can no longer rely on someone else to save her. I must do this, and I hope we both make it out alive.

I watch them from across the street. They're sitting at the dining room table having dinner. Bailey sits in her high chair, eating something the woman feeds her. The man takes a bite of his food while smiling at his wife and *my* daughter. They look like the perfect family, but I don't care. I want my daughter back, and I have no problem going above and beyond to make that happen.

I exit my car, debating if I'm making a mistake. If Telly knew what I was doing, he would have had a heart attack. Which is why I didn't tell him or Dafari what my plans were. I don't need a pep talk about how it's best to stay away from my daughter.

I approach the house cautiously. This looks like a quiet neighborhood—the kind where they have one of those groups who watch over it and report suspicious things. When I step foot on the front porch, I knock. I nervously shift as I wait for someone to open the door. The man flings it open.

"May I help you?" he asks.

Yes. You can give me back my daughter and have your own kids.

"Hi, I'm interested in purchasing your home," I reply.

I rehearsed this several times and have the script down to a science. I had to figure out the best way to get inside the home, and what better way than to offer to purchase their home? If they consider, they won't have a problem allowing me to take a tour. There are a few factors that led to this. One, I'm sure they could use the money. With him being a coach and her being a teacher, who knows how much debt they have? I was told that America is in something called a recession. People are out of jobs and making little to nothing to survive. The last factor is safety. Bailey was taken from this home, which means that it's not safe for her here. And if my instinct serves me right, they can't afford to sell this home and purchase another one. Otherwise, they would have done it the moment they got her back. My research showed that mortgage prices have almost tripled, and many can't afford to rent, let alone buy.

Confusion crosses his face. "I'm sorry, excuse me?"

"I'd like to purchase your home. Cash."

His eyes widen, and he steps forward. "What real estate firm are you with?"

"None. I don't need one."

"Is this a joke?" he asks.

"With all due respect, does it look like I'm joking?"

He crosses his arms. "How much?"

I already know the house is listed for well over three hundred thousand, so I have to make a substantial offer. "Six hundred thousand."

He chuckles. "How about eight hundred thousand?"

He's testing me, but I'm already one step ahead of him. "Deal. But only if I can take a tour."

"Now?"

"Yes."

"My family and I are having dinner."

I shrug. "That's my offer."

"Let me check with my wife."

He walks away but returns a few minutes later and opens the door wide. I step inside and am immediately hit with the smell of food. The woman enters the living room with Bailey in her arms.

"Your daughter is beautiful," I say as I fight the urge to snatch her away and run.

She smiles widely. "Her name is Bailey."

"Bailey, what a beautiful name."

Bailey stares at me and smiles. A small piece of me hopes it's because she remembers me, but I can't say for sure.

"We couldn't have our own kids, so we adopted her. The mother insisted we don't change her name, so we kept it. Besides, Bailey fits her perfectly."

"Yes. Yes, it does."

The woman looks up at me. "You have an accent. Where are you from?" she asks.

"I'm from Africa. My family just moved here, and we are searching for a home. I drove past this place, and it seemed perfect."

"Oh, how wonderful. Do you have kids?"

Yes. I have kids. And you're holding her right now.

"Yes. A daughter."

She squeezes Bailey tightly. "Daughters are wonderful, aren't they? I can't wait until I get to put Bailey in ballet and piano lessons. I was so distraught when I found out I couldn't conceive, but then God gave us this angel."

Her eyes sparkle with joy, and for the first time, I feel sorry for them. This is a loving couple who wanted the blessings of parenthood. These are the kind of people we look for to adopt the children from my orphanage back home. The look in this woman's eyes is pure love. This will make it much harder when it's time to take Bailey from her. Fuck! This is going to be complicated. The man steps forward.

"Are you ready for the tour, Mr. . . . I'm sorry. I didn't get your name."

My phone rings, and it's Telly. He called at the perfect time. "I'm sorry, I need to take this." I step away and answer the call. "Hey."

"We leave in the morning."

"Okay."

Bailey chooses that moment to cry.

"Baas, where are you?"

"I'm running some errands," I lie.

"Please tell me you didn't go over there. Baas, get out of there before you expose yourself and make this situation harder than it already is."

I don't want to leave, but he's right. I have to get out of here. Because the longer I stay, the harder it will be for me to walk away from Bailey. "I'm on my way." I end the call and turn to them both. "I'm sorry. I have something urgent to tend to."

The man nods. "Do you have a business card or something so we can contact you? We want to put you in touch with our realtor."

I take one last look at my daughter before I turn to him with my reply. "No, but I'll be in touch soon."

"I can't believe you went against my orders to stay away from Bailey right now."

"I don't take orders from you, Telly. You know that."

He pinches the bridge of his nose. "You and Dafari are impossible at times. You guys stress me the fuck out."

"We also pay you a sizeable amount of money," I remind him.

"Which is why I put up with you two."

"Listen. I'm walking into danger. I needed to see my daughter one last time, just in case I don't make it."

"What you did was risky," he replies. "But I understand why you did it."

Dafari steps onto the plane. "Sorry, I'm late. I had to calm my worried wife."

"Ebony has a right to be worried. Are you sure you're up for this? Telly, his men, and I can handle this," I assure him.

He looks offended. "Baas, did you sit back and do nothing when *I* needed help?" he asks.

I shake my head.

"Okay, then. I have your back just like you had mine," he replies.

We stand in the middle of the aisle with Telly and his men while he briefly overviews the game play for saving Shaya. It's all a blur to me. He may have his tactical plan in place, but the only thing on my mind is revenge. Jay will pay for putting Bailey and Shaya in harm's way. I will gut him just enough for him to bleed out over time and die a slow and painful death.

Shaya

I slept well last night, surprisingly. My body is doing a great job of letting me know when it needs rest. I got up early enough to boil an egg and slice some fruit. Jay is still asleep, and while I slice the fruit, I contemplate sneaking into his room and slashing his throat. I'm not a killer, but I have no other choice. If I accept my fate, it's only a matter of time before he expects me to sleep in the same bed with him. What am I supposed to do? Wait patiently for that day to come?

I hear his footsteps and place the knife I'm holding in the kitchen sink before I turn around to face him. He grabs a granola bar out of the pantry.

"You're up early," he says.

"I wanted to take a walk before it gets too hot."

He gestures for me to take a seat, and I do. I want him to say what he has to say quickly so I can get out of here. He walks around the table, sits down, reaches behind his back, and pulls a gun out of his waist. He places the gun on the table in front of him. His grip is tight as he watches me.

"I thought we had an understanding."

"We do," I reply.

"No. We don't, Shaya. This isn't what I had in mind. You won't talk to me. You refuse to eat, you're mean, and you constantly defy me."

I shrug. "So, what? You're going to kill me because of it?"

"Maybe. I wanted you to have freedom here. I wanted you to be free to roam the island and do as you please. All I asked was that you give me companionship. Just a little until we get back to where we once were. But you won't do it. So, here's what's about to happen. There will be no more freedom."

"What!" I shout.

"These are the rules now, and you will do as I say."

"I'm not doing that," I respond.

He shoots to his feet, walks around the table, and places the gun against my head. The steel is cold against my temple.

"You have no idea what I'm capable of, do you?" he asks.

I don't answer him because I'm too busy trembling at the thought of him pulling the trigger. He leans in and speaks into my ear.

"I have no problem ending your life, Shaya. And after I'm done, I'll go back to New York and kill that bastard baby of yours too, I swear before God!"

Tears stream down my face, and I bite my lip out of fear. This isn't a threat. Jay is serious. I can hear it in his voice. This is not the man I once knew, but none of that matters right now. "Jay, please. I'll do better."

"No, you won't. You're stubborn, Shaya. You've been that way since the moment we met."

"No. I'm serious."

I turn to face him slowly and look him in the eyes. He presses the gun against my head tighter, but I don't flinch.

"I will do better. I promise. I just needed some time, Jay. I miss my daughter and struggle with never seeing her again. Please, just give me one more chance. Please."

He stares into my eyes but doesn't respond right away. I can see the wheels spinning as he weighs his options. I can tell that he wants to give this a try. He wants to know if I'll stick to my word and be friendly to him. But he also doesn't trust me, and that's working against me. He was right when he said that I'm stubborn. We spent five years together, and he knows that once I have my mind made up about something, it can be difficult for me to change it. He slowly moves the gun away from my head.

"You get *one* more chance, Shaya. And it's only because I'm in a good mood today."

He places the gun back in his waist, and I release the breath I've been holding. "So, we're good? You'll leave Bailey alone?"

He takes a seat in front of me. "That depends on you. But for now, yes."

I could jump across the table and strangle him. I take a second to size him up and quickly conclude that I don't stand a chance. Jay is much bigger than me and physically fit. I couldn't hurt him if I tried.

"I'll do better, Jay. You have my word."

"Then we shouldn't have a problem."

He opens the granola bar and takes a bite before scrolling through his phone. I stay frozen in my seat, unsure of my next move. Do I get up and go for my walk? Or do I stay here and make small talk to show him that I'm serious? I decide on the latter.

"What plans do you have today?"

He looks up at me. "I have a few errands to run."

If he's running errands, that means he's going off the island. I need to see where he's going. "Mind if I come along?"

He shakes his head. "Maybe next time, if you act right."

"Okay."

I'm met with a tiny flicker of hope. If I play this right, there's a chance he'll let me come with him off the island, and I can escape him or, at least, call for help. He stands to his feet and shoves his phone into his back pocket. He takes one last look at me before he leaves the kitchen. "I'll be back in a few hours. Until then, stay out of trouble."

I decided to tour the house today for the first time. I had little interest in touring it before, but it's probably wise to know the blueprint. I start with the master bedroom that Jay sleeps in. I attempt to open the door, but it's locked because he doesn't want me to see what's inside. I walk farther down the hall and into an office. The mahogany desk is immaculate and neatly polished. I attempt to open the drawers, but they're all locked. I tug the handle on the file cabinet, and, as I suspected, it's also locked. He's made sure that I don't have access to anything that will help me get out of here. I turn to face the bookshelf; it's lined with every genre, both fiction and nonfiction.

I glide my fingers across the books as I read each title, carefully familiarizing myself with them in case I have the urge to get lost in one while I'm here. I quickly shake away that thought. My mind won't be relaxed enough to read a book. Right now, my mind is overloaded, searching for ways to get off this island. I constantly think about Bailey and Baas and how much I want to be with them. I think about my parents and how worried they must be.

I stop when I reach a familiar book. It was a book I gave Jay for our first anniversary. I pull it from the shelf and open it. Sure enough, my handwritten love note still lies inside. I open and read it and immediately feel sick. The message speaks about how much I love him and how I can't wait to spend the rest of my life with him. I shake my head at how stupid I was. I had no idea what love was when I was with Jay. I had no idea what it felt like to be in love until I met Baas.

Tears prick my eyes as I think about how much I've hurt him. I've been so busy dreaming of being reunited with him that I hadn't considered that he might want nothing to do with me once I make it out of here. And I can't say that I blame him. Baas gave me his heart, and I broke it into pieces. Maybe I shouldn't leave here at all. Maybe Bailey should be raised by the parent who didn't give her away. How could I look into those beautiful, brown eyes, knowing it was my fault her life was in danger? How can I ever explain to her that I kept her a secret from her father? She deserves better. Baas deserves better. They both deserve more than what I've given them.

Baas

It's hot, so hot that my clothes are sticking to my skin. We arrived on the island thirty minutes ago, and so far, there are no signs that Shaya and Jay are here. There are a few natives to our right, but they pay us no mind as they pull fish out of a boat and onto the shore. I look around and see a few small kids playing on the beach. Sadness washes over me as it reminds me of Bailey. I snap out of it. This is not the time to think about that. My only focus now is saving Shaya. Then we can focus on Bailey. Telly approaches me.

"There are two homes through those trees," he points toward the area.

I don't hesitate and immediately walk in the direction he's referencing.

Dafari catches up to me. "Telly and his men are capable, you know?"

"That's up for debate," I reply.

He places a hand on my shoulder, stopping me. "Hey, remember, you're a father now."

"What are you saying, Dafari?"

"I'm saying that I understand your urge to dive into the lion's den, but think about Bailey."

"I am thinking about Bailey. All that matters right now is saving Shaya. Bailey needs a mother more than anything. And if that means I have to risk my life to save hers, then so be it."

I'm frustrated. I'm hot, tired, and hungry. This is *not* how things are supposed to be right now. I was supposed to propose to Shaya. She was supposed to say yes. And we were supposed to live the rest of our lives happily together. I think about how angry I was when I discovered she had lied to me. I was furious, and honestly, I never thought I'd be able to forgive her and move past her deceit. But that all changed the moment I lost her. I no longer felt anger. I felt panic, pain, and worry. Now, all I want to do is save her. I want to hold her tightly and tell her that I forgive her. I want to tell her that nothing else matters to me except for her and Bailey. I want to apologize to her for being an asshole and vow to spend the rest of my life making it up to her and loving her.

Dafari continues to watch me. After a few minutes, he nods and continues to walk beside me. We silently walk through the forest, with Telly and his men trailing behind us. We stop when we reach a clearing. I see a single home ahead but no sign of anyone living there.

I speak in a low voice to Dafari. "Ambush or discreet? What do you think?"

He concentrates before he speaks. "It doesn't look like we can be discreet. There's no way we can approach the home without someone seeing us."

I look around the forest. "You're right. This is the only way in. Fuck! If we're not careful, they could see us coming."

I turn around to speak to Telly—and I'm met with the barrel of a gun. I look over at Dafari, who also has a gun pointed at his head. Dafari and I don't exchange glances, but we don't have to. We've fought side by side many times and can tell what each other thinks through our body language. He slowly shuffles. It's his way of telling me not to react hastily. I take heed and analyze the situation. Telly has four men behind him, guns drawn, which means we're outnumbered. Dafari and I could still attempt to take them down. These are trained men, but I highly doubt they could beat us. But is it worth the risk? Is it worth both of us being killed? I quickly conclude that the answer is no.

"What the fuck is this, Telly?" I ask angrily.

He smirks. "*This* is getting what's owed to me."

CHAPTER SIXTEEN

Baas

How the fuck did Dafari and I *not* see this coming? Did we really get so comfortable with Telly that we didn't see the signs of a traitor? Of course, we did. Our country has been working with Telly since Dafari was a kid. He's been an ally and a confidant over the years.

He and his men lead us past the house, shove us inside a vacant shed, and handcuff us to a pole. They withdraw their guns once Dafari and I are no longer a threat. Now, Dafari speaks.

"Telly, do you have any idea what you've just done?" he asks.

Telly laughs. "I know *exactly* what I've done."

I lunge at him, but the handcuffs pull me back. "Clearly, you know the consequences of this?" I add.

He shakes his head. "Oh, please. You two won't make it out of here for there to be consequences. I'll tell the people that you died trying to save Shaya. No one will bat an eye."

"Why?" Dafari asks.

He takes a step forward before responding. "I need the money."

I huff. "With all the money we've paid you over the years, you should have more than enough in your savings."

"I lost it all. I made some bad investments, and I owe a few loan sharks for a gambling debt."

"How much do you want?" I ask. At this point, I'm desperate and willing to give him anything to let us go.

"Let's start with $5 million."

"You could have just *asked* us for the money, Telly. You didn't need to go through all of this," Dafari says.

Telly smiles. "Where's the fun in asking? Do you know how good it felt to outsmart you two? Two big-shot men from a royal family who couldn't save one of their own."

"This was a game to you?" I ask angrily.

"Yes. And I win."

At this point, I become uninterested in Telly's motive and more interested in whether Dafari and I can deliver what he wants to him. Five million dollars will be tough to get since we're on a remote island. I look over at Dafari.

"Do we have it to give?" I ask.

We both know that the answer is yes. Five million dollars is a drop in the bucket for a billionaire. The purpose of my asking Dafari is to look into his eyes and see what he's thinking. It's a way for us to communicate silently. He watches me, shifting his eyes to my handcuffs before nodding.

"Yes."

The look of confidence in his stare tells me what I need to know. We will get out of here . . . by any means necessary. He has Ebony and Aiden to get back to. And I have to find Shaya to get back to Bailey. I turn to face Telly.

"What do we get in return?" I ask.

Telly's brows narrow. "This isn't a negotiation."

"We're not giving you a dime until we know you'll release us," I reply.

He throws his head back with laughter before he answers me. "You will give me *exactly* what I asked for if you ever want to see Shaya again."

"What does Shaya have to do . . ." I stop midsentence. I look over at Dafari, who looks at me. It registers to us both. "You. *You* were behind this?"

He smiles with satisfaction. "How else do you think Jay got away so easily?"

It all makes sense now. All this time, Dafari and I couldn't figure out how Jay was always two steps ahead of us. We racked our brains, trying to figure out how he could afford a private plane and leave the country undetected. Now, I'm seething with anger.

"You have given yourself a death wish, Telly." I glance at the other men. "All of you."

"Yeah, yeah. Do we have a deal or not?" he asks.

"Where is Shaya?" I ask.

"She's safe."

"Has she been harmed in any way?" I continue.

"Not to my knowledge," he replies.

I probe further. "Just one more thing, is she here, on this island?"

Telly smirks. "That's confidential."

He's fucking with me, and I'm close to losing my cool. But this is not the time for that. I've always been able to remain calm and rational in front of my adversaries. And this is no different.

"We will get you the money," I reply.

He nods. "Good. I'll be back to arrange for payment."

He and his men leave the shed, and I turn to Dafari. "How did we miss this?"

He shakes his head. "I have no idea, but he played us like a fucking fiddle."

I yank my arm angrily, but the handcuffs stay intact. "He knows too much about us. He knows how we work. *That's* how he outsmarted us."

"He won't get the chance to do it again, trust me," Dafari responds.

"We have to make it out of here first. Then we can plan his demise."

"So, what now?" he asks.

I don't have an answer for him because I don't know. I look around and see nothing available to help us escape. We can barely move a few feet beyond the pole we're handcuffed to.

"I don't have an answer right now, Dafari."

"It's okay. We'll put our heads together and figure out something. We *always* come out on top, Baas."

For some reason, I'm not convinced. Maybe it's because I've had no success finding Shaya or getting Bailey back. From the moment Shaya received that phone call, I felt like a failure. I'm a confident man. I stand steadfast in what I'm capable of. But with the love of my life still out there and me being captured, I'm starting to feel defeated.

"She's got to be here. Why else would he choose this island?"

"You raise a good point," he replies. "If he's working with Jay, it makes sense that he would lure us here."

"Once we make it out. I'm killing all of them on sight. Jay. Telly. And his men."

"Yes. But not until we're sure Shaya is here. Otherwise, we'll torture one of them until they tell us what we want to know."

Beads of sweat drop from my forehead as the temperature rises. Insects fly around us, and we shoo them away with our free hand. The place smells musty, like it's never been cleaned, and the pipes are rusted. There's one tinted window, and the floor is hard and uneven. They were smart to leave nothing near us. Everything is out of reach, including the trash. My brain goes to work. I've trained for moments like this, moments where I'm captured and need to escape. I've successfully escaped handcuffs before, but these are too tight. I won't be able to get out of these unless I have something to help me. A pin. Needle. I need something because Dafari and I are of no use bound like this.

"You know what we have to do, Dafari. We must get out of these handcuffs and fight for our lives."

"Yes."

"It's the only way," I reply.

"I know."

I'm glad to know he's on the same page, but I can hear the worry in his voice. He's worried about his wife and kid. I can tell that the possibility of him not returning home resonates with him.

"We will get out of here. Keep your head up, and let's do what we need to do to get back to our families."

He nods. "Damn straight."

Shaya

Jay returned in an hour. Just as I was about to take a walk, he walks onto the porch, and his eyes sweep me from head to toe.

"Where are you going?" he asks.

"Remember I mentioned I wanted to take a walk? You're back early. Why?"

"Don't question me. And I don't think it's a good idea for you to roam the island alone and unattended."

Roaming the island is the only escape that I have from this house. It's the only time I get to clear my head and have some time alone where I don't have to pretend to like him.

"I promise I'll be safe."

He grips me on the shoulder. "I said no. There are enough things here in the house to occupy you."

I want to smack him. No. I want to punch him. It's bad enough I have to share this house with him, but now he wants to forbid me from leaving. I almost resist. I nearly spit in his face and tell him to fuck off before I run off and down to the beach. But I have to keep my word. Otherwise, he could kill me and harm my daughter next.

"Okay. Well, will you take a walk with me?"

It's not the ideal way I want to spend my day, but something is better than nothing. He searches my eyes to see if I'm being serious before he answers me.

"Maybe. But not today."

"Okay."

I walk over to the hammock and sit on the edge as it swings from side to side. He watches me for a second before he speaks to me.

"Don't even think of defying me, Shaya."

I shake my head. "I'm not going anywhere. I told you that you had my word."

"Good."

He walks inside, and I lie back on the hammock and look out at the ocean. It's a beautiful day today. The sun shines brightly, but it's not too hot. A nice breeze blows, and the waves crash upon the shore slowly and delicately. The hammock rocks from side to side, and I take deep breaths, calming the panic inside me. What if he never lets me out? The front door swings open, and he peeps his head out.

"I made lunch."

He stares at me as he holds the door ajar. I slowly climb out of the hammock and follow him inside and into the kitchen. Two salads are placed on the kitchen table. He opens the cabinet, pulls out two bottles of dressing, and sets them in the middle of the table.

"I know you like Caesar, but I was told this is really good. It's a mango jalapeño dressing."

The first question that pops into my head is, who told him the dressing was good? The second question is, where did he buy it? The fact that he was only gone for an hour and returned with items tells me we're closer to civilization than I thought.

I reach for the mango jalapeño dressing. "Thank you."

I drizzle a little on my salad, still apprehensive about eating the food he's prepared for me, but I have no choice. I'm hungry. I haven't eaten much since I've been here, and I'm sure that if I stepped on a scale right now, I would have been down at least twenty pounds. I can feel the weight shedding from my body. I take a small bite of my salad, and it's surprisingly good. The lettuce is fresh and crisp, the cheese is robust, and the croutons are fresh and flavorful. It also tastes like he drizzled some fresh lemon juice over it. I chew slowly as he watches me with a smile.

"Good, isn't it?" he asks.

I finish chewing before I answer him. "Yes, it's delicious."

His smile grows wider. "You know I was never much of a cook. But I learned to master the art of a good salad."

I offer a smile, but it's a weak one. I focus on eating my salad and taking small sips of my

lemonade . . . just in case he poisoned me. When I've finished my plate, I drink the rest of my lemonade, which I've concluded isn't poisoned. Because if it were, I'd feel weird by now.

"Thank you for lunch." The statement alone drains my energy.

"See, it wasn't bad at all, was it? Soon, we'll be back to how we used to be."

I feel sick at the thought, and he must see the expression on my face because he frowns. "Does that bother you?" he asks.

"What?"

"The thought of getting close to me again? Being intimate with me again?"

I almost pass out when he says it. I'd much rather slice my throat than be intimate with him—ever.

"I need some time, that's all. I'm trying."

I fear my answer isn't good enough for him, but he nods.

"I understand. I will try my best to give you some time, but I'm a man, Shaya, and I have needs. As I said before, I won't force myself on you. That's not how I operate. But at some point soon, I'll expect you to be on board and enjoy it."

In his twisted mind, he thinks he's doing me a favor. But all he's doing is making me hate him more than I already do.

"I understand."

It's the only thing I can say to him at this point because if I'm not careful, I'll say something to anger him.

"Good. Oh, and you may as well get Baas and Dafari out of your head. They won't come and save you. As a matter of fact, they'll both be dead very soon. I just thought I'd get that out of the way so we both can move on."

My eyes widen. "What did you do?"

"That's no business of yours."

"We agreed you wouldn't hurt my family."

"No. I said that I wouldn't harm your daughter. I said nothing about the two of them."

I'm stricken with panic as I ask my next question. "Why, Jay? You got what you want. Why go after those who I love?"

"Because if I don't, they'll never stop looking for you. I can't live peacefully with that hanging over my head."

I shake my head as the tears fall. "No. Please, no."

"It's done."

I lose it. I grab the fork next to me and lunge across the table. I'm close but not close enough to harm him. He grabs my arm before the fork can reach his neck. "You bastard," I yell as I struggle to shove the fork into whatever area of his body I can reach. But he's stronger than me. He forces the fork out of my hand and drags me out of the kitchen by my arm. I try my hardest to escape his grip, but I'm unsuccessful. He opens the door to the room I've been sleeping in and shoves me inside.

"You can come out when you calm down."

He slams the door shut and locks it from the outside. I curl in a fetal position and sob.

I don't know how long I've been in this room. I've lost count. It could be two hours, or it could be two days. All I know is that I haven't slept. I haven't eaten anything or had anything to drink. I've been in the same position, crying my eyes out at the fact that everyone I love is in danger. If Jay succeeds, Ebony will never forgive me for this. She will be without her husband and soul mate, and Aiden will be without his father. Baas will die before I can make things right, and Bailey will grow up without knowing how much he loves her. And that's only if Jay keeps his word about not harming her. Eventually, the door opens slowly. I hear footsteps, but I don't look up. I feel him standing over me.

"Are you at least going to clean yourself? You haven't showered in two days."

Two days. That's how long I've been in this position. And that works just fine for me. I don't answer him because I don't have the energy.

"Shaya, get up!"

It's not a request. It's a demand. I take a deep breath and slowly uncurl myself while he walks into the bathroom.

"I'll turn the water on," he says.

I rise slowly as my headache worsens. When I stand, my head spins. I drag myself to the bathroom, and when I walk inside, I glance at the mirror. My hair is matted to my head, and I have bags under my eyes. The mirror quickly frosts from the steam from the shower, and I look away. My eyes meet Jay's, and he seems angry.

"We'll make breakfast when you're done," he says on his way out the door.

He brushes past me, and I sigh, relieved that he gives me privacy to undress. I step out of the clothes I've been wearing for two days and into the shower. The hot water relaxes me, and I close my eyes tightly.

"I'm so sorry," I say softly.

No one hears it, yet I feel I need to say it. The guilt of everything is too much for me to carry. It's weighing me down like I'm carrying a bag of bricks. I had a sliver of hope that I could make it out of here. I was determined to escape by any means necessary. But now . . . Now that Jay has taken everything from me, I do not doubt that my life will also end here.

Baas

I've been going stir-crazy for the past two days. We haven't seen Telly. One of his men brings us cold sandwiches and water but does not mention when Telly will return. I'm running out of patience, and we're running out of time. I'm deep in thought as I think about the fact that I could be close enough to save Shaya. Bailey and I need her. And I cannot fail. I haven't slept a wink since we've been captured because I keep thinking about her well-being. I can only imagine the toll this has taken on her.

Another thought pops into my head, and I try my hardest to shake it away, but I can't. Shaya is a beautiful woman, and any man would be tempted to sleep with her. Especially a man who already knows what she's like in bed. The thought of Jay violating her in any way makes me sick to my stomach. When Shaya agreed to run away with him, she sacrificed her own life to save our daughter. Who knows what else he's made her do? I grunt angrily, and it wakes Dafari.

"What is it?" he asks.

"Nothing."

"Baas, I know you. It's something."

"If he's touched her . . ."

"Hey, don't even think about that right now. Stay focused."

"How can I? What if he . . ." I can't even finish the sentence.

"We don't know what he's done. But right now, we have work to do. We need to get out of here and save her."

"I know."

"Listen. I know exactly what you're feeling. I felt the same way when Ebony was in danger. But you can't let the worry and anger consume you so much that you can't think straight. You, of all people, know what's at stake when you don't control your emotions."

I nod because I don't have the words to speak right now. Dafari is right. Emotions will get you killed. It's the number one rule I learned when I first started training. It's why I've been successful at my job. But I also never had to worry about emotion. My job was to eliminate a threat with no questions asked. And when I did so, I moved on as if nothing had happened. This situation is different. My anger is tied to other emotions I can't control, and although I'm trying, it's all new to me. I lean back and take a deep breath.

"I don't see how you can sleep at a time like this."

"It's hard, but do you remember what you taught me during our sessions?" he asks.

I take a minute to think before I reply. "Yeah. Your body needs rest for energy."

"Exactly. How can we take them down if we don't have energy?"

I look over at him. "And here I thought you weren't paying attention."

He chuckles. "I always paid attention."

I grab the plate in front of me and bite the sandwich. The bread is hard. The meat tastes old, and the cheese is thick. There are no condiments in it, but it doesn't matter. I'm not eating it for the taste. I'm eating it for the energy. I chew and swallow the pieces, even though the taste disgusts me. I grab the water bottle and gulp it down, even though it's warm. When I'm finished, I sit back against the wall.

Soon, the door opens, and Telly walks in with two men behind him.

"I apologize for the delay in my return, but I had an important matter to address," he announces.

Dafari and I remain silent while he continues.

"I have a burner phone. You get one time to call the person you need to transfer the funds into an account I have set up. If I even think that you're trying to screw me over, Shaya dies."

"How do I know she's not already dead?" I ask.

"Well, I guess you'll have to trust me, won't you?"

I shake my head. "No. I need proof. Why would we give you a dime without ensuring she's still alive first?"

My heart pumps hard and fast as I say the words—the adrenaline from the anger courses through my veins. Telly watches me quietly before he responds.

"Okay, then," he replies.

He takes his phone out of his pocket and hits the call button.

"They want proof she's alive." He listens to the other person's response. "Okay." Then he ends the call.

Before he can place the phone back in his pocket, it vibrates with a notification. He opens the message, looks, and then turns the screen toward us. She looks at the camera with confusion and exhaustion. She looks thinner in the face and dehydrated. She looks tired and worn out. It's heartbreaking, and I divert my eyes because I can't take seeing her like this.

"That's enough," I reply.

It tortures me to be so close to her yet unable to do anything about it. When I saw her, I felt relief that she was still alive. And I'm determined now more than ever to save her. He places the phone back into his pocket.

"So, we're good?" he asks.

"Yeah."

He places a black phone on the floor and slides it over to Dafari. "Make the call," he demands.

Dafari wastes no time grabbing it and dialing a number. The room is so quiet that I can hear Ebony's voice when she answers. He takes a deep breath.

"Ebony."

"Dafari, where are you? What is going on?" she asks frantically.

"I can't talk long, Princess. But I need you to do something."

"What do you mean you can't talk long? Dafari, you're scaring me," she responds.

I can hear the panic in her voice and the pain in Dafari's eyes as he tries his best to calm her.

"I need you to wire $5 million from the savers' account," he instructs her calmly.

The average person will hear the word "savers" and automatically think that Dafari means *savings* account. He does, but it's not a traditional savings account. After Dafari was captured, we opened an account specifically for ransom requests. Or instances where we needed to pull additional resources to save someone. Hence, the title "savers" account. Ebony's breath hitches.

"Dafari . . ." she doesn't finish her sentence because she knows someone could be listening. "Done. But you know it'll take at least a day."

It doesn't take at least a day. We can wire the funds immediately. But Ebony is smart enough to understand that an extra day can make or break a situation like this.

"Okay. I'll text the wiring instructions."

"All right."

He shuts his eyes tightly before he wraps up the call. "Kiss my son for me."

He doesn't give her a chance to reply. He ends the call and tosses the phone over to Telly. "Text the information to the number I just dialed. You'll have the money in a day," Dafari instructs.

Telly smiles widely. "Thank you for your cooperation."

He and his men leave, and Dafari and I remain quiet until we're sure they're really gone. He looks over at me.

"We *will* get out of here."

I nod. "Yes, we will."

He looks away, deep in thought, and I use my free hand to rub the tension I'm feeling in the back of my neck. We have one more day. One more day to save ourselves and Shaya. Neither of us knows how we will do it yet, but none of that matters. At this point, it's all about survival. All we can do is rely on our instincts and hope it's enough to save us all.

CHAPTER SEVENTEEN
Shaya

Jay was acting weird after my shower. Once I was dressed, he demanded that I pose for a picture. I stared into his phone as he zoomed his camera on me and snapped the shot. Then I followed him downstairs to cook breakfast. He decides on eggs, toast, and fresh fruit. He's made the toast already and is standing over the stove cooking the eggs.

"What fruit are we having?"

He jerks his head toward the refrigerator. "I'm going to cut up some fresh mango and melon."

I take a seat at the table. I'm about to relax, but the word *cut* screams in my head. If he's about to cut some fruit, that means he's about to use a knife. And that knife could be my ticket out of here. I survey the area but don't see one yet. He's humming while he stands over the stove, scrambling the eggs, and I straighten in my seat, watching his every move. When the eggs are done, he removes the pan from the burner and opens the drawer beside him. Sure enough, he pulls out a knife. He grabs the fruit from the counter to his left and proceeds to chop it. It seems easy in my head. Find a way to get close to him, grab the knife, and kill him. But as easy as it sounds, it seems like a difficult thing to do. But I'm left with no other choice. I must do this.

"Need some help?"

He stops chopping the fruit and turns around to face me. When he does, I give him my most genuine smile.

"Yeah, sure," he replies.

I stand and walk toward him. His grip on the knife remains tight.

"What can I do?" I ask.

"How about you make us some fresh squeezed orange juice?" he replies.

"Okay."

I grab two glasses out of the cabinet above us. I bump into him when I turn around to take them to the table. The glasses slip from my fingers and crash to the floor.

"Shit!" I say before kneeling to pick them up.

He follows suit and kneels in front of me. "Are you okay?"

Instinct causes me to shove a piece of glass into his eye. Blood gushes out, and it bulges as his hand grabs for the piece of glass protruding from it. I quickly grab the knife on the counter and lodge it into his shoulder. He reaches for me, and I back up quickly, moving out of his path as more blood gushes to the floor. He manages to stand but is unsteady as he tries to hold on to the counter in front of him. He gasps for air, and I slowly back away at the sight unfolding before me. When he drops to his knees, I make a run for it. I don't stick around to make sure he dies. I grab the bottled water on my way out and rush out the door and into the woods. I run. And I run. And I run until I'm too tired to run any further.

I stop to catch my breath and look behind me to make sure that he hasn't miraculously followed me. I twist the top off the water and take a sip. My thirst makes me want to guzzle the entire bottle, but I also need to save some in case I don't come across fresh water. I don't know how long I could be out here, but I do know that I'll last longer without food than water. I sit at the base of a tree and continue to catch my breath. I listen for the sounds of footsteps, paranoid that Jay has somehow found me. When my breathing is managed, I take one more sip before I rest my head against the tree.

"What now?" I ask myself.

Who knows what happens now. I could somehow make it out of here, or I could die out here in the woods. And if I die, at least I tried to return to Bailey. I look up at the sky. It's a bright, sunny day, but it doesn't feel like it. It feels cloudy and gloomy. I place the bottled water next to me, and that's when I notice the dried blood on my hands. Reality sets in at the thought that I may have murdered someone, but the remorse only lasts a moment. I had to do what I had to do. Jay hadn't harmed me yet, but eventually, he would have. I had to protect myself. I hold my head high and think about my next step. Home. I must get home. I don't know what Jay has done with Dafari and Baas, but I know they're in danger. I stand to my feet and look around my surroundings. It all looks the same. Trees. Grass. Shrubbery. And insects.

I have no choice but to keep walking until I find something or someone to help me get off this island. I hear something behind me, and I freeze. I lean down and pick up the branch lying in front of me. It's small but big enough to defend myself if need be. I stay very still, and I hear the noise again behind me. I whirl around and breathe a sigh of relief when I see the source of the noise. It's a squirrel.

As I walk forward, I drop the tree branch and wipe a bead of sweat from my face. I walk for what feels like hours with no sign of life in sight. The sun is starting to set, and soon, I won't be able to see my way around. Just as I'm about to take a rest, I hear water. I rush toward the sounds of waves until I find a clearing. I push my way through the remaining trees and grass until my feet reach the sand.

"Oh my God!"

I can't believe my eyes, but I rush toward it anyway, silently thanking God for hearing my prayers. When I reach the boat, I look inside it. There are weighted sandbags inside to keep the boat in place, along with a flashlight and life vest. I look out into the sea, fear crippling me from doing what I know I need to do. I fear the water. I can't swim, and drowning is one of my biggest fears. But this is my way out. So, I throw out the weighted sandbags, snap on the life vest, pull the boat to the water, and jump inside.

There is nothing to row it with. Only the waves from the sea can guide the boat, wherever that may be. The ocean is calm right now, and I'm grateful because the further away I drift from shore, the more nauseated I feel. I open the bottled water, take another sip, and lie on my back as I drift to the unknown. I stare at the cotton candy sky and cross my fingers that this boat can sustain whatever challenges the sea may bring. I'm no expert when it comes to aqua life. I know nothing about water and boats. But I'm smart enough to know I'm doomed if this boat gets so much as a tiny hole for any reason.

My eyes get heavy as the boat continues to sway lightly with the motion of the waves. Add in the cool breeze, and my body slowly shuts down. I feel myself letting go, but I try my hardest to stay awake. It doesn't work. I close my eyes and allow myself to drift asleep.

I'm dreaming. And it's a good dream. I'm in Mafachiko with Baas and Bailey, and we're having her birthday party. She and Aiden run around the yard as they play and laugh. Baas sits on the grass, and I sit between his legs, snacking on grapes. He strokes my hair and smiles at me. I smile back at him and mouth the words, "I love you." And then I wake up. It's pitch black except for the moon and bright stars above me. I can't see my surroundings, but I hear the waves as it guides the boat.

Fear slams into my chest at the thought of the unknown. I don't know what's out there lurking in the water beneath me. And if something were to attack, I wouldn't see it coming. I remember there's a flashlight here, and I feel around to find it. When I do, I press the button, praying it turns on. And it does. I shine the light around me, paying attention to any creatures that may be lurking. But I don't see any. I'm tempted to keep the flashlight on for the remainder of the night, but it wouldn't be wise. I have no idea how long I'll be out in the open water, and I shouldn't drain the battery on the first night, especially since I don't see an extra one. So, I turn it off.

I lie back down and listen to the still of the night. I don't know how long I've been asleep or how late it is, but I'm anxious for the sunrise to see what's around me. My stomach growls, indicating that I'm starving. I've tried my best not to think about food, but it's almost impossible when you're as hungry as I am. I have about three days before my body feels the effects of starvation. My best bet is to continue drinking my water until that's gone. And when I finish that, who knows how much longer I'll survive.

A noise startles me. It sounds like a loud splash. Like a big fish coming up for air and diving back into the sea. But how big? And does it like to eat humans? I turn the flashlight on again and shine it on the water before me. I can see a ripple where something is there. "Shit!"

I scoot back a little in the boat, but it's so small that I barely have anywhere to go. Whatever it is that's out there, it has an advantage. I'm stuck in here with no escape, and if it chooses to attack, I'll have to decide if I want to fight it off or jump into the water. I'm dying either way. I shine the light inside the boat to check again for any weapons, but I don't see any. I only have the flashlight and my bottle of water to defend myself. I look over the edge of the boat again, and this time, I see the cause of the noise. It's a big orange fish swimming beside the boat, right at the water's surface.

"Oh, thank God. You scared me, buddy."

He leaps out of the water and swims away. I fall back into the boat and turn off the flashlight. Then I place it next to me, close my eyes, try to relax and sleep away my anxiety. Hopefully, when I awake, it'll be morning.

The sound of chirping birds awakes me. When I open my eyes, I shield the sun from blinding me. Night one, and I'm still alive. If I can keep this up, I might have a chance. Considering the small space, I rise and stretch my body as much as possible. I try to rub the tension out of my neck, but it doesn't help. My back, shoulders, and neck are all achy, compliments of sleeping on a hard surface. When my eyes come into focus, I see land ahead. I almost don't believe it. I've heard that mirages are common when you've been in the water for long periods. But I've only spent one night in the water. And although I'm thirsty, I'm not dehydrated yet. I'm still in pretty good shape for someone stranded at sea. I feel pretty good except for my growling stomach, achy muscles, and slight headache.

I don't take my eyes off it out of fear of it not being real. The boat floats slowly, but it's floating in the right direction, which means I'll be on another island soon. I clear my throat because it's as dry as cotton. I grab the bottled water and take another sip. It's the best damn water I've ever tasted, and if I were confident that I could find fresh water on the island I'm approaching, I'd drink the whole bottle. But I have no clue what's there to greet me when I arrive, and until then, I'll save as much of this water as I can.

"Please let there be someone on this island. Please," I say out loud.

There has to be someone there, and hopefully, they have a phone I can use to call for help. Hopefully, they have food I can eat while I wait for someone to come and rescue me. Excitement and hope fill me as the boat floats closer and closer to the shore. I did it. I got away. Now, all I have to do is save my family.

CHAPTER EIGHTEEN
Shaya

I barely wait for the boat to touch shore before I jump out. I want to kneel, bow to the sand, and kiss it. Never in my life have I been this excited to grab a handful of hot sand and watch it fall between my fingertips. My sandals become heavy from stepping in the wet sand, but they don't weigh me down at all. I drag the boat as far up on the beach as I can. I don't have weighted sandbags to keep it in place, and if it washes away for any reason, I'm right back where I started, except with no roof over my head or food and drinks. When I'm satisfied with where I've placed the boat, I wipe my hands on the front of my jean shorts and remove my life vest. I look around. I see no one, and it scares me. It's daylight, but I grab the flashlight and my remaining water anyway.

I venture into a wooded area, careful not to make too much noise. These woods aren't as deep as the ones on the island I was on, so I can see through them better. I kill a mosquito that lands on my arm and frown when I see blood. I stop in my tracks. Mosquitos don't have blood. So, this is either from it biting an animal or a human. My heart beats rapidly. This could be a good sign. I keep walking . . . and that's when I see it. Two homes are straight ahead. I hurry toward them, tripping over a rock in the process. I don't know which one to start with, so I start with the one to my left. There are no curtains on the windows, so I peek through them. It looks empty inside, but I knock anyway. I wait for someone to answer, but no one does. Someone has to be here, right? Why else would there be homes here if no one lived in them? I move on to the next house. This one is a bit bigger and has a shed behind it. I knock loudly, hoping someone will open it this time.

Baas

I finally doze off but am awakened by the sound of loud knocking. "Dafari, do you hear that?"

His eyes pop open, and he listens carefully. "Yeah. Someone is knocking. Maybe they'll get suspicious and check the shed."

"Let's hope so."

"Who do you think it could be?" he asks.

I shake my head. "One of the natives, maybe? We did see a few when we arrived here."

"Yeah. Let's hope they aren't turned away."

We remain quiet as the knock continues, and then it stops. "Shit!" I utter.

We were so close to letting someone know that we were back here. I almost yell for help, but I don't want to risk it because we have no idea who is knocking. Yes, it could be a native. But it could also be someone that Telly is working with.

"They're leaving," Dafari says as he looks at me.

"I know. But let's stick to the plan."

He nods before he leans back against the wall and shuts his eyes. I do the same, but I don't fall asleep this time. I listen carefully. Just in case someone comes across the shed and decides to see what's inside.

Shaya

I knock one last time before the door swings open. "Oh, thank God."

I throw myself into Telly's arms and squeeze him tightly, soaking him with tears.

"Shaya! Thank God you're all right."

I pull away and can barely contain myself as I ramble about Jay and how I stabbed him. Telly watches me intensely before he stops me.

"Shaya, here, have a seat."

When I sit on the couch, he sits across from me.

"Telly, Baas and Dafari are in danger. Jay has done something with them."

"I know. My men and I are already on it, which is why I'm here. You're safe now, Shaya. Don't worry."

I wipe away more tears. "Thank you, Telly."

He rises. "You must be hungry. Thirsty. Would you like anything?"

"Yes. Water. Lots of water, please."

He disappears into the kitchen, and I take a second to catch my breath. It's the first time I've breathed evenly since being taken. Telly returns and hands me a tall glass of iced water. I gulp it down in seconds before passing the glass back to him. He places the glass on the table and turns around to face me.

"You said you stabbed Jay. Is he dead?"

I take a second to think as the vision of him gasping for air enters my brain. "I . . . I don't know. I ran before I could be sure."

"Okay."

"Why? Am I in trouble? Will I go to jail?"

He shakes his head. "No. It was self-defense."

"What about Baas and Dafari? Do you know where they are?"

"No, not yet. But we're on it."

Dread fills me. Baas said that Telly is the best. If he doesn't know where they are, then who else can help us?

"We have to find them, Telly."

He nods. "We will." There's a moment of silence before he speaks again. "We returned Bailey to her adoptive parents."

That feeling of loss washes over me. Along with the fear of never seeing her again. "Did Baas get to spend some time with her?"

"Yes. And he wasn't happy about giving her up. But he also knew that it was the best thing to do while we searched for you."

I blink away tears. "I want her back. I want all of them back."

I'm on the verge of tears again, but I hold them in this time. Telly may need me to help him find them, and what use am I if I'm crying every two seconds? I feel safe now because even if Jay somehow made it out alive and tracked me here, he wouldn't stand a chance against Telly and his men. Knowing I'm safe helps me focus on the more important matters. And that's finding the love of my life and my best friend's husband. I gasp when Ebony enters my mind.

"I have to call Eb. I have to tell her what's going on."

He shakes his head. "Ebony is already aware. I've been communicating with her from the beginning. She's pulling every resource she can on her end to help."

"But shouldn't I let her know that I am safe?" I ask.

"No. Not yet. If we tell her now, it could jeopardize the plan we have in place to save Baas and Dafari."

None of that makes any sense, but I'm also tired and unable to think clearly. So, I let it go. Besides, Telly is the expert at this kind of stuff. He's the one who helped Dafari when he was in trouble. And I trust him.

"I guess you're right."

He nods. "Won't you go get some rest? I'll catch you up to speed in the morning."

I yawn the moment he says the word *rest*. My body is finally giving out on me, and if I don't allow myself to sleep, I won't be able to focus tomorrow.

"I am tired," I reply.

"I can tell. The bathroom has fresh towels, and the guest bedroom is the second room to your right."

"Thank you."

His phone rings, and he steps away to take it. I rise to my feet and head to the bathroom, but I stop in the kitchen first to grab a bottle of water. I open the refrigerator, grab the bottle, and stop when I walk past the kitchen window. I stare at the shed, settled in the backyard, wondering what's inside. I shake my head, quickly bringing my thoughts back to focus. It's none of my business what's inside unless it can help us save Dafari and Baas. I take the water to the guest room and place it on the nightstand beside the bed. I'm anxious to shower, but I have nothing clean to sleep in. I walk farther down the hall to ask Telly if he has an extra set of pajamas, but I can hear that he's still on the phone. I'm about to walk away, but something catches my attention. He's whispering but loud enough that I can hear him.

I hear him say, "She's here." Followed by, "I'll take care of her."

Those words could have two meanings. Telly could mean that he'll take care of me in the sense of making sure that I am safe. Or he could mean it in a way that suggests he plans to eliminate me. Something in his voice tells me he means the latter. And my gut is telling me that he's hiding something. I softly tiptoe back to the guest room and close the door. I lock it before I sit on the edge of the bed. Were Telly and Jay working together? If so, why? What reason would Telly have to betray Dafari and Baas after knowing them for so long? I need answers. And I'm going to do whatever I need to do to get them.

CHAPTER NINETEEN
Shaya

I didn't shower last night. I was too afraid to put myself in a position that would put me at a disadvantage. Telly knocked and asked if I was okay, and I yelled through the door, telling him I was. I told him I was too tired to shower and needed to get some rest. I can't let him know that I find him suspicious because there's no telling what he might do. Telly is smart, and he's strategic. I don't know much about his world, and there's a slight chance he could outsmart me if I don't do this right. I'm up early, hoping to beat him to the punch, but I'm disappointed when I walk into the kitchen and he's making coffee.

"Hey, how'd you sleep?" he asks.

"Not too well. I'm so worried about Baas and Dafari."

"I understand. But don't worry. We're going to find them."

"Tell me, what leads do you have?" I probe.

"So far, none. But my people are on it," he says before placing a cup of coffee and a breakfast sandwich in front of me.

I take a bite of the sandwich. "What about my parents? Are they still safe?"

He nods. "Yes. They're still in the secure location Baas placed them in."

"I'd like to call them."

He holds my gaze for a second before he responds. "That's probably not a good idea right now. Until we can find who's behind this, you need to refrain from contact with anyone."

He averts his eyes when he says it, and it confirms my suspicions. He's hiding something. Which means he most likely was working with Jay.

"Thank you, Telly. It's just . . ." I take a second to let a tear slide down my face for added effect. "I just hope they're all okay."

He gives me a small smile. "I know."

I finish my sandwich in silence. I should win an Oscar for my performance. He has no idea that I know he's lying to me. It's one of the first things Baas taught me during our time together. Never show your hand. Never show what you're thinking. Mask your emotions and play along to your advantage. I gather my composure and take a sip of my coffee. When I'm finished, I quickly contemplate my next move. I can only play along for so long before Telly realizes I'm up to no good. He stands to his feet.

"I have some emails to check, but there's food in the refrigerator if you're hungry. I'll be in the living room."

He leaves me at the kitchen table. I stare out the window at the shed. There might be something in there I can use to protect myself. Most sheds have tools like chainsaws and hammers. But I can't check and see with Telly being so close to me. I'll have to wait until he leaves the house or falls asleep. This house is immaculate, with nothing out of place and nothing that is remotely helpful in fighting off an attacker. But that's okay because, one way or another, I *will* find Baas and Dafari. And when I do, Telly will pay.

I've been stuck in this house all day, and it's starting to feel like I traded one capture for another. Telly has been checking emails and taking calls all day with barely any feedback for me. When I do ask questions, he gives me vague, nonchalant answers. I've been reading magazines and doing crossword puzzles to keep myself busy. I've also been paying attention to Telly's patterns and body language. He keeps his cell phone in his right pocket because he's right-handed, and his password is facial recognition. He's been on edge as if he's waiting for something important. I can tell by how his fingers fidget and how tense his shoulders are. I can also tell that I've interfered with his plan. I was an unexpected guest who wasn't supposed to show up. But now that I have, he needs to improvise. He has a gun. Maybe more than one. But for now, I only see one placed in his holster. I can't determine what kind it is, but I know it can kill. Otherwise, he wouldn't be carrying it. I place the magazine down beside me.

"I think I'll take a walk to clear my head."

"No!" he says immediately.

My eyes widen at his abrasiveness.

"It's just . . . It's not safe. Shaya, I already have enough on my plate with looking for Dafari and Baas. I don't need anything happening to you again."

"I understand."

What I want to say is that he's a liar. I want to hold him down with a knife and demand that he tell me everything. But I must take baby steps. I have to wait for him to slip. I keep talking.

"Telly, I can't tell you how grateful I am that we have you."

"I'm just doing my job."

I stand to my feet because sitting across from him starts getting to me. "I think I'll go lie down for a bit."

"Yes. It would be best if you rested all you can. I'll let you know if I hear anything else."

I leave the living room and lock myself in the guest room again. It's the only way I feel safe. I lie on the bed as my mind swirls with questions, concerns, and thoughts. Tonight, I will sneak out of here. I will go to the shed in the back and grab anything to help me. Telly won't see me coming, and it'll be too late by the time he does.

I doze off, and now it's late. I don't know how late because I'm in a room without a clock. But I think it's late enough for Telly to be asleep. I slowly open the door and peep out into the hallway. I'm not wearing shoes because I must be as quiet as possible. I tiptoe down the hallway and freeze when I reach the living room. Telly is asleep on the couch. I didn't anticipate this, but I won't let it stop me. He's snoring loudly, so I walk softly past him and to the front door. I turn it slowly, but it doesn't open. I yank it, but it doesn't budge. I realize he's locked the door, and the only way to unlock it is with a key. Shit! He's making sure that I can't get out. I turn around and make sure that I haven't awakened him. When I confirm that I haven't, I walk past him slowly and into the kitchen. I try the back door, and that too is locked. For a second, I panic . . . until my eyes land on the kitchen window. It's right above the kitchen sink, and I'd have to climb on top to open it, but it's my only way out. I take one last look into the living room before I hop onto the sink. I lift the window slowly, pause, then check to see if he's still asleep. I lift it up, hoping the incoming breeze doesn't knock anything over in the kitchen. I climb out of it quickly and onto the back patio. After that, I softly lower the window, leaving a slight crack, and run to the shed as fast as possible.

When I reach the door, I turn around one last time. Since I don't see him following me, I open the door and walk in. It's dark inside, and I'm breathing hard as I grip the door tightly just in case he tries to open it and drag me out. Suddenly, I hear a noise behind me, and I whirl around, but I can't see anything, which scares me even more. I step forward, and my foot gets tangled in something, causing me to fall. I yelp when I hit the ground. Two shadows move in front of me. I don't know what or who they are . . . until I hear his voice.

"Shaya?"

I gasp. "Baas?"

I don't hesitate. I climb to my feet and rush in his direction.

"I'm right here," he guides me.

I follow his voice until my hand lands on him. I don't know which body part it touches, but I don't care. All that matters is that I've found him. I somehow find my way to the upper portion of his body, and he pulls me to him, embracing me tightly.

"Thank God you're all right," I say.

His hands roam my body, checking for any injuries. "Are you okay, sweetheart?"

"Yes. Yes, I'm okay. Who did this?" I ask.

"Telly betrayed us." Dafari's voice speaks loud and clear.

"I knew it. I could feel something wasn't right," I reply.

Baas grabs my hand. "Baby, listen to me. I need you to get out of here."

"What? No. What about you and Dafari?"

"We have a plan. But I need you out of harm's way and into safety."

"I can't. I have no way off this island except for a tiny boat I can't even row."

"I'd rather you take the boat than stay here and get hurt . . . or worse," he argues.

I shake my head. "No."

Dafari interjects. "Okay, you two, we don't have time for domestic disagreements." He pauses for a minute. "Baas, you know there's no way in hell she will leave us here."

Baas squeezes my hand. "How many men are in the house right now?" he asks.

"Just Telly," I reply.

"Any weapons?" he continues.

"I saw a gun on his holster, but that was it."

He gives me another tight hug and places his lips on mine. I've missed those lips, and I melt in him. He takes a deep breath, releases me, then speaks low and firm.

"Sweetheart, we need you to do something."

CHAPTER TWENTY

Baas

I almost thought I was dreaming when Shaya stumbled into the shed. When the door opened and shut, Dafari and I didn't know who had entered. It was dark, and we would have attacked if the person had come closer. But then I heard her voice. I wasn't sure if I was imagining it, but I called out her name anyway. And when she answered, I wanted to cry tears of joy. She was alive. And that's all I've been hoping for this entire time. She holds me tightly, and I don't want to let her go. I want to keep her chained beside me to make sure no one ever hurts her again. But realistically, I know that can't happen. Besides, how can I protect her with only one free arm? I continue speaking.

"We need you to get the key to these cuffs."

She thinks for a second before she responds. "I haven't seen any, but he most likely has them in his pocket."

"You need to be careful; he's not alone, sweetheart."

"He's alone right now," I respond.

"Then you need to move quickly. He has about five other men from his team with him."

She nods. "I'll get the key."

"Once you get it, I need you to return here quickly. Sweetheart, get the key and run. The sooner Dafari and I are released, the sooner we can protect you."

"He's locked me in. I only got here because I climbed out of the kitchen window while he was sleeping."

"You need to get back fast before he realizes you're gone."

She leaves my side, and I can hear her feel her way around the shed, looking for anything to help her. She returns to my side with something cold and hard in her hand. A tear drops from her eyes and onto my arm.

"I'll get you both out of here—I promise."

I plant my lips on hers, and when I release her, I brush the back of my free hand across her cheek, reveling in the feel of her skin. "I love you."

"I love you too."

She releases me quickly and stands to her feet. When she opens the door, I get a tiny glimpse of her silhouette from the moonlight. The door closes shut, and I fall back, breathing heavily.

"Fuck!"

"She will be okay," Dafari says.

"We don't know that. I just put her back in danger, and if she gets hurt, it's my fucking fault."

"Baas, you asked her to go away, and she refused. Shaya loves you, and there's no way she would save herself and leave us here. You know that."

"Yes, I know."

"I didn't realize until now just how alike she and Ebony are," he adds.

"I guess that's why they're best friends." Horrible thoughts enter my head. "I can't lose her, Dafari. Bailey and I need her."

"I know. But one thing I've learned about my wife and her best friend is that they're resilient and headstrong."

"And stubborn," I add.

Neither of us is in a situation that calls for laughter, but we chuckle anyway. I can tell we're both in our thoughts as the room grows quiet, hoping this goes the way we both want it to go so that we can go home and return to our families. The thought of it gives me hope and also motivation. Because now that I know Shaya is safe, it's time to get out of here and put my family back together.

Shaya

They're alive! Baas and Dafari are alive! I'm screaming with joy inside that they haven't been harmed, but if I don't do something soon, they will be. Baas mentioned that Telly had men with him; however, I haven't seen them. But that doesn't mean they won't come back soon. I thought it was hard enough trying to elude Telly. But now that I know others are involved, it's even more challenging.

The purpose of climbing out of that window was to find a weapon to protect myself so I could get off this island. But that was before I found them. Now, I'm getting the three of us off this island. I climb the steps to the deck and look through the window. Surprisingly, Telly is still stretched across the couch, asleep. I slowly lift the window, and once it's opened wide enough, I gently place the hammer inside before climbing through it. Then I close it, grab the hammer, and prepare to attack. But when I turn around . . . Telly is gone.

He grabs me from behind in a chokehold. I release the grip on the hammer to loosen his arm from around my neck, and it drops loudly to the floor as I struggle to breathe.

"You shouldn't have done that, Shaya."

I struggle to get out of his grip. He's strong, and I'm no match for him, but I use all my strength to fight back. I have a chance to have my family back, and he will *not* take this from me. I find enough power to reach and dig my nails into his face. I use pressure to drag them down the front, scraping the skin and causing blood.

"Fuck!" he screams as his grip loosens.

I somehow manage to get out of his hold and make a run for it. But he grabs me by the ankle, and I fall. He pulls me back to him, but I reach for the leg of the kitchen table and hold on for dear life. He pulls, and I kick. The table slides as we struggle, causing items from the top to fall to the floor. A coffee mug falls in front of me, and I grab it. I allow him to pull me back closer to him, and when I'm close enough, I twist my body and smash the heavy mug over his head as hard as I can.

He grabs his head, releasing me from his grip. I struggle to get to my feet, rush to the counter, and grab the first knife from the knife block. I spin around just as he's managed to get up and reach me. I shove the knife into his chest. He looks down at it in disbelief and tries to pull it out, but he's unsuccessful. He stumbles back before crashing onto the kitchen table. The table collapses underneath him, and he lands on top of it. Blood soaks the front of his shirt and spills out of the corner of his mouth.

I wait a second before I move closer to him, and when I see he's grown weaker, I use the opportunity to grab the gun out of his holster and point it at him.

"Where are the keys?" I ask. He doesn't respond, so I place the gun at his temple. "Give me the keys, or I blow your brains out."

He tries to speak, but he's unable to. His eyes lower to his pockets, indicating they're in there. As I dig through the left pocket, I keep the gun pointed at his head. Nothing is there. I slide my hand into his right pocket and find them. I yank them out quickly, stand to my feet, and keep the gun pointed at him. He's barely clinging to life, and I'm certain he won't be able to stop me from leaving now. I rush to the front door and fiddle with the keys when I reach the doorknob. I try key one and am unsuccessful. I try key two, and that won't even fit inside. But when I insert key three . . . It slides in, and I can unlock the front door. I run as fast as possible toward the shed, swing the door open, and step inside.

"I got them!" I yell.

"Flip the light on your left," Baas says.

I flip the switch, and the shed lights up. I'm about to shut the door when someone runs toward me. It's hard to see, but I can see well enough to know the person is coming after me. I aim the gun and shoot. I miss the intended spot: the chest. The bullet hits his thigh instead. He collapses, but not before firing at me. The bullet hits the shed door.

"Shaya, keys!" Baas yells.

I lean down and slide the keys to him while I guard the door with the gun. If anyone comes my way, I'll shoot without question. Four more men come from out of nowhere with guns raised.

"Baas, they're coming. Hurry!"

I start shooting, hoping to hit at least one of them until Baas and Dafari are free, but I'm missing them. I feel something penetrate my shoulder, followed by a sharp pain, and I fall to my knees.

"Shaya!"

Baas rushes to my side. He quickly moves me out of the way and runs out the door with Dafari right behind him. I press my hand tightly against the wound, hoping to stop the bleeding. I watch in horror as Baas and Dafari fight off Telly's men. There are four of them, and I worry they'll overpower Dafari and Baas. But as I stare ahead, I realize I have no reason to fear because Dafari and Baas easily fight them off, ultimately grabbing their guns and killing them. When the last one falls to the ground, Baas turns and looks at me. He's in a state I've never seen. His expression is intense. His eyes are dilated, and his chest rises and falls with adrenaline. He looks at the men lying around him before he and Dafari turn around and walk toward me. I smile at the thought of us finally being safe . . . but that smile turns into a frown when I see who's running behind them. I scream at the top of my lungs.

"Baas, behind you!"

Baas

Shaya screams for me to look behind me, but by the time I do, it's too late. I turn around just as Jay hits me with an object. It knocks me to the ground and causes my head to spin and throb. Dafari jumps in front of me as I stagger to my feet. The two of them struggle as I try to join the fight. A gun goes off, and I freeze. My eyes open wide when I see Dafari stumble back and collapse to the ground.

He's still. And it's enough for me to ignore the excruciating pain in my head to make sure that Jay doesn't finish him off. I rush him and knock him to the ground. I punch him hard enough to bruise my knuckles. He punches back but only grazes my chin as I dodge it. He somehow manages to flip me on my back, and before I toss him off, he holds a gun in my face. I look closely at him, wondering if Shaya caused the patch across his eye.

"I killed your buddy over there. Next, I'm killing you. And then, Shaya and I are going on a little adventure. Hell, I may even bring Bailey along."

Anger shoots through me at the sound of him saying my daughter's name.

"Are you *really* this desperate that you have to *force* a woman to be with you?" I can tell my words strike a nerve because he frowns. "Face it, Jay. She wants nothing to do with you."

He pushes the gun deeper into my face. "She would if it weren't for you. I was supposed to win her back. But you swooped in and stole her from me."

I need to be careful with how I choose to respond to him. After all, he has a gun in my face. If I say something to set him off, he could kill me, and this all would have been for nothing.

"You hurt her, Jay. That's why she left."

I can see the wheels spinning in his head because he knows I'm telling the truth. "It was a mistake," he says.

"Jay, you can kill me right this second. You can even take Shaya away again. But she will *never* be yours. Her heart will *always* belong to me."

I can see the rage swirling in his eyes. This is it. This is when I overpower him and get rid of him for good. But I don't get the chance. A shot goes off, followed by him collapsing on top of me. I shove him off and take the gun from his limp hand. I take one more shot to ensure the job is finished, then run toward Shaya. She's still aiming the gun when I reach her. I gently remove it from her hand and pull her in tightly.

"It's okay. You're okay."

I release her and check her wound to ensure it isn't fatal. It's not. The bullet went straight through.

"We need to help, Dafari," she says.

I rush to his side and check his pulse. When I see he still has one, I'm relieved.

"Shaya, see if Jay has a phone on him."

She rumbles through his pockets until she finds one and quickly dials a number. I can't hear whom she's talking to, but I can hear the panic in her voice. I speak to Dafari.

"Hold on, brother. We're getting you help."

He doesn't answer me, but I hope he can hear me. Shaya joins me. "Is he . . ."

I shake my head. "No. But we need to get him medical help soon."

"I called Ebony. She's getting us help. They'll ping this phone and come for us."

"Okay."

We sit and wait, guarding Dafari and hoping help reaches us in time.

CHAPTER TWENTY-ONE

Shaya

One Week Later

Ebony pulls me in as soon as she walks inside. "I thought I'd never see you again." We hold onto each other tightly, shedding tears of happiness.

I release her. "How's Dafari?"

"He's well. He just needs lots of rest for the next few weeks."

Ebony managed to ping Jay's phone and contacted the local authorities to come and help us. They were able to provide immediate medical attention to Dafari, saving his life. We were quickly transported to a hospital, where we were treated and kept for observation for a week. Ebony wanted to be there, but Dafari forbade her from coming. He wanted her and Aiden safe, and the only way he could ensure that happened was for them to stay put until he was well enough to come home. We were finally released and took the first flight back to Mafachiko.

"Eb, I'm sorry for dragging you guys into this. All of this was my fault."

She shakes her head. "Shaya, stop! None of this was your fault."

"She's right," Baas says from behind me. "Hi, Ebony."

He gives her a quick hug before throwing his arm around my shoulder.

"How are you?" she asks.

"Better," he replies before kissing me on the head.

She smiles. "I'll let you two rest."

"We'll come by tomorrow," I reply.

She hugs me once more before I walk her to the door and see her out. When I close it behind me, I take a deep breath. Baas approaches me, grabs my hand, and we walk into the sitting room. He strokes a piece of hair out of my face.

"Do you feel okay?" he asks.

I place my hand over the bullet wound. "Yes. They patched me up pretty good."

"Not physically, sweetheart. Are *you* okay?"

I nod. "I'm okay."

"Are you sure? Because if not . . ."

I place my hand on his knee. "Baas, I'm okay."

His eyes bore into mine. "When I lost you, all I could think about was how horrible I treated you."

"Baas—"

"I need to say this, sweetheart."

"Okay."

"All I could think about was how horrible I treated you. You needed me, and I turned my back on you. I'll never forgive myself for it."

Old emotions surface, but they leave as quickly as they come. "I should have been honest. I should have never made such a big decision that affected you without your input. You were angry, and you had every right to be."

"I've contacted our lawyer to get Bailey back."

I knew this was coming. And honestly, I'm surprised he waited this long. "What happens now?"

"They're arranging a meeting with her adoptive parents, and we'll go from there."

"Okay."

"Shaya, I want us to be a family."

"Me too."

He stands to his feet and drops to one knee. I gasp as my hand flies to my mouth in shock. He places his hand inside his pocket and pulls out the same tiny, black velvet box I saw fall to the floor that day that seems so long ago. He opens it, and my eyes widen when I see the diamond. It's more beautiful than I could have imagined.

"Shaya, I can't imagine my life without you or Bailey. I love you and want to spend the rest of my life showing you. Will you be my wife?"

Tears rapidly stream down my face. "Yes."

He removes the ring from the box, slides it on my finger, and it fits perfectly. He rises, sits beside me, and places his lips on mine. Heat sweeps through my body, and the kiss intensifies. It feels like forever since he's touched me, and my body yearns for more. I lean into him, swirling my tongue with his and wrapping my arms around his neck. I pull away from him and search his eyes. I want this. I want him. But he rejected me the last time I tried to get close to him. For good reason, of course, but I don't want to assume he's ready to go there with me.

"What's wrong?" he asks.

I want to tell him to make love to me, but I'm too scared to make the first move. I shouldn't be afraid, I know. He just proposed to me, and I highly doubt that he would have if he had no intention of ever touching me again. When I don't answer, he places his palm against my cheek.

"Talk to me, sweetheart."

"I want you. But I wasn't sure if you were ready. For *that*, I mean."

What I'm saying registers to him.

"You should never have to wonder if I want you. I will always want you. And I'm so fucking sorry for pretending otherwise."

He doesn't give me time to respond. He takes the lead and removes my clothes. When I'm completely naked, he stands to his feet and sheds his. My body is on fire, but the chill in the air cools me. Baas kisses me from head to toe. My body shutters when he reaches the inside of my thighs. I can't wait any longer. I look down at him and tell him how much I need him.

"Baas, I *need* you."

Baas is a patient man in the bedroom. He takes his time with me, ensuring he gives every inch of my body the attention it deserves. He can make love to me for hours and never waver. But he doesn't keep me waiting. He gives my thigh one last kiss before he rises and hovers over me.

"I need you too, baby."

I moan as soon as he enters me.

"Spread your legs for me," he demands.

I open them wider, allowing myself to take him deeper. I cling to him as he moves in and out of me, nibbling on my ear. "Oh, Baas."

"Yes, baby."

The rumble of his voice sends goose bumps down my spine. Our bodies move in sync as he makes love to me. As he quickens his speed, my core tightens. I grip the sheets beside me and moan with ecstasy as I come.

"That's right, sweetheart."

He stills as he comes inside me. Then he leans down and kisses me softly on the lips.

"I can't wait for you to be mine."

I smile. "I already am."

"No. Officially, mine."

I laugh softly. "I can't wait either."

Baas

New York

I'm worried, but I don't allow Shaya to see it. She would worry too if she knew, and one of us must remain calm. I've been walking around as calmly as possible when inside of me, I'm very anxious. My lawyer told me that these kinds of cases are difficult. Judges are reluctant to remove a child from a home after it's already become attached to its adoptive parents. Then there's the issue of the paperwork that Shaya signed. It specifically states that her right to Bailey is irrevocable.

I'm unsure if she knew exactly what she was signing, but it's too late to ask her now. The only thing we can do at this point is to find out how we can convince the judge that Bailey belongs with us. My lawyer's first suggestion is that I file for sole custody of my daughter based on the fact I didn't know she existed. But that comes with a risk. The judge would question Shaya and ask why she failed to tell me she was pregnant and considered adoption. Shaya lied on the paperwork. She stated that she was unsure who the father was. She also said that she was uncertain of my whereabouts and could not tell me that she was giving our baby up for adoption. Of course, this was also untrue. She will be in trouble once the judge realizes she falsified legal paperwork.

We sit nervously at the table while waiting for the adoptive parents to arrive. Shaya bites her nails, and I lower her hand to stop her.

"It's going to be okay."

The wooden doors open, and the couple walk in, followed by their lawyer. Our lawyer stands to his feet.

"Mr. and Mrs. Smith, thank you for coming," he says.

Mr. Smith takes one look at me and raises an eyebrow. "Wait, I know you."

I've already filled my lawyer in on my impromptu, inappropriate visit to see Bailey. I knew they would recognize me the minute they laid eyes on me, and I didn't want any surprises. My lawyer nods.

"Let's take a seat and get started."

They sit, and their lawyer speaks as soon as they do.

"My clients would like to make it clear that they have no intention of giving Bailey back."

"Then why are they here?" I ask.

I can't let my anger get the best of me, but fuck, it's hard. How dare these two strangers walk into this room and tell me what they will and won't do concerning my daughter. This is already off to a bad start, and I don't like it. Mrs. Smith looks directly at Shaya as she responds.

"We're here out of sympathy for her mother. We won't give her back, but we're open to allowing her to have a relationship with both of you once she's old enough to understand."

My mouth opens to speak, but Shaya places her hand softly on my knee. She speaks for us instead.

"This is all my fault. Baas had no idea that Bailey existed. I didn't tell him the truth, so he wasn't allowed to have a say in my decision."

Mr. Smith speaks. "Surely, you don't think that we should be the ones to suffer because you chose not to be honest."

I shoot to my feet with my hands placed firmly on the table. "Watch your mouth."

"Baas, have a seat, please," my lawyer says.

I lower myself into my seat but don't take my eyes off Mr. Smith. He needs to know that I won't tolerate disrespect to Shaya or me. He backs down and diverts his eyes, and I look over at Shaya, who is pleading with me to behave. She wants me to apologize but knows that won't happen. My lawyer speaks.

"That's right. My client did not tell the truth, which started this ripple effect; however, now that the truth is out, we have a parent who wants and deserves to raise his child."

Their lawyer speaks. "The Smiths have been the only parents Bailey has known for six months. It isn't fair to remove her from her surroundings and into unfamiliar territory."

I speak because I can't help myself. "*We* are her parents. There will be nothing unfamiliar about us."

Mrs. Smith speaks as her eyes water with tears. "Yes. You are her biological parents. And you will always be her parents. But it takes more than that to raise a kid. We are the ones changing her diapers, feeding her, and bathing her. We sing her to sleep and care for her every day." She looks directly at Shaya as she continues. "You had your chance to be her parents, and you didn't want it."

Tears stream down her face, and her husband consoles her. But her tears don't move me. I don't care how sad this makes her. All I care about is getting my baby back. I can tell that was a blow to Shaya because I can feel her stiffen beside me. But she speaks anyway.

"I know. And I appreciate you both for being there for her when I couldn't."

My lawyer speaks. "Let's all take a deep breath. I'm sure this is a lot for all of us, and we want to come to a decision that is best for everyone."

The only decision I want is to legally get Bailey back so we can move on with our lives and be a family. Their lawyer skims the paper in front of him.

"Your clients live in Africa?" he asks.

"Yes. But they have no problem traveling back to the States while the case is pending," our lawyer answers.

Their lawyer shakes his head. "This poses a risk. If we allow them to see Bailey and spend time with her, who's to say they won't take her to Africa, and my clients will never see her again?"

Shaya shakes her head. "No. We would never do something like that."

Their lawyer skims the paper again. "I think it's best that all visits be supervised until the judge rules."

Shaya looks at me frantically, and I intervene. "That's ridiculous. We should get to spend time with our daughter without outsiders watching our every move."

My lawyer speaks up for us. "I assure you, my clients have no intention of taking Bailey out of the country."

Their lawyer turns to them. "What do you two think?" he asks.

They look at each other before Mrs. Smith speaks. "We believe you."

Shaya and I both exhale with relief before I ask my next question. "When will we get to see her?"

Their lawyer responds but doesn't make eye contact with me. "The judge has granted visitation once a week for an hour until a ruling is decided."

Once a week. I *only* get to see Bailey *once* a week. An hour isn't long, and I strongly want to request more time. But I've already pushed my limit today, and I don't want visitation off the table altogether.

"Great. When?" I ask.

"As early as this evening, if that works," their lawyer replies.

"That works," Shaya and I both reply in unison.

There's no way in hell either of us will pass up the opportunity to see Bailey. The room grows quiet—both sides of the table still high on emotions and tension.

"How's six p.m.?" their lawyer asks.

Shaya speaks alone this time. "Perfect."

Shaya

I don't know why I'm so nervous. One would think I didn't carry Bailey for eight and a half months and go through seven hours of labor with how I'm acting. Bailey is my daughter. She's a piece of Baas and me, and I'm nervous I will mess this up worse than I already have.

"Shaya, you're pacing."

I spin around to face Baas. "Did you babyproof the rooms?"

"Yes."

"Covers on the sockets?"

"Yes. Baby, remember they already did a walk-through. If anything were missing, they would have mentioned it."

"Right. Okay. Did you turn the temperature up a little? It's chilly out today."

He nods. "Yes. Everything has been taken care of, sweetheart."

"Okay." I think to myself for a second. "What if she cries?"

"She's still a baby, honey. She *will* cry."

"I know. But what if she cries, and I have no idea how to get her to stop? What if she won't let me hold her? What if she hates me?"

He rises and walks over to me. When he reaches me, he places a hand on my shoulder.

"You will be okay, sweetheart. You're her mother."

Tears prick my eyes. "I know I'm her mother, Baas. But am I *really*? These people have been taking care of her day in and day out. They know her. They know what she likes to eat and what toys she likes. I don't know anything. I—"

He pulls me into an embrace and kisses the top of my head. "Shh, don't worry. We'll figure this out together."

The doorbell rings, and I gasp. It's time—time to face my daughter and see if I'm really fit to be her mom. I appreciate Baas supporting me and having confidence in me, but the truth is that I'm scared shitless. I never imagined myself being a mom. I was so focused on work and my own goals that I couldn't imagine being responsible for another human being. But then, I found out I was pregnant, and that changed my mind. I fell in love with my baby. I would place my hand against my belly and talk to her. I imagined what she would look like when she made her entrance into the world. I wanted to be there for her. I wanted to be her mother. But I couldn't. Not at that time.

"Can you please get the door?" I ask Baas.

He nods before he walks over to the door and opens it. The social worker walks in carrying Bailey, and my heart melts. There is my daughter. Bundled up in a blue jacket with pink hearts and a pink hat on her head. She hands Bailey over to Baas, and my heart melts even more. Watching Baas hold her makes me emotional. He walks the social worker to the door, and she reminds us that we only have an hour before she leaves. When he closes the door behind her, he removes Bailey's jacket and hat and walks over to me. I hadn't realized that I was standing frozen in time until he reached me.

"Do you want to hold your daughter?" he asks.

Yes. A million times, yes. But I don't say the words. I open my arms. He places her in them, and I burst into tears as her bright brown eyes meet mine. Our baby is gorgeous. She has a head full of thick, black, curly hair. Her skin is a deep brown and smooth to the touch. Her lips are full, just like her father's, and she has my nose.

"Hi, my sweet little girl."

I pull her to me and kiss her cheek. She giggles at the touch, and I know then that Baas is right. It's going to be just fine.

I look up at Baas. "She's perfect."

He smiles. "Yes, yes, she is."

CHAPTER TWENTY-TWO
Shaya

The hour is rapidly approaching, with us having about twenty minutes left with Bailey. We took turns feeding her dinner, which consisted of sweet potato puree and mashed banana, and then we gave her a bottle, which she guzzled in no time. Now she's lying in my arms, staring up at me as she slowly drifts to sleep. Baas sits next to me, enjoying the view.

"I knew it. I knew she would be okay."

I smile down at her. "She wasn't the least bit fearful or anxious. It's almost like she knows us."

"In Mafachiko, we believe that is the case. Babies know their parents, even if they've never met them. There's a connection there unlike anything else in the world. Of course, this isn't always the case, but it happens more often than not."

I continue to stare down at my daughter. "I can't believe I'm holding her. Like, she's really here with us."

He kisses me on the cheek. "I know."

Bailey finally falls asleep, and I hand her to Baas. "I've been hogging her this whole time."

He shakes his head. "I wanted you to have this time with her more than anything. I'm happy watching you bond with her."

I pull her back to me quickly, fearful he'll change his mind. He's her father, and he has a right to spend as much time with her as I do, but if I'm given the opportunity to hold onto her just a bit longer, I will take it. Bailey smiles in her sleep, and I wonder what she dreams about. I don't want to take my eyes off her. In fact, I could spend a whole day watching her sleep. Soon, the doorbell rings, and I know it's time for her to leave. My chest tightens, and I dread giving her back. But I know I have to. I look up at Baas.

"I'm not ready."

"I know, sweetheart."

He rises from the couch and walks to the door to allow the social worker in. We exchange pleasantries as I carefully place the coat and hat on Bailey. I lean down, kiss her cheek again, and hand her over to Baas. He does the same before handing her over to the social worker. Watching her walk out the door with Bailey guts me, and I almost don't think I can keep it together. But I do. When Baas closes the door behind her, I don't break down. I don't cry. I simply look at him and say, "That was tough."

He places his hand behind his neck. "Yeah, tell me about it."

We both plop down on the couch, and I snuggle beside him.

"I don't know how I'll be able to do that every week, Baas. Being so close to her but having to give her back is painful."

"I know. But it's what we must do until the case is over."

"What if the judge sides with her adoptive parents?"

"They won't," he says with confidence.

"How do you know?"

"Because I can feel it, Shaya. Everything points against us, but deep down, I can feel it. Because Bailey belongs with us . . . in Mafachiko."

I snuggle closer to him. "And if we get her back, will we allow the Smiths to see her?"

He looks down at me. "Is that what you want?"

I shrug. "I mean, it doesn't feel right to exclude them completely after all they've done."

He doesn't respond, but I can tell he's thinking long and hard about my comment. A few minutes pass before he replies.

"I agree. They deserve to have a place in her life if they want. We will ensure that happens if Bailey is given back to us."

I twist around and face him. "I love you."

He leans in and kisses me on the lips before he throws his arm around me. "I love you too, baby."

Today, I'm spending the day with my parents. I haven't had much time to catch up with them since I returned, and I missed them. Baas refuses to let me out of his sight, so he tagged along. Once we returned home, we sat them down and told them what had happened and why they were kept in a hidden location. I'm with my mother in the basement, going through a trunk of my old baby stuff.

"I can't believe you kept all this."

She laughs. "You're my only child. Of course, I kept it."

I pull out a white lace dress with ruffles. "This is cute."

She turns around and places her hands on her hips. "That was the dress you wore to your baptism. You were about six months old."

"That's close to Bailey's age now."

She watches me for a second. "Honey, have you thought about what you would do if this doesn't go how you want?"

"No, I haven't thought about it because it hurts too much. I'm scared, Mom."

"I know. And I don't want you hurting any more than you already are."

"I shouldn't have done it. I shouldn't have given her up. I regret it every day of my fuck—" I stop when I realize I'm about to swear in front of her. "Sorry, I regret it every day."

She smiles at me. "We all have regrets, honey. Give yourself some grace."

"I'm trying."

"Do you and Baas plan on having more kids?"

"Honestly, I'm not sure. We haven't talked about it much lately."

"I see."

I can tell she wants to say something. "What is it?"

"Nothing."

"Mom!"

"Okay. I want you to understand that everything happens for a reason, sweetheart. You and Baas may want Bailey back, but have you ever stopped to think that maybe she was a blessing to the woman who couldn't have children?"

I have thought about it. And that's what makes this situation much worse. When I first gave her up, I was thrilled to know she went to a couple who tried and couldn't conceive. It did make me think that it was the universe confirming that I was making the right decision. The Smiths were blessed with Bailey. Now, I'm trying to take that blessing away from them.

"I do think about it, Mom."

She nods and then changes the subject. "Enough of that. Let me see that rock you have on your finger!"

Baas

Shaya's father hands me a lemonade before sitting across from me at the kitchen table. There's an awkward silence as I sip my glass, and he drinks from his water bottle. When he finishes, he leans back in his chair.

"So, you and my Shaya are getting married, huh?"

I make direct eye contact with him. "Yes, sir."

"Hmm."

I take another sip of my lemonade before I reply. "Let me take the opportunity to apologize for not asking for your blessing first. After everything we'd gone through, I had to ask her as soon as possible. Tomorrow isn't promised."

He nods. "That's right. You did the right thing."

"Thank you, sir."

"But . . ."

I knew the questions were coming, and honestly, I don't mind. Shaya's parents don't know me very well, and I want them to feel as comfortable as possible with me being their son-in-law. He shifts in his seat.

"I need to know that nothing like this will ever happen again. We almost lost our daughter. I'm her father, and my job is to protect her. But now that you're asking for her hand in marriage, I need to know you can take it from here."

I pause before I respond. "Sir, I can't promise you we won't be tested again. Being a part of the royal family can create enemies. But I promise you that no matter what happens, my priority is my family. Shaya and Bailey will always be protected, and I will gladly give my life for theirs."

He takes a sip of his water but keeps his eyes on me. When he's finished, he cracks a smile.

"Well, okay, then. Welcome to the family."

CHAPTER TWENTY-THREE

Baas

After we spent the day with Shaya's parents, we decided to grab some dinner and have a night in. I would love to take her to a fancy restaurant, but we're both still on edge and don't want to be around a crowd. We're trying our best to find our normal, and I can tell that it's a lot harder than either of us expected. We're seated at the dining room table with soft music playing in the background and candles lit throughout the room. I had the chef bring us dinner, which consists of a creamy shrimp pasta dish with a side of garlic bread. Shaya glances at me from across the table but barely says anything.

"Are you okay?"

She nods. "Yeah. Just a little tired."

"We can cut dinner short and go to bed if you like."

She smiles. "That's not necessary. I'll be okay."

She smiles again, but it doesn't reach her eyes this time. It's forced, and I know that although she says she's okay, she isn't. But I don't want to push. One thing I know about Shaya is that she needs time to process things and deal with her emotions. If I push too hard, it'll only end with her shutting down and me feeling frustrated.

"Are you sure?" I ask.

"Yes. Besides, dinner is delicious, and I'm not even close to finishing my meal."

"Okay."

We continue to eat our dinner and speak a few sentences here and there, but this is different from what I imagined for tonight. I don't like when my lady hides the fact that she's upset. She should be able to come to me and know that whatever is on her mind will be received. After our meal, we do the dishes together and head to the bedroom. I had hoped we'd be tearing each other's clothes off by now, but I have a feeling that won't happen tonight. When we reach the bedroom, I grab her hand.

"Shaya, something is bothering you. I can tell. Talk to me, sweetheart."

She stares at me for a second before plopping down on the bed. "I've been thinking."

"About?"

"The petition we filed to get Bailey back."

I take a few steps closer to her. "Okay, what about it?"

"I think we should let it go."

At first, I think I misheard her. But when I zero in on her expression, I know I haven't. "I'm sorry, what?"

"Hear me out, Baas."

"Hear you out? Shaya, are you saying that we shouldn't fight for Bailey?" I almost lose my balance when she nods.

"You want to give her back, just like that?"

"No, I don't. But, Baas, you must admit what we're doing is wrong."

"How? How is it wrong for us to want to raise our daughter? How is it wrong for me to want to be a father to her? There's nothing wrong about wanting my family together, sweetheart."

"I want that too, but not at the expense of snatching her away and creating a grieving mother."

I cock my head to the side. "If you let her go, *you'll* grieve her, will you not?"

The realization slams into me like a truck as I say the words. *Let her go.* Those were the very words of the Seer. She saw this coming.

She nods. "Yes."

"So, you're willing to push your own grief to the side to spare hers?"

"Yes."

It would be an admirable thing to do if it didn't involve my daughter being raised in another country by someone other than us. But Shaya is not making sense, and I don't like where this is going. I can't do it, even at the direction of the Seer.

"No."

"Baas, this is not just your decision."

I want to tell her that this *is* my decision. Because the last time she decided for me, it didn't end well. But I would be saying that out of anger, and it would crush her. The anger soars through my veins, but I keep it at bay because the last time I was this angry with her, I said some hurtful things. Shaya is going to be my wife. And that means I must protect her at all costs. Physically, mentally, and emotionally.

"Shaya, I understand you want to do the right thing. But how do you know that *this* isn't the right thing?"

"Because it doesn't *feel* right."

I don't think there's anything I can do to change her mind at this point. And as much as I want to stomp my feet and demand that she go through with this, it's useless. She stands to her feet and throws her arms around my neck.

"I know this isn't what you want."

"No, it isn't," I reply.

We're supposed to be happy right now. We're safe, and Shaya has agreed to marry me. But I'm not happy because my family isn't complete without Bailey.

"Can you take a second to see it from my point of view?" she asks.

I don't know how or why Shaya believes I can step foot on that plane and head back to Africa without our daughter. She knows me better than anyone else, except for Dafari. So, she should know better. She should know that leaving without my daughter isn't an option for me. But I owe it to her to listen. To really hear what she's saying.

"Let me think about this."

She nods. "Okay."

Shaya

I had been thinking about it since my mother and I had the conversation in her basement. She was right. I did something good, and now I'm trying to undo that good for my own selfish reasons. I knew what I had to do, but I also knew that Baas would not be happy about it. I could see the smoke coming from his ears. He was so angry. He wants his family. But what he isn't realizing is that family comes in all forms. The children at the orphanage. Dafari, Ebony, and Aiden. They're family as well. This is tough for me too. I have a chance to get my daughter back and live my happily ever after with the man of my dreams. But how can I do that if I constantly have visions of a crying mother?

I barely slept last night and could tell that Baas was restless. He tossed and turned all night, refusing to get close or cuddle with me. I can't say that I blame him. I've taken him on an emotional roller coaster since I've been back in his life, and I hate it. I want a happy life with Baas. I want the happily ever after. But I also have to have a clear conscience. I'm making coffee when he enters the kitchen.

"Good morning."

"Good morning," he replies.

I can't tell if he's still angry, but I can tell something is bothering him. I pour him a cup of coffee and hand it to him.

"Thank you," he says.

I pour myself a cup and take a seat across from him. I glance at the rose gold engagement ring as I drink from my cup. It's beautiful and sparkles underneath the kitchen light. I suddenly become anxious. There's a slight chance Baas may change his mind about marrying me now. And this would be the second time.

"Baas—"

"Don't," he replies. "Not right now, Shaya."

"Then when?" He stands to his feet and walks over to the sink. "Baas, this is important. The longer we wait, the harder it will be."

He turns around to face me. "Sweetheart, it will be hard for me regardless of how long we wait." He takes a deep breath. "Do you not want her?"

The pain in his voice kills me, and I hate hurting him. I rise and join him at the sink. "Of course I do. I always have."

He searches my eyes before he replies. "If I'm being honest, Shaya, it doesn't seem like you do."

I knew he would feel this way. And for a second, I almost wonder if he's right. But deep down in my soul, I know that he isn't. I know what it feels like to carry a child and give her up. I know what it feels like to worry and wonder about her daily. I know what it's like to love your baby from afar. Whether she's with me or not, Bailey is my daughter. I love her with every piece of me, and this decision has no bearing on that. I place my hand in his.

"I can see why you would think that, but it isn't true."

He watches me for a second before nodding. "I know that you love her."

"Yes. And nothing will ever change that."

"I want what's best for her too, Shaya. And I believe what's best is for her to be with us. But . . ." He thinks for a second. "I thought about what you said last night. And I can understand your point."

"Thank you for seeing things from my point of view."

"I still need a little time. Just give me that," he replies.

I rise on my tippy toes and kiss his cheek. "Okay."

I told Baas I needed some air. He was hesitant about me going out alone but eventually agreed. Without Telly, we don't have protection, and he certainly doesn't trust anyone else to watch over me but him.

I thank the Lift driver before I climb out of the car and stand in front of the home, debating if I'm making the right decision. I conclude that I am. This is a big decision I'm making, and I have to be 100 percent sure. I ring the doorbell, and it isn't long before Mrs. Smith opens it. Her mouth parts in shock before she speaks.

"Shaya, what are you doing here?"

"I'm sorry for dropping by unannounced, but can we talk?"

"How did you find our address?" she asks.

"The court petition."

"Ah, yes." She opens the door wider. "Come on in."

I walk inside and follow her to the living room. Her home is inviting and beautifully decorated with warm colors and accents.

"Have a seat," she gestures.

I sit on her beige, plush couch and wait for her to join me. When she does, I immediately start talking.

"First, thank you and Mr. Smith for being so good to Bailey. Children don't always find good homes, and I'm grateful that Bailey got such loving parents."

"We do love her." She grows teary-eyed when she says it.

"I know you do," I reply.

She scoots next to me. "Lenny and I met in the eighth grade and have been inseparable ever since. He's my best friend and soul mate and gives me the world. But there's one thing I've never been able to give him."

"A child," I answer.

She nods. "I had fibroids. They were so big and caused me so many problems that I had to have a hysterectomy. I was twenty years old when it happened."

"I'm so sorry."

"For so long, I felt inadequate. Can you imagine it? The one thing your husband desires the most, you're unable to give him?"

I shake my head. "No."

"We had been waiting for a baby for a long time and almost gave up hope. But then we got the call. A six-month-old was available, and our intake counselor thought she would be the perfect fit." A tear slides down her cheek. "Our prayers had been answered, and we were so grateful that God blessed us with such an adorable and sweet baby."

"I wanted to keep her. I really did. I just had so much going on at the time with her father and me, and it seemed like the best thing to do at the time." I think back to the day I walked into the adoption center. "I almost didn't go through with it."

"I understand."

I didn't expect us to connect the way that we are. Honestly, I thought she would be angry with me. But she's not angry at all.

She's kind, compassionate, and understanding. She's everything I would want the woman raising my daughter to be.

"I spoke with her father. I think we should allow you to continue to raise Bailey. You've been the only mother she's known for the past six months, and it just doesn't feel right snatching her away from that."

Her face lights up. "Really?"

"But . . . I can't promise that he'll agree. This is different for him. He didn't know about her. He had no say in the matter, and his choice to raise her was taken from him. It won't be easy for him to let her go."

"I understand."

I rise to my feet. "Thank you for hearing me out."

"Would you like to see her?"

I freeze. Of course, I want to see her. I want to hold her in my arms and whisper how much I love her. But I'm also scared that I'll change my mind. Maybe it's best I don't tempt myself.

"Um, maybe I shouldn't."

She grabs my hand and smiles. "Come on."

I follow her down the hall and into the first bedroom on the right. She opens the door, and I smile at the sight. The room is painted lilac with white hearts plastered on the walls. A fuzzy white rug lies in the middle of the floor, and a mahogany crib is placed on top. A purple rocking chair sits in the corner with stuffed bears on it, and a toy chest sits beside it, which I'm sure is filled to the brim with toys. We stand over the crib and watch Bailey sleep. She's on her back with a pacifier in her mouth.

"She gets more beautiful every time I see her."

Mrs. Smith looks over at me. "I see where she gets it from."

The baby is sound asleep, wearing a pink onesie, with her tiny finger wrapped around the yellow blanket right beside her. Soft music plays in the background, and the room is dimly lit.

"She looks so peaceful."

"She's probably the only baby in history who loves naptime. The ladies in my mom circle say their babies fight it every time. But not Bailey. She goes right down when she's tired."

I lean in and grab her little finger. The warmth of it makes me smile. She stirs a little but doesn't wake up, and I laugh.

"She must be dreaming," I observe.

"Yeah, she sometimes smiles in her sleep."

I let go of her finger and take a step back. "Thank you. Thank you for letting me see her."

She nods. "You're welcome."

Baas

We have another mediation day today. Usually, I'm fired up and ready to attack, but today is different. In light of Shaya's wishes to pull the petition, I don't know what to feel. I don't know how to be. It was on my mind all last night, and I hate being stuck in the middle. I want my baby back, and I've made that clear since the moment I found out about her. But I started to see Shaya's point once I thought about it.

Then there's the matter with the Seer. She told me to let her go. And now, I realize that she's talking about Bailey. I don't know why, but I know that her instruction comes with good reason. If she's telling me to let her go, it's for a purpose, and I need to think long and hard before I go against that purpose.

But it's hard. I run an orphanage back home. I see the joy the parents feel when they're given a child. Some of those parents have tried for years to conceive. Some have kids but want to be a blessing to other kids. No matter the reason, I know the joy it brings them. They become immediately attached to them, and the thought of losing them is painful. I'm in awe at how Shaya can be so selfless. She's pushing her wants to the side to bless another family.

The room is quiet as our lawyers skim the papers before them.

"The first visitation week went well, so we see no need to make any changes," their lawyer states.

We should have been given more than visitation once a week, but I digress. We took what we could get until all of this was settled. Shaya places her hand over mine. She must feel the tension rolling off me. But one look at her, and the storm calms inside me.

"There's some news we'd like to share," Shaya announces.

She watches me as she says it, and her hand stays firm over mine. I know what she's about to say. I expected it today. But her saying it in this room, in front of the Smiths and their lawyer, makes it too real for me.

"Now?" I ask.

"Yes," she answers.

Their lawyer nods, and Shaya continues. "We want to pull the petition."

Our lawyer whips his head around. "What?" he asks.

"We just decided a few nights ago," I add.

He looks over at the Smiths and their lawyer. "Can I please have a minute with my clients?"

They rise from the table and leave us alone in the mediation room. "What are you two doing?" he asks.

"They're the only parents she's known. We can't just take her from them," Shaya says.

He looks at me. "What do you think about all of this?"

I turn to Shaya. "I don't like it. But I understand it. She's right. Giving a blessing and then taking it away would be cruel."

He looks frustrated. "You two do know that once you've pulled the petition, there's no turning back. A judge won't grant custody to parents who can't decide whether they want their child."

I slam my fist on the table. "I don't like your tone." I'm already on edge, and he's making it worse. When I've calmed my breathing, I continue. "We know what we're asking you to do. We've thought about it and weighed every option before coming to this decision, so when we tell you that we want you to pull the petition . . . We want you to fucking pull the petition."

He leans back in his chair. "Okay. But let me tell you what this means. If you pull this petition, you are essentially reverting back to the original terms of the adoption agreement. Since it's a closed adoption, that means that there can be no contact with Bailey unless she's old enough to reach out to you first."

Shaya nods. "Yes. We know."

He continues. "The most I can do is draft another petition asking the court to modify the terms of the adoption agreement. This would mean the Smiths must send you pictures and keep you abreast of Bailey's progress."

Shaya turns to me. "I don't think that's necessary."

"No. But there is one amendment I'd like to ask the court to add."

"What is it?" our lawyer asks.

"When Bailey turns sixteen, they must tell her that she was adopted and who her parents are. We will leave detailed instructions for them."

He nods before he writes it down. "Anything else?" he asks.

"No," Shaya and I say in unison.

"Okay," he replies.

He rises and walks to the door while Shaya squeezes my hand. He opens it and allows the Smiths and their lawyer back into the room. They take a seat, and he speaks for us.

"My clients have decided to drop the petition."

"Oh, Thank God," Mrs. Smith responds with tears.

Mr. Smith looks at us. "Thank you."

Our lawyer continues. "There is one condition. When Bailey turns sixteen, you must tell her that she's adopted and allow her to contact them should she wish."

They look at each other. "Sure, we can do that."

"Okay. Well, it seems we're done here. Anything else we need to discuss?"

We shake our heads. "No."

The Smiths shake theirs. "No."

CHAPTER TWENTY-FOUR

Three Months Later

Baas

Mafachiko

"**D**on't jump into . . ." It's too late. Kema jumps into the pool before I can even finish my sentence.

Shaya laughs out loud. "You had to know it was coming."

I pull her in and kiss the top of her head as we watch the kids enjoy the new pool we have built. We've been back home for three months, and Shaya and I immediately threw ourselves into the orphanage. I guess it was a way for us both to deal with the pain of letting Bailey go.

Shaya became the face of the orphanage, advocating for more families to offer homes to children in need. And since she has, our adoption rate has increased by 60 percent. Even older children are being adopted, which is usually a challenge. Between the orphanage and my duties to Dafari, I've been busy, but not too busy to spend time with Shaya and the kids. I've become more involved in a way I hadn't done before. My role before wasn't as involved. That was all Naomi. As long as the place ran smoothly and the numbers were up, I thought I was doing my job.

But recently, I realized there's more to it than that. These kids need role models. Both male and female. And that's what Shaya and I aim to do. I implemented counseling sessions. I want the kids to be able to say how they really feel without regard to what people may think. An unbiased counselor is a perfect way for them to do that. I started game nights, where we get together once a week and play games as a family. We also eat dinner with them as a family a few nights a week. Shaya takes the girls on spa dates, where they get their nails and feet done, and she also takes them to the salon. Her favorite thing is to cook with them in the kitchen. She loves it.

"They'll be out here all night if we let them."

"I know. But it's hot today, so it's a good way for them to cool off," she replies.

I turn to face her. "Did you decide on the cake yet?"

She shakes her head. "No. I didn't like either of them."

"But Yuri is the best baker in Mafachiko," I explain.

"So I've heard. But everything was too sweet."

Shaya doesn't eat sweets much. When she does, it's usually light and fluffy.

"Maybe we could go with something lighter like a lemon cake, light on the icing. Or we can always get two. It's your day, sweetheart, and you can have whatever you want," I respond.

"That's not necessary, honey. One cake is fine. I'll figure out something. You know I rarely eat sweets unless it's that time of the . . ."

She stops speaking. "What's wrong?"

She shakes her head. "Nothing. I just thought of something." A second goes by, and she continues. "You know, I might just choose the lemon cake, after all."

I smile. "Good."

Our wedding day is fast approaching, and it's been hectic, to say the least. More on Shaya's part than mine because she wanted to plan her own day. I brought in the best planners and decorators, but Shaya and Ebony have gone crazy. They have taken on this task by themselves with little to no input from the people I've hired. The only person they've taken input from is the seamstress who will customize Shaya's gown.

But whatever my girl wants, she gets. Shaya has her mind made up about how she wants our wedding. I've added my input here and there, but for the most part, it's all up to her.

"I've been thinking," she speaks.

"About?"

"What do you think about having an empty chair for Bailey? We could place her picture on it as if she were here."

I don't hesitate to answer. "I think that's an amazing idea."

There's a hint of sadness in her eyes as she takes a deep breath, but then she smiles at me.

"I knew you'd like that idea."

I pull her in close to me. "Have I mentioned that I can't wait to marry you?"

She giggles. "Yes. Every day. And I can't wait to marry you, either."

"You'll officially be mine."

She shakes her head. "I've always been yours."

I lean in and kiss her, holding her so tight I think I may break her. When I release her, I look into her eyes.

"Shaya Osei. It has a nice ring to it."

She smiles widely. "It does, doesn't it?"

Shaya

When Baas shared with me that he wanted me to be the face of the orphanage, I admit it had me nervous. The idea of putting myself out there left me feeling overwhelmed. I know nothing about running an orphanage other than what I've witnessed during my brief time there with Baas, and I want to do my best.

I pace in front of the bathroom and chew my nails. Three minutes and I'll know for sure. Can it be positive? Of course, it can. But if it is, how will I feel? How will Baas feel?

I've been feeling off lately. I've been extremely tired and a little cranky, and my tastebuds have been weird. But I thought it was related to the stress around the wedding. But then Baas mentioned the cake today. I don't eat sweets except once a month when my period comes. Only this month, I didn't have one. I check the time and have one more minute left. Ebony's text messages are coming through at a rapid speed, demanding updates. I'm surprised she hasn't come over yet to read them with me in person.

I can't remember how I felt the first time I was pregnant. I had so much going on that I ignored my symptoms. All I know is that my body doesn't feel right, and all signs point toward me being pregnant. Finally, the last minute is up, and I walk inside the bathroom. I grab the test from the sink and look at it. It reads positive! Baas and I are going to be parents again. Guilt slams into me as I think about Bailey. Would she think it's unfair that I'm keeping this baby after giving her up? Will she resent us for raising this child but allowing someone else to raise her? I'm consumed with emotions as I think about what my firstborn may think once she's older.

Baas knocks on the door. "Shaya, are you okay? I got your text."

I crack the door enough that I can see him. "Yes, I'm okay."

"What's the urgent matter? Are you sick?"

I open the door widely and allow him to step inside. "No, I'm not sick."

He sweeps me from head to toe. "Well, what's wrong?"

I hand him the test. He looks down at it, then back at me. "Is this saying what I think it's saying?"

I nod.

He lifts me up and spins me around. "You have no idea how happy this makes me."

When he places me down, I reply, "So, you're okay with this?"

"Why wouldn't I be?"

"Do you think Bailey would be upset that we didn't keep her but raised this child?"

He shakes his head. "When she's old enough, she'll reach out to us and ask questions. We'll tell her everything, and she will understand."

"Okay. Baas?"

"Yes, baby?"

"We're going to be parents again."

He smiles. "We've always been parents, sweetheart."

He hugs me again, and my thoughts revert to Bailey. Baas is right. Once she's old enough to reach out to us, we can explain everything, and I'm sure she'll understand. But a small piece of me is scared that she won't. Will she wonder why we didn't fight hard enough to keep her? Will she be upset that we left her in another country? I look up at Baas. "Should we tell the Smiths? That way, when the time comes, she can know she has a sibling."

He shakes his head. "Let's wait. They'll be plenty of time to tell her when that day comes."

"Have you thought about putting a detail on them?"

"No, I don't trust anyone. You see what happened with Telly. It's too risky. For now, no one should know she's the daughter of royalty."

"I agree."

"It's okay to miss her sweetheart," he adds.

"I know. And I miss her terribly."

It's here. My wedding has finally arrived. I stare at myself in the mirror as Ebony helps straighten the crown on my head. "You look beautiful, Shaya."

I look at her through the mirror. "Thanks, Eb."

My mom walks over. "Don't forget this," she says.

She hands me a diamond ring with a blue stone. "My something blue," I reply.

"Yes. It was your grandmother's. She wore it at her wedding, and I wore it at mine."

"Thank you, Mom."

I fan my face. "Okay, you two. You're going to make me mess up my makeup."

Someone knocks at the door, and Ebony rushes over to it.

"No, you can't come in," I hear her say. She turns around. "Shaya, can you please tell your stubborn soon-to-be husband that seeing the bride before the wedding is bad luck?"

I rise from my seat quickly, shielding my face. I stand off to the side of the door so that he can't see me. "Baas, what are you doing here?"

"I have something for you," he replies.

"It can't wait until after the wedding?"

"No."

Ebony exhales loudly with frustration. "Baas, if you ruin this . . ."

"Eb, it's okay. I won't let him see me."

She nods. "Okay. We'll leave you two alone."

She and my mother leave the room, and I'm left alone. I open the door, but my back is turned, so Baas can't see me.

"What is it?" I ask.

"Here."

He slips his hand inside the crack and hands me something. It's a white envelope, but I don't know what's inside. I open it and slide a photo out . . . of Bailey.

I gasp. "Oh my God."

She's grown. She's standing now, and her hair is longer and fuller. She stares directly at the camera, laughing, and I can see she has two front teeth. She looks like me.

"Baas . . ." I whisper. "How were you able to get this?"

"I had our lawyer also add this as a condition of the agreement with the Smiths. I knew this day would come and that Bailey wouldn't be here. So, I wanted to make certain you had something of her to make your day special."

"It's the perfect wedding gift, honey. Thank you."

"It is indeed. I'll get Ebony so she can return and have your makeup fixed."

He walks away, and I sit at the vanity with the picture in my hand. My baby is growing to be so beautiful. It's been three months since I last saw her, but it seems like a lifetime ago. Tears stream down my cheeks, and I can feel the makeup sliding off with it. I don't wipe them away out of fear of smudging my face. I bring the picture to my lips and kiss it. I close my eyes and imagine her being here with us to share on our wedding day. Ebony and my mother burst into the room with the makeup artists.

"He chooses to make you cry right before you walk down the aisle," she growls. "What did he say to you, Shaya?"

I shake my head as the tears still fall. "Nothing. He gave me this."

I hand her the picture, and she takes a look. My mom joins her. "Is that . . ."

"Yes. It's Bailey," I reply.

Ebony places her hand against her chest, then looks at me. "This was worth the messy makeup."

I laugh through happy tears. "Yes. It was definitely worth it."

CHAPTER TWENTY-FIVE
Baas

I can't stop the overwhelming feeling of emotions as I watch Shaya walk down the aisle. The palace is beautifully decorated in a mixture of rose gold and pink. I'm wearing a gray suit with a pink tie, and Shaya is wearing an ivory dress that makes her look like a goddess. She walks gracefully down the aisle with her father beside her, holding her arm. The lyrics *This Is Why I Love You* play through the speakers, a song she chose by an American singer. It summed up how I felt about her when I first heard it.

Our close friends and family surround us, as do people from the village we've invited. It's customary to choose a select few to attend royal weddings. When my bride reaches me, the officiant asks who gives her away, and her father replies that he does. He lets her go, and she makes her way to me. We turn to face each other and hold hands. Everything after that is a blur. I remember us saying our vows. I remember us promising to love and honor each other. I remember her crying and me wiping her tears away.

I was too engulfed in the moment. I was too distracted by the amount of love and devotion I feel for this woman. And when we both said, "I do," I could barely wait for the officiant to tell me I could kiss her. I pull her to me swiftly, placing my lips on hers while the crowd behind us claps loudly and cheers us on. When I release her, I whisper in her ear, "Are you ready to start our new life together, wife?"

She smiles at me. "I can't wait, husband."

Shaya

My wedding was exactly how I wanted it to be. The day was perfect. I stare out at the ocean that's lit under the stars, eager for my new life with Baas. We're heading to a beautiful five-star hotel tonight. We'll spend our wedding night there, and Dafari will introduce me to the people of Mafachiko tomorrow. It's customary with weddings of the royal family.

Once we're done, we'll head to Greece for our honeymoon. Baas told me we could go anywhere I wanted for our honeymoon, and I chose Greece. I've always been fascinated by the country and can't wait to see it firsthand. He approaches me from behind.

"Are you okay?" he asks.

"I'm on a beautiful yacht with my sexy husband and carrying his child. Is that a serious question?"

He chuckles as he spins me around and cages me in. "You took my breath away today."

I blush. "Thank you."

He leans in to kiss my neck. "I wanted to take you right there at the altar."

I swat him. "Your mind is so filthy."

"Isn't that what you love about me?"

"Yes. It's *one* of the things I love about you."

"Too bad you're already pregnant because that would have been the goal tonight."

"The doctor says I'm six weeks."

"How's your body feeling?" he asks.

"Good. A little tired, but that's it."

"Our child will officially be a native of Mafachiko."

"And what about Bailey?"

He nods. "If Bailey wishes."

"What do you mean by that?"

"There's a chance Bailey won't want anything to do with this. And it would be her choice."

"Yes. I hadn't looked at it that way."

He places his hand on my belly. "Dafari and I have trained additional men."

"Are we going to war again?"

"No. But we must be prepared after what happened with him and us. We'll both have a task force. Specifically assigned to protect our families."

"So, basically, I'll have a babysitter?" I ask.

"It's to protect you."

"What about Bailey? She was taken once. What if—"

He interrupts me. "No one knows about Bailey yet. And we're going to keep it that way. Now, if she decides to come here, that will be a different story."

His words weigh on me. I never considered that Bailey may never choose to reach out to us. In my mind, I thought she would as soon as she got the opportunity. I thought it was every adoptive child's dream to find out who their biological family is. But if the Smiths do a good enough job and she's happy and healthy, there would be no reason for her to come and find us. And if that happens, I have to respect that. No matter what, it's her decision, and we have to be okay with it.

"Okay. Thank you for keeping us safe."

"Now that we've got that out of the way, I'm dying to see what's under this silk robe."

I smirk. "Nothing."

He picks me up. "That's precisely what I was hoping you would say."

Baas

"I have something for you two," Dafari says.

Shaya was introduced to the people today, and they all seemed to love her. Dafari and I were grateful for such a warm welcome because we know this can be a lot to someone not used to our way of living.

"Dafari, you've already given us enough," I reply.

He hands me a piece of paper, and I read it. "A deed?"

"Yes. Crim, as you are aware, is a rising country. It needs proper management, and I haven't been able to give it the attention it needs over the years. This is my wedding gift to you and Shaya. You will be king of your own country, and she queen."

I shake my head. "This is too much."

"No. It isn't. You have everything it takes to be a good king, Baas, except for the royal blood. I can change that, and I'm doing so today. Crim needs a king. A dedicated king. And that king is you. I've arranged a crowning ceremony for you both."

I never thought that I would be king of anything. Yes, I have close ties with the royal family, and yes, I know the ins and outs of what it takes to run a country. But you see, men like me don't become kings. I'm an orphan who got lucky and became best friends with a future king. I dedicated my life to him and his family, and we became brothers. I didn't care about what he could do for me. I didn't care about the influence I had. I was just glad to be a part of a family since I had lost mine.

"I won't let you down."

"I know you won't."

"I present to you, Queen Shaya!"

I watch as Dafari places the crown on Shaya's head, and I swell with pride. It's been nonstop since we returned from our honeymoon last week, and today is our crowning ceremony. The people of Crim clap and cheer us on, but I'm not surprised. They love us. We spent an entire day touring the country and meeting the people. We connected with them and shared our vision for the future. They were warm and welcoming. They were also glad to have a king and queen who cares about their well-being. After Shay and I are crowned, Dafari approaches me.

"You've served me well, Baas. And it will be strange not having you by my side."

I place my hand on his shoulder. "Dafari, I will *always* be by your side."

He pulls me in a man hug, but not a long one. When we break apart, he looks around.

"This is probably the first time we've had a crowning ceremony for both a king and queen."

I look over at Shaya, who's talking to Ebony. "Me in love. Who would have thought?"

"Definitely not me," Dafari answers. We laugh out loud, and he continues. "But I'm happy for you both."

"So, have you replaced me yet?" I ask.

"No. Not yet, but I'll need your help finding the right person to replace you."

We shake hands. "Done."

Shaya makes her way over to me, and Dafari nods before he walks away. She looks at him, then back at me.

"What were you two talking about?"

"My replacement," I reply.

"I'm sure that's tough for him."

"Yes, it is."

"How do you feel about all this?" I ask.

"It's bittersweet. I'm sad to leave the role I've had since I can remember. But I'm excited about our future together. I'm still in shock that you and I will rule a country."

She smiles. "Me too. King and queen. You and me."

"Yes. You and me, sweetheart. It's probably too late to ask now since you're already wearing the crown, but are you okay with all this?"

Shaya

I can't believe my eyes. Me a queen? Women like me don't become queens. Ebony became one, but by accident. But no one gifts a country to someone and makes them a queen . . . except for Dafari. His loyalty and love for his best friend is astounding.

"Yes, I'm okay with this. And I know I can do anything with you by my side. But . . . I know nothing about being a queen, Baas. If I'm being honest, I'm really nervous."

He pulls me in. "It's simple, sweetheart. A queen should be kind. She should be compassionate, poised, supportive, and strong. She should be everything you already are, Shaya."

My eyes water as he continues. "You can't teach those qualities. You either have them or you don't. And you have them, which is what made me fall in love with you."

I throw myself at him and hold him tight. I'm nervous. I have no idea what I'm getting myself into, and I don't want to disappoint Baas. But I do know that I will take this role seriously. He releases me.

"We're going to be okay."

I nod. "I know."

Dafari calls for him, and he kisses me on the cheek before he walks away. I look around and admire the beautiful garden we're in, and then I look over at Ebony as she holds Dafari's hand. She looks at me and winks. Aiden runs around, playing, oblivious to the matters of adults. I place my hand on my belly, anxious to meet my baby. I have their names picked out already. If it's a girl, we will name her Imani. If it's a boy, we will call him Kofi. I sit on a nearby bench and smile at the sight before me. Just a few years ago, I was about to marry a crazy man, and Ebony was on the run. Neither of us could have imagined this was how our lives would become. We're both in love with men who worship the ground we walk on, live in this beautiful, magical country, and have been given motherhood's blessing. Life can't get any better than this, and I plan to be grateful for it every day of my life.

CHAPTER TWENTY-SIX
Shaya

Five Years Later

I open the cake container and pause. "Kofi!"

I hear the patter of his feet as he runs into the kitchen. "Yes, Mom."

"Did you eat some cake after I told you not to?"

He shakes his head no.

I cross my arms and stare at him. "So, what's that around your mouth?"

He wipes it with the back of his hand, smearing the chocolate on his shirt sleeve.

"I don't know."

I walk around the counter and kneel in front of him. "Kofi, what did I say about lying?"

He lowers his head in shame as he answers me. "Lying isn't good caraca."

"Character," I correct him.

Baas enters the kitchen shirtless and sweaty from his morning run. I take a second to sweep him in. This man doesn't seem to age. He runs his fingers through Kofi's hair and makes it messy.

"Hey, little man."

"Hi, Daddy."

When he looks at me, he sees my expression. "Uh-oh, who's in trouble? Him or me?"

"Did you see his face?"

He leans down and looks. "Have you been eating chocolate this morning?"

"Yes. He snuck a piece of cake . . . and lied to me about it."

Baas's expression turns serious. "Kofi!"

"I'm sorry, Daddy."

"Lying will not be tolerated."

I grab a wet cloth and wipe away the chocolate. "Your clothes are on the bed. Brush your teeth and put them on so I can take you to school."

He runs upstairs, and Baas laughs out loud. I cock my head to the side. "Don't laugh. He won't take us seriously."

"I'm sorry. But did you see the look on his face?"

A laugh escapes me. "Yeah, I did. Poor thing thought it was the end of the world."

"He's stubborn like his mother."

"Yeah, right. If anyone is stubborn, it's you."

He nods. "You do have a point."

"Are you hungry? I was just about to make breakfast."

He places his hand on the small of my back. "Yes. But not for food."

My body heats at his touch. "After I take Kofi to school?"

He smirks. "Yes. But I'll take him today."

I kiss him before I head upstairs to get Kofi ready. Thoughts of Bailey enter my brain as I climb each step. I wonder how smart she is and if she likes school. I think about her daily and wish I could have seen her off to her first day of school. I open the door and watch Kofi struggle to get his school uniform on. I haven't told him about Bailey yet. He's smart, but he's too young to understand. But I will tell him about his sister one day when I think he's old enough.

Maybe they will meet each other. Perhaps they will grow close. I can only hope and dream of someday having my children under the same roof. I walk inside.

"Need some help?"

"No, Mommy, I got it."

He's adamant about doing things on his own. He likes to show that he's a big boy and can dress himself as his father does. Kofi looks up to Baas and adores him. He takes every opportunity to mimic him, and it's the cutest thing.

"I can't find my shoes, Mommy."

"That's because you're not wearing your glasses."

"I don't like them," he replies.

"Why not?"

"Because the kids at school tease me about them."

For a second, I lose all humility at the thought of someone teasing my baby. He is a prince, and how *dare* someone be bold enough to tease him? But I know that's the protective mother in me because no kid is exempt from being teased.

"What do they say?"

"They call me four eyes and say I'm not a prince. They say a prince would be able to see without glasses."

I grab his glasses from the nightstand and put them on him slowly. Then I kneel in front of him. "Honey, you know that's not true, right?" He doesn't answer me. "Your father is a king, which makes you . . .?"

"A prince," he answers.

"That's right. If your father can be a king and wear glasses, then so can you, right?"

This time, he smiles. "Yes."

I kiss him on the cheek. "Don't listen to them. And if they keep it up, they'll have me to deal with."

He straightens his spine. "No, Mommy. Daddy says men face their problems head-gone."

"It's head-*on*, sweetheart. Do what you must to defend yourself, and if you need help, we're here."

"Okay."

He grabs his shoes and throws them on before running out of the room. He's probably going downstairs to tell Baas about what's happening in school. I plop down on his bed and look around his room. I chuckle at how wise Kofi has gotten. He's a straight-A student and has advanced to the first grade. It has nothing to do with the fact that he's royalty and everything to do with him breezing through kindergarten work. The teachers said the work wasn't stimulating enough for him, and he was bored in class.

In addition to his studies, he's excelling in martial arts and weapons training. Baas has been preparing Kofi to be king since he was born. And I allowed it because I would never interfere with the teachings from father to son. But the more I watch it unfold, the more I can't help to think that he's forgotten about Bailey. She has a claim to the throne as well. And as his queen, I have a say about who succeeds us.

Mafachiko has a history of tradition. No woman had ever run a kingdom until Dafari designated the crown to Ebony. The elders weren't happy, and they took her through hell. That won't happen on my watch. If Bailey wants to be queen, then she has that right. And I won't allow anything or anyone to stand in her way.

Baas

My son is a mini version of me. From the way he talks down to the way he laughs. I beam with pride every time I lay eyes on him. He's my greatest gift, other than Shaya and Bailey. My thoughts shift to her. I wonder how she's doing and how she looks. I miss her terribly, and I know Shaya does too. Sometimes, I see a look of sadness on her face, and I know she's thinking about her. I can also tell when she spends time with Kofi that she thinks about Bailey.

I came close to breaking the agreement and putting a detail on her. But I changed my mind. She was taken once for money, and no one should know who she is. It's safer this way. But moving on with our lives and knowing that she's living her life without us is still a tough pill to swallow.

I've just dropped Kofi off at school, which was an experience, as always. I try my best not to cause a distraction, but it never works. The kids get so excited to see me that they crowd around me. Most of them ask me questions like what is it like to be a king. Or they ask me questions like, is Kofi really my son? And I make sure that they all know that he is. He doesn't know I'm aware he is being teased at school. There's little that goes on in my territory that I'm not aware of. So when the kids ask me if he is my son, I not only tell them yes, but I also tell them that he is next in line to be king.

I walk through the door, excited to spend much-needed alone time with my wife. The house is quiet, and for a second, I panic, thinking something is wrong.

"Shaya!" I call out.

"In here."

I exhale with relief when I hear her voice. We're safe. And I can say with confidence that we will remain safe. But with everything that has been thrown our way in the past, one can't be so sure. I walk down the hall and into the sitting room, where I hear soft music. The curtains are drawn, and candles are lit. A blanket with wine and a basket on top of it is in the middle of the floor. Shaya sits on the edge of the couch with her legs crossed, wearing only a tiny piece of fabric. I grow hard at the sight of her. She stands to her feet, revealing the sexy lingerie she's wearing. I almost lose control. I want to bypass any plans she has for us besides me making love to her. But from the looks of it, she's put some effort into this setup, so I need to appreciate it and her.

"You look stunning."

"Thank you, husband." She walks over to me and throws her arms around my neck. "It's been some time since we've had a romantic date, don't you think?"

"Yes, too long."

As hard as I am, I'm also taken aback at how incredible she is and the little things she does. I shake my head.

"What is it?" she asks.

"I'm one lucky man."

She smiles widely. "I'm the lucky one."

"I love you, Shaya. Today, tomorrow, and always."

She nods. "I love you too. Until my last breath."

EPILOGUE

Bailey

Sixteen Years Later

My parents said that they have something important to talk to me about after school. I haven't been able to focus because I keep wondering what it could be. Do they know I snuck out to go to Marcie's party? Or maybe they know that I cheated on my math exam last week. Either way, I'm in trouble and most likely will be grounded. Which means I may not be able to make it to the school dance next week.

Jilly leans over and whispers, "Josh told Adam he likes you."

I look over at Josh, who smiles at me. When I turn back to face Jilly, I whisper loudly, "I thought he was going out with Kesha."

She shakes her head. "Nope. They broke up."

The bell rings, and I quickly grab my books and walk with Jilly to my locker. "He's cute and all, but I'm nobody's rebound."

She holds her hand out. "Okay?"

I tap mine with hers. "Period."

I grab my book from my locker and sigh when I close it. "My parents said they have something to speak to me about. I think they found out I snuck out last week."

"Shit!"

"I know."

"Your parents are cool, though. I doubt you'll be in that much trouble."

I laugh lightly. "You don't know my mom."

"Ahh, yes, I do. I spend the night at your house like every week."

"And she's on her best behavior when you're there," I reply.

Jilly laughs. "Mrs. Smith can't be that bad."

"She's not bad. She's just smothering. I swear she would follow me to the bathroom if she could. She has to know where I'm at and what I do every second of the day, even when I'm in school. What parent does that?"

"They just love you and want to make sure you're safe."

"Safe from what? I turned sixteen yesterday, and they treat me like a baby."

Jilly nods. "I'll admit, your parents are kind of strict."

"Right. You'd think I was a troubled kid or something, the way they keep track of me. It's getting annoying, and I can't wait until I'm an adult so I can live my own life."

Our school counselor, Mrs. Ramos, approaches us. "Bailey, could you come with me, please."

"Am I in trouble?" I ask.

"No."

Jilly watches on as I follow Mrs. Ramos to her office. When I enter, two police officers are already there.

"What's going on?" I ask.

"Have a seat, Bailey." Mrs. Ramos says softly.

I lower myself into the seat but don't take my eyes off the police officers. Mrs. Ramos glances at them before she speaks.

"Bailey, there's been an accident."

"What kind of accident?"

"Your parents."

"What? Are they okay?"

One of the police officers steps forward and speaks. "I'm sorry to tell you this, but your parents didn't make it."

I don't immediately process what he's saying. I'm numb and in shock and ask him to repeat himself to clarify. "Are you saying my parents are . . ."

He nods. "Your parents are deceased."

I should be crying right now. I should be stricken with grief. But I'm in disbelief that my parents are really dead.

"Is this a joke?" I ask.

Mrs. Ramos shakes her head. "Honey, that's not something we would joke about." I look into her eyes, then over into the police officers' eyes. They're serious. "Is there anyone we can call for you? Any other family?"

I shake my head. There is no other family. My parents were all I had. I was close to them both and can't imagine my life without them.

"I can stay at a friend's house," I quickly announce.

I'm close with Jilly and her parents. And I'm sure they won't mind me staying with them until I figure out how to live independently. I'll need a job to pay rent, but that will be hard while attending school. Mrs. Ramos looks at me with sad eyes.

"I'm sorry, honey, but that's not how it works. I'll have to call a social worker."

"No. That's not necessary. I have friends I can stay with. I don't need a social worker."

My heart beats rapidly, and it's becoming harder for me to breathe. Between the news of my parents and now this, I'm close to having a panic attack. One of the police officers steps forward.

"It'll be okay. We're here to help."

Tears fall from my eyes because I know where this is going. I'm being put into foster care. I've gone from living in a middle-class neighborhood with loving parents to being placed in foster care with God knows who. Mrs. Ramos picks up the phone, and I watch in horror as she calls social services to come to the school and escort me out.

I've been at the social services office for two hours now and am both frustrated and tired. I have questions about my parents, but no one will answer me. I have questions about what happens next, and they all ignore me. The social worker, Kari, seems nice. But I've learned long ago that you can't trust someone just because they seem nice. She finally returns to her office with a folder in her hand. I speak as soon as she takes a seat.

"Please, I want to see my parents."

"I don't think you're old enough to visit the morgue without an adult."

"Well, could you come with me? Please?"

She shakes her head. "I'm sorry. I can't."

She opens the folder and reads through some paperwork. "Hmm," she says. She then types something on her computer, and her eyes go wide. "Well, *this* changes things."

I sit quietly and allow her to do what she's doing because, by now, I have no energy left. She drops her pen and looks at me when she writes something down.

"Bailey, it seems your foster care placement will have to be put on hold for now."

"Really? I can stay at my friend's house?"

She laughs softly. "No, honey. It's because we found your next of kin."

I scrunch my face. I literally have no next of kin. Both of my parents were only children, and both of their parents are dead. It's been me and them all my life. No big family dinners. No family reunions—nothing. Just me, myself, my mom, and my dad.

"Who?" I ask with curiosity.

She smiles at me. "Honey, you were adopted. We have contact information for your birth parents."

THE END

ACKNOWLEDGMENTS

I grew up as an only child in a two-parent household. I didn't know what it was like to have siblings except for my first cousins, who were close enough for me to call them brother and sister. At forty years old, I found out I had a biological sister. My dad had been in a relationship before meeting my mother, and he had no idea the woman was pregnant when they split up. She kept the baby a secret and gave her up for adoption at birth. It was a shock to me, and my father and I were so anxious to meet her. I was curious if we would get along, if we looked alike. I wanted to know everything about her.

When we met, I got to hear her story and what it was like for her growing up. Adoption isn't easy for the parent or child, and I am so grateful that she was given to a loving and wonderful family who helped shape the woman she is today.

Angel, I love you, and this story is for you.

To my publisher, Black Odyssey Media, THANK YOU. Your belief in me and my work helps keep me driven to succeed in a very tough industry. Thank you for your unwavering support and motivation.

ABOUT THE AUTHOR

L. R. Jackson was born and raised on Maryland's Eastern Shore. She's a fun and spontaneous Gemini with an addiction to wings and a passion for food. By day, she works in Corporate America; by night, she dreams of Alpha Males and Romance.

When she's not working, she can be found reading, cooking, traveling, and, of course, writing. She lives on the East Coast with her daughter.

She has a huge appreciation for her readers and loves to hear from them. You may contact her via:

Facebook: authorlrjackson
Instagram: @authorlrjackson
@mdgirl1979
Email: authorlrjackson@gmail.com
Website: www.authorlrjackson.com

WWW.BLACKODYSSEY.NET

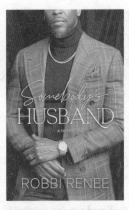

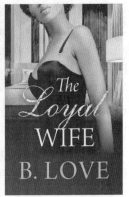

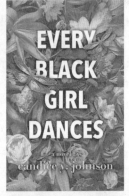

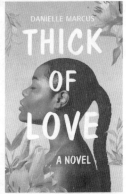

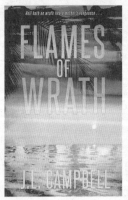